SMAS
HED

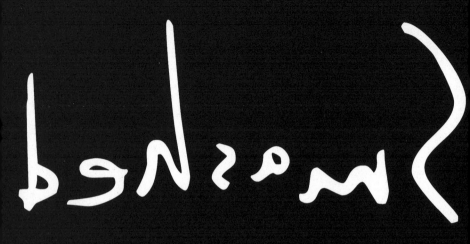

Smashed

LISA LUEDEKE

Margaret K. McElderry Books

New York London Toronto Sydney New Delhi

Smashed

LISA LUEDEKE

Margaret K. McElderry Books

New York London Toronto Sydney New Delhi

MARGARET K. McELDERRY BOOKS
An imprint of Simon & Schuster Children's Publishing Division
1230 Avenue of the Americas, New York, New York 10020
This book is a work of fiction. Any references to historical events, real people,
or real locales are used fictitiously. Other names, characters, places, and
incidents are products of the author's imagination, and any resemblance to
actual events or locales or persons, living or dead, is entirely coincidental.

MARGARET K. McELDERRY BOOKS is a trademark of Simon & Schuster, Inc.
For information about special discounts for bulk purchases, please contact Simon &
Schuster Special Sales at 1-866-506-1949 or business@simonandschuster.com.
The Simon & Schuster Speakers Bureau can bring authors to your live event. For more
information or to book an event, contact the Simon & Schuster Speakers Bureau at
1-866-248-3049 or visit our website at www.simonspeakers.com.
The text for this book is set in Bell MT.
Manufactured in the United States of America
2 4 6 8 10 9 7 5 3 1
Library of Congress Cataloging-in-Publication Data
Luedeke, Lisa.
Smashed / Lisa Luedeke.—1st ed.
p. cm.
Summary: Maine high school senior Katie Martin is set to win a field hockey
scholarship until her life is derailed by drinking, a car accident, and an angry classmate.
ISBN 978-1-4424-2779-2 (hardcover)
ISBN 978-1-4424-2795-2 (eBook)
[1. Emotional problems—Fiction. 2. Alcoholism—Fiction.
3. High schools—Fiction. 4. Schools—Fiction.] I. Title.
PZ7.L97654Sm 2012
[Fic]—dc23
2011030515

FIRST
EDITION

* * *

For Putnam, with love

* *

*

Acknowledgments

To Linda Pratt, editorial adviser, agent, friend: You are extraordinary at what you do. Thank you for taking all my calls and talking me off the cliff more times than I can count; for loving the work, and getting the work; and for your wise editorial advice. It would not be the same book without you. To Gretchen Hirsch, my wonderful editor: Thank you for your enthusiasm and humor, for expertly guiding my revisions, and for pushing me further than I thought I had it in me to go. I miss you already. To Michael McCartney for the absolutely best knockout cover design an author could hope for. I'm amazed every time I look at it. And to my new editor, Emily Fabre, who stepped in with grace, energy, and skill, my sincere thanks.

To Janet Freeman: Thank you so much for being my very first reader; you said all the right things. To Laura Rankin: My deep appreciation to you for reading and recommending this book early on—and for sharing Linda with me. It's made all the difference.

Huge thanks to my authors and NCTE friends for all your love, support, and friendship—and for promising to wave my book around on your travels. You are the best. A special thank-you to Kylene Beers for reading an early draft and helping me start sending it out. Your support gave me courage.

To the Division I field hockey coaches who talked to me about recruiting rules and likely scenarios, thank you for helping make my book accurate.

To Putnam, thank you for supporting my writing, always, even though it makes your life harder, and to Lily, for understanding that writing makes Mama happy. And to Catherine Cauthorne—for all you do and have done, my sincere gratitude.

Sometimes when I'm driving I see things that I don't want to see.

Things that aren't really there: A flash of my car careening off the road. A tree trunk smashing into the windshield, spraying sharp bits of glass, like bullets, into the car. A bloody body slumped, lifeless, beside me. Sometimes it's a moving picture, like a movie, sometimes a solitary image—a snapshot, a tableau.

I shut my eyes but they won't go away, won't stop. Flash, flash, flash. They intrude, like a thief breaking into my mind, stealing my sanity.

It's been happening ever since I got here.

For a long time, I tell no one.

When I finally tell the doctor at the university, she says there's a reason this is happening.

"Yeah," I say, "I'm going crazy."

"No," she says. "There's nothing crazy about it. These are symptoms of trauma. Normal reaction to trauma."

"Normal" is no longer a word I use to describe myself. I look at her, blink once, consider what she's said. Where I come from, people don't talk about things like that. Trauma is a topic left to *The Oprah Winfrey Show.* The closest thing in Deerfield, Maine, to admitting anything bad happens is a bumper sticker that says SHIT HAPPENS.

There are a lot of counselors here at school, but Pam is the only one who's a doctor, so they send me to her. I think she's reserved for the worst cases. So I tell Dr. Pam a few things to see how she'll react. At first I like how she nods at me, never looks surprised. But after a while it annoys me, so I tell her more to see if I can shock her. She looks very concerned, but that's it. No shock.

Dr. Pam tells me it's not so strange, this whole business of seeing things I don't want to see, of thoughts and visions circling through my mind again and again like a merry-go-round out of control. She talks about war veterans who flash back to Afghanistan or Vietnam at the sound of fireworks on the Fourth of July, who get jumpy when they hear a hunter's gunshot—even a car backfiring.

"It's not like I was in a war."

She is still for a moment before she speaks. "No. But you thought you killed someone once. And you thought you were going to die." She pauses again. "Twice."

Twice.

The word echoes in my head. I can't even remember the first time. But the memory is lodged like a bullet in my brain; it's lurking in there somewhere. If it came out, maybe I could get rid of it. But I don't want to remember any more than I already do.

I glance at her wastebasket, sure I will throw up. I want to run, but I can't. I've been sentenced to these weekly sessions with her. It's a condition of my playing hockey here. Plus, Pam's not surprised that I'm seeing things. For the first time, I wonder if she could actually help me.

"It's called post-traumatic stress disorder—PTSD," she says.

I don't care what it's called as long as I'm not crazy.

Something else happened, too. Like a nightmare, but I was awake. Awake but in a dream, another vision that I couldn't control, couldn't escape from. It was happening all over again and I couldn't breathe, couldn't get away. . . .

My roommate found me, in our room, yelling at no one she could see.

But there are some things I keep to myself for now, and Dr. Pam says I don't have to talk about anything until I'm ready.

"What if I'm never ready?" I ask.

"That's okay," Dr. Pam replies.

Ha. I remember my first counselor, Gail, and I don't believe that for a minute. But Pam's been nice to me, so I give her the benefit of the doubt. What other choice do I have, really?

She asks me to start at the beginning, a year ago, when I was seventeen.

It seems like a lifetime ago.

summer

1

The summer before my senior year I hooked up with Alec.

Alec Osborne: tall, cute, built. The guy every girl wanted and every boy wanted to be. That's how it seemed, anyway. He was captain of the football team, captain of the baseball team. Damn, he was captain of the *debate* team. Even the teachers looked at him with awe. He was *it* in our small high school.

But this is the honest-to-God truth: I never saw why. I never knew what they saw in him—the pack of friends that swaggered with him through the halls, the girls, his teachers. To me it was bizarre, his appeal. I couldn't see it. He was a big jock; that helped his case. But it was more than that. He could sway people, win them over. But not me.

That's what I thought, anyway.

Alec's friends were football players mostly, or basketball, or baseball, or all three. They were good-looking. But they were arrogant, too. Not *all* the guys who played sports—that's not what I'm saying. Just these guys Alec hung out with. There were plenty of good guys who were athletic. My best friend, Matt, for one. And field hockey means everything to me; it's my *life*. No, playing football wasn't what made Alec the way he was. I'll never understand what made Alec the way he was.

Anyway, we went to the same parties, had a few of the same friends. Both of us were totally devoted to our sports. We had those things in common; that was it. He'd never been part of my plans. But back then, what I planned and what I did weren't always the same thing.

Sometimes that was a problem.

You can make your head spin asking yourself why you did something. Something your gut tells you is trouble. But there are some questions that don't have answers—not good ones, not ones you can live with. This is what's true: I let myself get sucked in by Alec, even when I knew better.

And I did know better.

It started early that summer, in June. I've gone over it in my head a hundred times.

"Nine!" Matt hollered as I emerged from the water. He held up nine bony fingers as if that made it official.

"*What*? That dive was *so* a ten!"

"Sorry," he said, poker-faced. "Toes not quite pointed on the touch. Gotta deduct one for that. If I don't, what does a ten really *mean*? What is a ten really *worth*? I mean, if I allowed *that* . . ."

"Shut *up*." I laughed and swiped my arm across the lake's

LISA LUEDEKE

surface, sending a mini tidal wave in his direction. Water flew up and over where he sat on the side of the dock, his long legs dangling over the side.

"Shouldn'ta done that," he said, grinning, and hopped in, arms and legs flying, chasing me all the way to the ring of buoys and beyond, straight across the lake.

Breathless, we collapsed in the shallow water on the opposite side. Kids' voices echoed across the lake's surface. Our little town beach sat in one of the lake's narrows, and a ten-minute swim got you to the other side. Not far, but a world away when the beach was crowded and noisy, which it was on this first truly hot day of the summer.

Matt leaned back, his elbows sinking into the wet sand. His legs stretched out into the lake, toes poking out of the water.

I propped myself up next to him, then lifted my chin to the clear blue sky. "There goes Cassie."

Matt looked up. A tiny, silent airplane passed slowly overhead, leaving a thin white trail in its wake.

Cassie, the third member of our trio, who any other summer would have been sitting here beside us, had left that morning for London. There, she'd spend the summer with her aunt and cousins seeing and doing things I could barely imagine. I'd lived in Maine all my life. I'd been to Boston twice. By car. That was as far away as I'd ever been.

"Must be nice," Matt said.

I kicked at the soft sand under my feet, sending smoky clouds through the water. "No kidding."

We were stuck here like the rest of our friends, working two jobs, trying to save money for college.

"I'll miss her," I said.

"I'll miss her *boat.*"

"*Matt.*"

He laughed. "She's insane in that boat."

I pictured Cassie—all five feet two of her—at the wheel of her parents' motorboat, red hair lit up in the sunshine, grinning as she gunned the throttle and took off down the lake. We loved going fast in that thing, the wind tangling our hair, our loose T-shirts flapping in the breeze.

"Remember this?" Matt threw his arms dramatically across his chest in a big X and leaned back in the water, laughing.

I shoved some water at his head. He *knew* I remembered.

It had been June and Cassie had just moved here, so we were about thirteen. The three of us had ridden in Cassie's boat up to the widest part of the lake and shut off the motor as far from any shore as we could get. I'd dared them to jump in with me, and we'd plunged into the dark blue water in shorts and T-shirts. Matt came up hollering. The water was still only about sixty-eight degrees on the surface, and when you jump off a big boat, you go down *deep.*

"It's like the ocean!" Cassie yelled, pulling herself back on board.

Exhilarated by the cold, I went back under, then opened my eyes and swam until my breath ran out.

"You're crazy!" Cassie said to me when I came up again. She

was hugging herself, shivering in the sunshine. "Are you really staying in there?"

"It doesn't feel that cold," I said.

"That's because everything's *numb*," Matt said.

When I climbed back into the boat, my thin white T-shirt—under which I'd worn *nothing*—had turned transparent. I threw my arms across my chest in the big X.

"Don't worry." Matt turned around and grinned. "There's nothing to hide."

"*Men*," Cassie said, rolling her eyes, and tossed me a life jacket. We *all* remembered what Cassie now referred to as "the wet T-shirt incident."

"*Men*," I said to Matt now, but Matt's attention had shifted, his whole demeanor changed.

"Shhh," he said, and touched my arm, signaling me to stay still.

I followed his eyes to a line of ducklings that had just emerged from some brush, swimming in the shallow water behind their mother. While the mama duck hovered protectively, the baby ducks dove for food.

We watched them, silently, until they finished, lined up once more, and swam away.

"Reminds me of your family," I said.

"We'd need Dad and Grandma taking up the rear," he said. "And Mom's protective of the twins, not me."

"That's because you don't need protecting."

"Not anymore," he said, and a shadow crossed his face. Sometimes I forgot how bad it had been in middle school, when Alec Osborne's sidekick, Scott Richardson, had relentlessly bullied Matt. It was so many years ago—and Matt could hold his own in any situation now—but he'd never gotten over it.

"*Definitely* not anymore," I added. "Let's swim back."

The beach was quiet, only a few stragglers left. The air had cooled and the mosquitoes were starting to swarm in the shade under the tall pine trees where Matt and I sat on a bench putting on sneakers and T-shirts.

"Damn things," I said, and swatted another one. They could eat you alive in June. "Let's get out of here." I ran to grab my bike.

When I wheeled it around, Matt was standing still, skateboard tucked under one arm, his eyes fixed on the dirt parking lot across the road.

"What the hell is *he* doing here?" he said.

I followed Matt's gaze to a blue and silver pickup truck, the handles of a lawn mower sticking up in the back. Alec Osborne sat behind the wheel. He lived in Deerfield, ten miles away, where there was a bigger lake and a nicer town beach.

"Who cares?" I said, and I meant it. I had no use for Alec.

"I do," Matt said. "I can't stand that guy."

"No one can."

"*That's* not true," Matt said, "and you know it." He jumped on his board.

I climbed onto my bike and began to pedal slowly, watching Matt as he weaved down the lake road on his skateboard just ahead of me. His balance seemed effortless. With each turn, his long, slender body bent gracefully, a tall blade of grass in the wind. The breeze blew his bright blond hair back from his face.

Something made me hang back. I stopped pedaling, letting Matt get farther ahead. Then, I don't know why I did it—curiosity, the strange sensation that someone was watching me, the pull of something I didn't understand—but I looked back toward the beach as we rode away. And for an instant, my eyes locked with his: Alec Osborne had stepped out of his truck and was standing still on the pavement, staring up the road after me.

2

I dashed out the door at six forty-five the next morning, the screen door banging behind me. Across the street, Matt's father's logging rig was already gone; the two of them had left before dawn. They'd log until midafternoon, then head home in time for Matt to get to his night job, busing tables at the single fancy restaurant in Deerfield.

In our ancient barn, my bike leaned against a wall covered with cobwebs. I glanced at my watch; in fifteen minutes, I'd teach my first swimming class of the summer. I got on my bike and rode.

The cool air blew my dark hair back, whipping it in the wind. Ten minutes later, I flew past Cassie's house; seconds later I was at the beach, my face damp from a thin mist that hovered in the morning air.

The Junior Lifesavers were first, my twelve-year-old brother, Will, among them, griping as they jumped into the cold water. With each class that followed, the kids got younger and the sun rose higher. The mist rose off the lake and disappeared. By noon, I was finished and the afternoon was mine. Summer was officially here.

But the hours stretched out in front of me with nothing to do. I was already restless, bored. Matt had always worked long hours with his dad in the summer, but Cassie was usually around. We should be buzzing down the lake in her boat, I thought. I wondered what she was doing in England right now. Not sitting alone on a beach, I was sure of that.

"Hey, Katie."

The voice startled me. Turning, I squinted into the sun. Alec Osborne stood against the chain-link fence that separated the beach from the lake road, smiling at me.

"Hey," I said, surprised.

Weird. If we'd passed each other in the hall at school just two weeks before, we wouldn't have said a word. But here, surrounded by mothers and little kids, we were the only two from our high school anywhere in sight, and he was standing three feet away from me. Here, it would be rude not to.

"What are you doing out here?" I asked. It was a perfectly normal question. There was nothing to do in Westland, nothing you couldn't do in Deerfield, anyway, a town four or five times the size of ours.

Alec placed his hands on the fence and swung both legs over in a single, graceful leap. "I've got a job fixing up a stone wall that got mauled by a snowplow last winter." He dropped a backpack onto the sand. "I've got a little business," he said.

"Landscaping, light maintenance work. Whatever people want, really."

He took a couple steps and sat down next to my towel, which surprised me even more than the fact that I was having a conversation with him.

"You get to make your own hours, then."

"Yeah, that's the best part," he said. "Green feet are the only drawback."

We both looked at his feet at the same time; then he caught my eye and we laughed.

"I've only had these sneakers for a couple weeks. You'd never know it." He flipped off his shoes, peeled away sweaty socks covered in grass stains and dirt, and wiggled his toes.

"Want to go for a swim?" His smile was warm, disarming.

I couldn't think of a single reason why not.

"Ladies first," he said. I took the lead off the diving board and he followed, both of us coming up for air near the chain of buoys that encircled the swimming area.

"You're a good diver," he said.

"I practice. Matt coaches me—so he likes to think." I laughed and treaded water. "He dives like a frog, so what does he know?"

Alec's head bobbed, his eyes scanning the trees on the far side of the lake.

"You ever swim across?" he asked.

"Sure. All the time."

"Let's go," he said, and started swimming before I could reply.

Sitting in the shallow water on the other side, Alec stretched his arms up toward the sky, then sat back. "Nice swim," he said. "It'd be tough getting across the lake in Deerfield. It's, like, three miles wide. This is like having your own private beach." He gazed down the long lake, then turned back to me. "So, where do you live?"

"Not too far. Caton Road. It's just past the store, a mile or so from here."

Alec nodded, like he knew where I meant. "We built a new house a couple miles from school, in Deerfield. It's a new development. My stepmother's dream house, supposedly. She's got her pool now, but who wants to swim in chlorine with all these lakes around? All she does in the summer is sit by that pool and tell me what to do."

"You don't sound like you like her very much."

"She's a bitch," he said.

I looked away. It was a harsh word to describe your mother, *step* or not.

"Where does your real mother live?"

"She's dead."

Across the lake, little kids screeched and splashed each other, their voices carrying across the smooth surface of the water. What should I say? What *could* I say?

"I'm sorry."

"It was a long time ago," he said. "I was four."

"I'm really sorry," I said again. "Losing a parent—that's . . . it's awful." My voice faded to a whisper. "It's the worst."

I should know, I thought, and a familiar feeling gripped me, a fist clenched tight in my gut. For a moment, the lake—everything around me—disappeared. I was free-falling into a gaping dark space where nothing lived, a hollow place that nothing could fill.

My father had pulled his truck out of our driveway five years before, after a fight with my mother, and vanished. There had been one card, on my brother's birthday, then nothing. Nothing. I didn't know if he was dead, but sometimes believing he was beat the alternative—that he hated us enough to leave and never look back.

"Ever go out to that island?" Alec asked.

"What?" I blinked and looked where Alec was pointing.

Off to our right the land opened and the water spread out a mile wide. In the middle, a small, tree-covered island rose up, an oasis of green in the deep blue water.

"Yeah," I said. "Matt likes to shoot pictures out there."

"Sounds nice." Alec caught my eye and held it. My face flushed and I glanced down quickly. The memory of Alec looking up the lake road at me the day before zipped through my mind and disappeared.

"Your dad took off, didn't he?" Alec said.

I nodded, then turned away, silent. You don't have to open your mouth in a small town. Everybody knows everything about you, anyway.

When I turned back, he studied my face. "I thought I heard that," he said. "That sucks."

For moment, our eyes met.

"Let's go back," I said, and dove into the water.

Emerging from the lake, Alec not far behind, I spotted Matt through the trees. Leaning against his skateboard, he stood glaring at Alec.

"Matt!" I called.

"Hey, Matt," Alec said, shaking water from his hair. "Nice board."

Matt didn't reply. For an instant no one spoke.

"You got back early," I said. "Want to go swimming?"

Matt looked at Alec, then back at me. Silence.

"Want to go for a swim or *what*?" I asked him again.

"I've got a lawn to do," Alec said. "I'll see you later." He walked toward the spot where his backpack sat next to mine on the beach.

"See you," I said.

Alec had hopped the fence and reached his truck before Matt spoke. "What the hell was *that*?"

"Yeah, what the hell *was* that?" I said.

"*You* don't like him either. Or, you didn't last time I knew."

"He just showed up here, Matt. He asked me to swim across. It was no big deal. There was nobody else around."

"He's an idiot," Matt said.

"How do you know? Do you even know the guy?" My words surprised me, even as they spilled out of my mouth.

"What's to know? The way he struts down the hall at school?

The way he uses girls? The way his buddy Scott Richardson tried to kill me in seventh grade by suffocating me in a snowbank?"

"That his mother died when he was four?" I said.

Matt looked at me like I had lost my mind. "And *that* means . . . ?"

"It means you might not know him as well as you think you do. Maybe *none* of us do." I turned and walked across the beach toward my things, then headed for my bike. I was tired and hungry and irritable. I didn't want to think about dead mothers or disappearing fathers or argue with Matt about who was—or wasn't—a nice guy. When Matt had an opinion, he stuck with it. There was no use arguing, anyway. Especially over Alec Osborne.

I climbed onto my bike and rode away without waiting for him, but Matt followed, pushing hard with his back foot to pick up speed until his skateboard rumbled along beside me. We passed Cassie's house, then turned onto Main Street, where the store, the church, the town hall, and the post office sat clustered around an island of green and a statue of a Civil War soldier. Five minutes later, we turned down the dead-end road where we lived.

"Katie!" Matt called after me as I sped ahead of him. I'd reached the spot where the road separated our two houses. I stopped and turned to look at him.

"I'm sorry," he said. "It's not your fault Alec showed up."

Matt's face was grim. I thought about what he'd said back at

the beach, about Scott trying to suffocate him in that snowbank—
his buddy Scott, he'd said. They were best friends, Scott and Alec,
practically inseparable at school. None of us—Cassie, me, Matt—
ever liked them. But with Matt, it went deeper. To Matt, anyone
who hung out with Scott Richardson was a bully, too.

"It's okay," I said.

I looked at my empty house, a small Cape, at least a hundred
and fifty years old, paint peeling, windows black against the late
afternoon sunlight. A hollow feeling crept through me.

Matt's eyes followed mine. He knew I hated staying home
alone at night, knew I'd rather do anything else—even work—
to avoid it. But my night job at the Big Scoop hadn't started yet.

"Sorry I can't hang out tonight," Matt said. "I've got to
work. . . ."

"I know."

"Is Will at the McSherrys'?"

"Yeah." My little brother would spend the night at his best
friend's house again. He stayed there a lot these days. The
McSherrys had a barn full of animals and five kids—what was
one more? They loved having him. And who could blame Will
for wanting to be part of their family?

"Your mom working?" Matt asked.

I nodded. "Then at the boyfriend's."

Matt shook his head. "I'll come over if I get off early, okay?"
He reached out, wrapped his long arms around me, and squeezed
me tight.

I wondered if he knew how much I needed that.

3

Suddenly, Alec was everywhere.

That's how it seemed, anyway. He came to the beach a few more times that week, parking himself next to me in the sand like we were old friends, not two people who had coexisted at the same high school, at the same parties, for three years without speaking three words to each other. He showed up as I finished my last lesson, talked about rebuilding stone walls, and asked questions about teaching kids to swim. And he listened—like he was actually interested in how using a hoop helped get the littlest kids to dare put their faces under the water.

Who is *this guy?* I thought.

By three o'clock, he'd be gone, his *siesta* as he called it, over, and missing Matt by a half hour.

Now he was at the Big Scoop, his blond hair visible above the crowd, his glance catching my eye across the room as he talked to a couple of my field hockey buddies: Megan, our goalie, and Cheryl Cooper, varsity sweeper. During the school year,

Megan, Cheryl, Cassie, and I hung out, went to the same parties. Megan was the class ringleader—if she hadn't made the party happen, she was the first one to know: when, where, who. Then she spread the word.

Cheryl was Megan's silent sidekick. Moonfaced and muscular, with short blond hair, Cheryl was more a presence than a personality. As our sweeper, she stoically defended the expanse of field in front of Megan's goal and was the last line of defense a player had to get through before she could get at Megan. Cheryl's steady, reliable, no-flash play caught opponents off guard because she was also fiercely determined—and she *won*. Her dependable defense had earned her the nickname "the Rock."

"You can't score without getting past *the Rock*, and *the Rock* ain't moving," we liked to say.

Stiflingly hot and packed with customers, the Big Scoop was deafeningly noisy. I leaned my head toward the opening in the glass window, hoping to better hear what the customer in front of me was trying to order. Behind her, I saw our hockey coach, Coach Riley. Her face lit up when she saw me; she smiled and waved. Her skin already tanned, her gray hair cropped short, she stepped up to the counter next.

"You girls should get together this summer and scrimmage," she said after she'd ordered, nodding toward my teammates. "You'll be that much stronger come fall."

We were favored to win our division title this year, and we all wanted it as much as Coach Riley did. "That would be great," I said. "We just need to figure out a time when no one's working."

"It can't be an official practice or we're breaking the rules. You girls will have to do it yourselves."

"We'll figure it out." Smiling, I handed her a cone. "I'll call everyone," I said—and I would. It wasn't just the division title I wanted, it was the state title. This was our senior year, and we were going to get it.

That night after work, I drove out to Cheryl's summer camp on Sunset Lake in Deerfield. Her parents were away for a few days, and cars already crowded the dirt road and tiny driveway near the cabin. A steady thud of music carried from the screened porch out across the lake.

In the kitchen, ice and beer filled the sink. I opened one and took a long pull. With each swig, the tension flowed out of my body a bit more. There was nothing like a beer to end the day. I loved the feel of the bubbles going down my throat, the warmth that spread through my belly.

With each beer, my mind let go a little bit, too, my worries fading away. So what if I went home to an empty house? Who cared if my mother wanted to be with her new boyfriend more than she wanted to be with her own kids? By the third beer, the hollow space in my gut, that space that I dreaded more than anything, had disappeared.

Alec came up behind me, put his hand on my right bicep, and squeezed. "Scooping all that ice cream's a workout. You should alternate arms—it's better than free weights."

"No kidding," I said, and laughed, heat rising in my cheeks.

"You guys are set up to be state champions in hockey this year," he said, leaning back against the pine paneling.

"You think?"

"Are you kidding? No contest. Especially with scorers like you and Cassie. Isn't Yarmouth losing, like, seven seniors from last year? They were your only real challenge."

"You're right," I said. "I can't believe you know that."

"I was at all your games last year. You should pay more attention to your fans," he said.

"I will." He caught my eye, and I looked away.

Out on the porch, a game of quarters was in full swing. "Martin's up next," Megan hollered. "Where's Katie Martin?"

"Looks like you're wanted," Alec said.

"Nah, I've got to work in the morning. I shouldn't even be here."

"Katie!" It was Megan again.

"What the hell," I said. "One round won't hurt." I moved out onto the porch with the others.

"What *time* is it?" I said to no one in particular, weaving toward my car in the dark behind the camp.

Suddenly, Alec was there again. *Omnipresent Alec*, I thought to myself, laughing silently at my own little joke.

"It's after one," he said, falling into step beside me. "What's your curfew?"

"No curfew," I said, my words a childish singsong. "Nobody home, nobody cares."

He took the keys out of my hand. "You can't drive like that."

"I can drive fine."

"I'm taking you. We'll pick up your car tomorrow."

I looked at him; I could barely make out his face in the dark. He took my elbow and steered me toward his truck. *Whatever*, I thought, letting him guide me. All I really wanted was to sleep.

The next morning I slept through my alarm. Swinging my backpack over my shoulder, I pulled my bike out of the barn, hopped on it as I ran, and rode off toward the beach.

Stupid, stupid, stupid, I thought as I wheeled around the corner and down Lake Road. If I had my car, I'd be driving it right now. I loved riding my bike; it was exhilarating, especially in the early mornings. It was great exercise, too—part of my plan to keep in shape for field hockey. But it was too late for even a fast bike ride to the beach this morning. I hadn't been thinking straight. I hadn't been thinking *period*.

I glanced at my watch. It was past seven already. Why had I taken this stupid job, anyway? Who gets up at six thirty when there's no school? The parents who had dragged their kids out of bed for Junior Lifesaving and driven them to the beach at this hour would not be pleased. I looked at my watch again: eight minutes late and counting.

I leaped off my bike at ten past. "Sorry," I said to whoever was listening.

Will stood among his friends, looking puzzled and then slightly embarrassed. Parents in sweatshirts and shorts sat at a picnic table, drinking coffee from Styrofoam cups. A couple of them glanced over at me, eyebrows raised.

"Get in the water. Hurry," I said to the kids. The parents would have to get over it—and so would Will. I'd never be late again.

I pulled down the shades, shutting out the harsh afternoon light. My head hurt, my stomach hurt—every part of me felt like crap. Alec had said he'd stop by the beach in the afternoon and take me to pick up my car, but I'd left minutes after my last lesson. If I was going to throw up, it would be in a cool, dark place of my own.

I had no idea how much time had passed when the phone rang, waking me. Pulling back a shade, I saw the light had faded slightly outside the window; the sun sat lower and to the west. Curled up on my bed, I'd been asleep for four hours. I reached the phone on its fifth ring.

Omnipresent Alec.

I felt terrible turning down Alec's offer of help, but I couldn't go get my car from Cheryl's camp, not now. Matt's family was expecting me for dinner in half an hour, and I'd promised Matt I'd look through his photographs with him after that. There were hundreds of them, and if he didn't start weeding them out now, he'd never have a portfolio ready when he needed it in the fall.

"No problem," Alec said. "Are you working tomorrow night? I could drive you out to Cheryl's before that. You'd get to work and have your car to drive home after your shift. I'll come by at three o'clock."

"You're amazing, Alec. *Thank* you," I said, and hung up.

Had I really just told Alec Osborne he was amazing?

"You look sick," Matt said. "You should go home."

"I'm okay," I said.

"You don't look okay. Even the twins noticed you hardly ate anything."

"I'm *fine*," I insisted, sitting down on his bed.

What else could I say? I could lie and tell him that I was sick—the flu or something—but I already felt bad enough without a lie to my best friend topping off my brilliant last twenty-four hours. But I couldn't tell him the truth: that I'd been out drinking until two in the morning, that I had the beer hangover from hell, and that I'd been so smashed the night before that Alec Osborne had driven me home—that, in fact, my car was still at Cheryl's camp.

No, that wouldn't fly with Matt. Never mind the Alec-driving-me-home part; Matt thought drinking was a complete waste of time. If I told him the truth, I'd have to listen to another one of his drinking-is-for-idiots speeches. Even without a pounding headache, I couldn't endure that.

Besides, this was important. Photography was to Matt what field hockey was to me—his passion, maybe even his future. He'd been snapping pictures for years, and right from the start he'd had an eye for unusual things. He'd shoot a bug from inches away, or a crumpled candy wrapper, or a drain pipe that ran down the wall of our school. He'd lie down on the ground and take a picture of the side of the building, looking *up*.

He knew going to art school was probably crazy, that the chances of making a living taking pictures was pretty slim, and that his parents worried about that. But he had to try. Selecting photos for a portfolio was the first step.

I took a sip of water from the glass I clutched and tried once again not to throw up. "Come on," I said to Matt. "Let's look at some pictures."

"This could use a little trim," Alec said. He was standing on the edge of my overgrown lawn the next day. Neglected for two weeks, the grass had become overrun with hundreds of bright yellow dandelions.

"Yeah, a *little* one," I said.

He laughed. "You ready?"

Alec's unmistakable blue and silver pickup truck, lawn mower in the back, sat like a circus elephant in the driveway. I might as well have had a loudspeaker pointed at Matt's house blaring the news of Alec's appearance at my house. Matt and his father were not yet home, but the sooner we left, the better.

"Thanks again," I said as we pulled out of the driveway. "My mom is never around, and I wouldn't have had any other way to get to work tonight."

"Where's your mom?" he asked.

"She's a nurse in Portland. Maine Medical pays better, especially when she works nights and overtime, and she's trying to save for my college. In case I don't get a scholarship."

"For field hockey?" He caught my eye. "You'll get it," he said, like he knew—just *knew*—I would. Why did *he* have such confidence in me?

It was like he could read my thoughts. "I've seen you play plenty of times," he added. "Believe me, you'll get one."

"Anyway, my mom is stressed out about paying for my college."

"She's got a long commute."

"She doesn't drive it every day. She started staying down there after she met this doctor. We hardly see her anymore."

"I hope you like him better than I like my stepmother," he said, turning onto the main road.

"No worries there. I never even met him. A couple years ago, she started going on this dating spree. The guy she sees now is, like, doctor number five or six. I met one of them once—he actually came out here—but then she broke up with him for a surgeon. It turned out later that he was married."

"The one she broke up with?"

"No, *he* was nice. The surgeon." *Why was I talking so much?*

The windows were down, but it was hot and sticky. Maples and oaks, their lush, green leaves heavy in the dead air, stood motionless in rolling fields. The occasional house rushed by. In between, long stretches of pines and birches closed in around the road, a thick, scraggly forest grown in where farmland used to be. Alec turned on the air conditioner and we closed the windows, racing silently along the bumpy back roads toward Deerfield.

"What's your stepmother like?" I said finally.

"She never changes." In Deerfield now, we pulled onto the narrow dirt road that led to Cheryl's camp. "She moved in, like, the day after my mother died, and she's been a pain in the ass ever since." He glanced over at me. "When she first came home with my dad, I thought she was the maid or something—no joke. What does a four-year-old know? One day my mom was in the hospital, the next day she was gone."

"That's awful, Alec."

He parked in the tiny dirt driveway at Cheryl's camp; we climbed out of the truck and walked down toward the water.

"My dad married her right away," Alec said. "It turned out, she'd worked with him for years—was his *secretary* or some bullshit cliché like that. They'd known each other way before my mom got sick. I hated her for that. Just fucking hated her. It got so bad that in eighth grade she tried to sign me up for boarding school. Part of me wanted to go just to get out of the house. We looked at some good schools. I could have played on a better football team, gotten into a better college."

"Why didn't you go and get away from her?"

"I almost left. But then I thought, why should I let her drive me out of my own house?" He paused and skipped a rock across the lake's surface. "I stayed around just to spite her."

The rock hopped six times and disappeared into the water.

"I'll be out of here next year for college, and I don't care if I never see this place again," he said.

I looked out across the shimmering lake and couldn't

imagine ever feeling that way. "I love it here," I said softly, more to myself than to him.

He looked at me suddenly, as if he'd just remembered I was standing there. "You know what I mean," he said. "I can't wait to get out of my house."

That I could understand.

That night, I pulled into my driveway just after midnight. My headlights swung across the lawn, landing on my empty house. Coming home late at night still spooked me, and I'd been so anxious about Alec picking me up that I'd forgotten to leave the porch light on.

I shut off the car but left on the headlights, my heart picking up speed. Something was different, not as I had left it; I could feel it. I ran for the door, flicked on the kitchen and porch lights, and ran back to the car. Stopping short on the edge of the lawn, I realized what it was: the grass.

The grass, which eight hours earlier had been a rough mess, up above my ankles, had been trimmed down to a smooth three inches. *Matt?* I thought. It was something he would do, knowing how busy I was with two jobs. I looked at his house and smiled. Who else would do such a nice thing unasked?

But as I walked back toward the house, an image of a blue and silver pickup truck, lawn mower in the back, crept into my mind and lingered.

Alec?

Will dashed past me, feet pounding across our porch's old floor-boards. Leaping over the granite steps, he landed with a thud on the grass and ran toward the car idling in our driveway, his best friend, Ben, in the backseat.

"Hey, get back here!" I called after him.

Will tossed his duffel bag on the ground next to the car and turned toward me, rolling his eyes.

"No leaving until you hug your big sister. That's the rule," I said sternly.

Will made his way back to me, dragging his feet in a display of exaggerated hardship. "Do I *have* to?"

"You do." I hugged him, then looked him straight in the eye. "Behave yourself," I said. "These are nice people."

Will rolled his eyes again, but we both cracked a smile. This was our routine. Of course he'd behave himself at the McSherrys. But I was one of Will's moms, too.

"Okay if we keep him a couple of nights?" Mr. McSherry

asked. He knew I worried about leaving Will home alone when I worked at night.

"Sure," I said. "Thank you."

"Call us if you need anything at all," he said, and met my eyes before they pulled away. The McSherrys worried about me, too.

The trim grass felt cool between my toes. I glanced at the small perennial garden my mother had planted years ago—it had been weeded, too, by whoever mowed the night before—and walked around the perimeter of the house. *What would my father think if he saw our house like this*, I wondered. The white paint was chipped and peeling, and a hole in the screen door had been patched up with thick gray electrical tape to keep the bugs out. My mother said he was lazy, but at least he'd kept the place up. I ran my fingers along the wood and wondered if I could somehow handle the job of scraping and painting it myself.

But who was I kidding? I couldn't even manage to get the lawn mowed. It was evening now, and I still had no idea if Matt or Alec had done it. I'd called my mother to ask her if she'd paid someone to do it, and she'd laughed.

"*Paid* to have the lawn cut and the garden weeded? We're not the hired help kind of people, Katie. Where'd you get an idea like that?"

"Never mind" was all I said.

Above Matt's house, the sky turned pale gold, then dusky blue. The only sound besides the peepers was a car in the distance, moving slowly down the road that ran by our houses. There was no traffic through here; about fifty yards beyond us, the road turned to dirt. Matt was at work. One of his parents was coming home, I figured.

A moment later Alec's pickup truck appeared, the handle of his lawn mower poking up high above the bed of the truck. Alec hadn't come to the beach that day, but here he was now, at my house—just showing up. My heart skipped a beat. Why was he here?

His smile was easy when he climbed out of the cab. "I don't suppose you've got a glass of ice water for a desperate man? Today was a scorcher."

"Sure. Sit down on the screened porch away from the bugs. I'll be right back."

Inside the house, I turned off the music I'd left repeating on the CD player an hour ago. Not many kids my age listened to Janis Joplin—or even knew who she was. I imagined he didn't either.

In the small mirror over the kitchen sink, I caught a glimpse of myself. I'd had no shower after the beach, leaving my dark hair curlier than usual. Running my fingers through it made it worse. A stray elastic I found next to the dish soap would have to do; I pulled it up quickly. Who was I kidding, anyway? I was a lost cause, at least for tonight. And why did I even care?

Back on the porch, I handed Alec a tall glass and switched on the fan that sat atop a table in the corner. A breeze wafted across the porch.

"Nice," he said, looking around. "I bet you spend a lot of time out here."

"This is my favorite place in the house," I said. "Sometimes I even sleep out here," I said, then wished I hadn't. I could feel my face coloring. "When my mother's home, anyway," I added.

"Actually, if you're not expecting your mom anytime soon, I've got a cooler in the truck. . . . Care for a beer?"

I hesitated. A beer sounded great right now. I glanced across the street at Matt's house. Lights had flicked on, and no one lingered outside. Matt was busing tables at McCormick's.

"Why not?" I said.

We drained our water glasses. Alec poured the beer and then tucked the empties back into his cooler. I took a sip. It tasted great, ice cold. It flowed through my body, relaxing every limb. Nothing calmed me like a drink. Beer, vodka, wine—it didn't matter; it all did the same thing. Anxiety drifted away, words came more easily. For a fleeting moment, all seemed right in the world.

"Oh my God," I said suddenly, like I'd forgotten something of vast importance. "Did you . . . ?"

"What?"

My face flushed. "Never mind . . ."

He grinned. "Your lawn? You're welcome."

"I meant to ask you at the beach today, but you weren't there."

"How'd you know it was me?"

"I didn't, really. But I don't know a lot of guys who are driving around Westland this summer with lawn mowers in the back of their trucks." I smiled. "I really appreciate it. I don't have much time with my two jobs."

"That's what I figured."

"And weeding the garden . . ."

"It was no problem—really. Glad to help."

"Well, thank you."

Alec held up his hand to stop me. *Don't gush*, I thought to myself. He'd meant it when he said it was no problem, I could tell. Sure, it was something Matt would've done, but I was used to Matt. Alec's help had come out of nowhere.

Alec sipped his beer. The sun had turned his face brown, and his blue eyes were a startling contrast. He was so comfortable, so relaxed here on my porch, his legs stretched out casually across the floorboards in front of his chair. There was something disarming about that, about his ease with me. It put me at ease, too.

The sky was dark now. I turned on a light and got a bag of chips from the kitchen. Alec poured two more beers.

"So what were you listening to when I showed up?" he asked.

"Oh, old stuff—Janis Joplin. You probably never heard of her."

"I have. I just never really knew what she did."

"She's great," I said. "I discovered her in my dad's old record collection years ago. Now I think I have everything she recorded before she died."

"Show me sometime?"

"The collection? Sure."

We talked about music—who we liked, who we didn't. I said the Fly was the best band in the world, and he agreed.

"I heard they're coming here this fall, to Portland. Cassie and I are getting tickets no matter what."

"Good luck," he said, and laughed. "Everybody's saying that."

The moon rose in the sky, higher and higher above Matt's house. It was late now, but I didn't care. The fan purred in the corner, rotating on its base, blowing warm air. It was easy sitting here with Alec, easy talking to him. I put my feet up on a nearby chair, and Alec poured me a third beer.

We sat quietly for a long time, the summer night still and quiet, no sounds but the fan whirring and the peepers peeping in the pond behind Matt's house.

Then I felt his gaze, his eyes on my face. He was studying me, taking me in.

"So, your mom's never here," he said finally. "Do you ever see your dad?"

"My dad?" There was a familiar ache in my throat the second I said the words.

"Yeah," he said quietly.

"He's gone. He took off." Alec knew that much already.

He nodded, waited.

I looked away. When was the last time someone had asked me about my father? When was the last time someone had really wanted to know? Cassie, probably, when she'd moved here. But that was years ago. I wasn't used to talking about my dad.

I looked out into the darkness. The beer was cold in my hand. Drops of moisture trickled off the glass and onto my leg. Alec was looking at me, waiting patiently, waiting like he had all the time in the world and would gladly give it to me.

No, I hadn't talked about my father in a very long time. But that night, to my surprise, I did.

* * *

The day my father left had been an ordinary day in November: cold, rainy, bitter. The unraked leaves clumped like mushy brown pancakes on the dying grass. I was twelve, in the middle of seventh grade; Will was just six. My father was lying on the couch watching football, empty beer cans cluttering the coffee table in front of him, while my mother sped around the house on her day off from the local hospital, vacuuming, doing laundry. The last time I'd walked by him, he'd been asleep, mouth half-open, snoring loudly.

The rain had gotten us off the hook with stacking the woodpile that day, but Mom asked us to go upstairs, clean our rooms, and strip our beds. Downstairs, I heard voices rising. I threw my sheets in a pile on the floor and shut out the sound of their words.

There were some loud bangs, then the front door slammed, and my dad's truck revved up and sped out of the driveway. Standing by my bedroom window, I watched him pull away. For all I knew, he was headed to the store for another six-pack. I never in a million years thought that would be the last time I'd see him.

November passed painfully slowly that year, with no sign of him and no word. He'd left before, but the longest he'd ever gone missing was two and a half days. This time, it was like an alien spaceship had come down and just zapped him off the earth: there he was driving his truck, then *poof*, he was gone. Vanished. He left no trail.

A week passed, then another, and another. I was convinced my father would have come home by now if he could and that something terrible must have happened to him—something we knew nothing about. But my mother had different ideas. She called him Mr. Undependable and talked like he'd show up any day now, the way he had in the past. I was furious at her for not worrying, too.

When Will and I begged her to call the police, she'd say, "They know about your father. Believe me, he'll show up when he's good and ready and not a minute sooner."

Those first few weeks, Mom had a sharp gleam in her eye. She was ready to blow. Will and I could both feel it. But by January she was scared, too. Her hands shook when she put our dinner on the table and washed the dishes. Mail had stacked up on the counter, unopened. She'd look at it out of the corner of her eye, sometimes even shuffle through it, but then she'd throw it down, pour a glass of wine, and sit on the couch, staring into space. Without our father, she couldn't pay all the bills that were piling up, and she swore the refrigerator, which had been rumbling loudly for several weeks, was about to die. She had been biding her time until he would walk through that door and she could let him have it. But she was beginning to wonder if he was ever going to show up at all.

When Will and I worried that he'd been hurt in an accident, my mother claimed my father was alive and well, that much she knew, though she insisted he'd never contacted her. As the months passed, we convinced ourselves he had to be dead—until

Will got a birthday card from him in April. Mom never showed us the envelope. She claimed he hadn't settled anywhere yet, so the postmark made no difference.

"It was from one of those Midwest states," she said. "I can't even remember which one." She handed the card to Will and walked away.

The spring after my father left, Ron Bailey started coming around to visit my mom. They'd known each other all their lives, graduated from high school together just two years before I was born. Mom said he'd asked her to go out with him a few times when they were teenagers, but she'd always put him off.

"I guess he just wasn't exciting enough for me," she said. Her anger over my father had drained her; she was quiet now, depressed. On her days off, she lay in her room, coming downstairs only to pour herself another glass of wine. Empty bottles piled up in the recycling bin; dishes and laundry went undone. Some days, she didn't even bother to get dressed.

"Will you go out with Ron now?" I asked.

"What makes you think he asked me?" She turned her head away and lay back on her pillow.

"I'm not stupid, Mom," I said.

"You know," she said, "I think I just might."

It was not the answer I wanted. I liked him and everything, but my father had been gone less than eight months, and if he came back and Mom was dating Ron Bailey, my father might just turn around and leave again. The truth was, I had a secret fantasy—bigger than getting a birthday card from my father in the mail. In my daydream, my father would make a grand entrance at my birthday party in June. He'd arrive looking healthy and handsome, bearing gifts, good excuses, and pleas for forgiveness. Ron just wasn't part of the family reunion I had in mind.

She went out with Ron a few times despite me. I glared at him when he came to the house and refused to talk to him, infuriating my mother.

"Katie Martin, you stop acting rude," she'd say, when he was standing right there.

"It's okay, Sandra," he'd say softly, compassion in his eyes.

There was a lot about Ron Bailey I liked, though I couldn't admit it. But my mother broke it off after a few weeks, anyhow.

"I'm not ready for a man in my life," she'd said. And that was the end of it.

When my birthday finally came and went and my father didn't even send a card, I spent the whole night locked in my room, crying.

My mother stood outside my door, knocking and questioning me impatiently.

"What's wrong, Katie? For God's sake . . . Did something happen today?"

I wasn't going to tell her my dream about my dad. It was obvious she wouldn't get it. It was my first birthday after he'd left, and she had to ask me what was wrong? No, I wasn't going to tell her. I wasn't going to tell anyone.

I tucked inside myself, like a turtle retreating into her shell.

I protected my brother and kept to myself. I stopped mentioning my father's name.

No one would know how I felt about my dad but me.

I got up abruptly and left Alec on the porch, taking the empty potato chip bag into the kitchen. Talking about my father made my throat ache. I wanted to go to bed, to be by myself. I'd never meant to say half as much as I did, and now I felt exposed, stripped to the core. I threw some empty beer bottles into the recycling bin. Who cared if my mother saw them? She barely lived here. As far as I was concerned, what I did was no longer any of her business.

Alec had followed me silently into the kitchen. Washing the glasses at the sink, I sensed him behind me, then felt his hands rest gently on my shoulders. I paused, my hands trembling, afraid I'd start to cry, but I had to do something. I turned and looked into his face.

"I didn't mean to upset you," he said, "talking about your dad."

"I did all the talking," I whispered, my voice unsteady. "Not your fault."

His hands fell down around my waist. I took a deep breath, and we looked at each other. It felt like we'd been friends for a very long time. We understood each other; we both felt it. I looked away, and for some time we just stood there in my kitchen, until my body relaxed into his and he held me.

When we kissed, it was long and slow. A river of heat flowed through me, a powerful yearning. I reached for him, pulling him close, and he lifted me up onto the counter, his lips brushing my hair, my cheeks, my neck. His fingers, rough from yard work, slipped across my belly, lifting up my bra until he could slide one hand, then the other, underneath it. I exhaled, my face lost in his soft hair.

"Let's go upstairs," he whispered, and suddenly everything was moving too fast.

Is Matt home? I wondered. And then Matt's voice sounded in my head, refusing to shut up: *I can't stand that guy.*

"You should go," I said.

Alec paused. "Are you sure?"

I nodded.

He took my hand and led me back out to the porch. There, he kissed me again, picked up his cooler, and headed for his truck. "I'll call you," he said.

Across the street, a light flicked on in Matt's house. My eyes fell to his driveway. Sitting in the dark was the car Matt had driven to work that night. He was home.

He couldn't have missed Alec's truck in front of my house. He'd probably even seen us kiss on the porch. *He'll flip out,* I thought. And for a moment I wanted to take back the whole night, start it all over again from the minute Will got in the McSherrys' car and left. I'd hide in my room when Alec pulled into my driveway, pretend I wasn't home. I'd read a book, go to bed early. And in the morning, Matt and I would still be best friends who had no use for Alec Osborne. Nothing would change.

I touched my lips, still swollen from kissing. It was too late for that.

6

Sun streamed through my bedroom window. I blinked and ran through the night before in my mind. Alec on my porch. Alec in my kitchen. Alec saying *Let's go upstairs.*

Well, at least I hadn't done that.

Not that part of me hadn't wanted to. *A big part,* I thought. But Matt—I couldn't stop thinking about what he'd say. And I'd always sworn to Cassie that I was going to wait for the right guy, the right time, the right place; that I wasn't going to do it in some backseat with just anyone, you know? My parents may have screwed up their relationship, but I still believed in love. I was holding out for the real thing.

A wave of butterflies sailed through me. What was I feeling? Excitement? Anxiety? Some bizarre mix of the two?

My heart knocked heavily in my chest.

Downstairs, my eyes rested on the kitchen counter. Had I really sat there, making out with Alec? What had I done? What was I *doing*?

I had no idea.

I took a bowl of cereal out onto the porch and sat. It was ten o'clock, the sky perfectly blue in the morning light. I longed to talk to Cassie. If anyone could help me, she could. Matt was immovable when it came to Alec or any of his friends—but Cassie? She'd talk it over with me, help me figure this out. That's how she approached things. And she'd listen.

We'd made fun of Alec together, Cassie and me. "Part the Red Sea, Moses—they're coming through!" Cassie would say in her southern preacher imitation when Alec and his buddies came marching down the hall in a pack, Alec in the lead, so smug, Scott smirking at his side.

I'd burst out laughing, but Matt would just glare at them.

How long ago had that been? Two months? Three?

But everything was different now. I'd told Alec all about my father, and he'd listened so well, had understood when I'd gotten upset. His mother had left, too, just in a different way. The pain, the empty place inside that never goes away—he knew those things. For once, I felt like someone understood—not just because they were my friend and wanted to understand, but because they'd *been* there. That was the relief: talking to someone who'd been there, too.

Maybe this all made sense. Maybe there weren't two Alecs, the one from school and the one I knew this summer. Maybe the way Alec acted at school was a cover-up, a way of keeping people at bay, a misguided attempt to look normal and *be* normal when only he knew how empty he felt. I could understand that: I lived it.

Across the street, Matt appeared and waved. In a couple hours, we'd be packing up for the camping trip we were taking out to the island. We'd been planning it since we'd managed to get the same night off. If Matt had seen Alec at my house, there'd be no escaping an argument.

I had to try to make him understand.

"He's after you," Matt said quietly, his eyes fixed on the water that stretched from the beach outward to the circle of buoys.

I pulled my paddle through the water, propelling us forward. Behind me, in the middle of the canoe, a couple of daypacks, two sleeping bags, a two-man tent, and way more food than we needed for one night lay piled in a heap.

"What?" I wasn't sure I'd heard him right.

"Alec."

At three o'clock, it was still hot, the beach still crowded with kids, their shouts ricocheting across the lake. My eyes scanned the water as we passed. There—what Matt saw: Alec's head bobbing up and down out beyond the diving board.

"He's not usually here on Saturday," I said, then realized my mistake.

But he didn't seem to hear me. Alec had Matt's full attention. "He sees us," Matt said.

I lifted a hand high to wave, but Alec, who appeared to be staring right at us, turned and swam toward shore. My stomach knotted; I looked away.

"Cocky bastard," Matt said.

"He just didn't see us, Matt."

"How could he *not*?"

Above our heads, the late afternoon sun shone. Ahead, the lake opened wide, our island in the middle of all that blue, tiny waves lapping its shore.

"He was at your house last night and now he acts like he doesn't see you."

My heart dropped. So he knew. "It's no big deal—it was no big deal last night."

"I doubt that," Matt said, but it was more to himself than to me.

We didn't speak for several minutes after that; we didn't need to. It was a silent truce. A temporary truce. Warm wind blew through my hair. I took the paddle out of the water and rested.

"Mind if we float?" I looked back at Matt. "It's so beautiful."

He shook his head.

I lay back on our gear and closed my eyes. I cared what Matt thought—that was the problem. His opinion, his friendship—those things meant something to me. He was one of the most caring people I knew, but he was also solid, unflappable. He had his head on straight; his own mother even said so.

Matt was the first person I ever talked to about my father leaving, all those years ago. I'd kept it inside for months, all through the long, horrible school year that was seventh grade. I hadn't talked, and nobody had asked. Not nicely, anyway, not in a way that made you want to tell them how it felt to have your father just walk out and never come back or call or write or tell you that he was alive or why he did it—just left you to think it was because of *you.*

But that summer after seventh grade, Matt did.

"Your parents got divorced this year, huh?" Matt had said, tilting his head to one side. We'd been at the beach on a bench that's away from the swimming area, shaded by some trees.

"Yeah, I guess so. I mean, my father left last November." My throat tightened and ached.

"Do you see him ever?" Matt asked.

"Not really, not much. No."

He kept quiet, just looking at me, waiting for me to speak again.

"Actually, not at all." I took a deep breath and blurted it out. "I don't even know where he is. I figure we'll maybe hear from him when he gets settled someplace. That's what my mom says."

"That must be hard," Matt said, like he meant it.

I stared at my left foot, which I was digging deep into the sand with my big toe. Tears had welled up in my eyes and I didn't want to look up. Neither one of us said anything for a few minutes. Then Matt asked me to go in the water.

I'd been so grateful. Grateful not only for the chance to escape into the water, but also that Matt knew what I needed at that moment—to escape to someplace I couldn't be seen.

The rest of that summer, Matt patiently walked to the mailbox with me day after day, watched me open it, and watched my eyes fill with tears. He learned to hate my father, hate what he'd done to me. He had no patience for that.

"What kind of father leaves his kids without telling them where he is?" Matt blurted out one day.

But I wasn't ready to hear bad things about my dad. It didn't fit with my dream of his coming back to us, like a white knight, with a perfectly good explanation for everything.

"There's a reason," I said, my voice trembling. "You'll see."

Matt pursed his lips and nodded, wrapped his arms around me, and held me tight. With Matt, I was always safe. I knew it then, and I knew it now.

With Alec, how could I be sure?

It was cool enough on the island to have a campfire without roasting ourselves, but just a small one. We'd dug a hole out there years ago, placed stones around the edge, and built our fires in the same spot ever since. With that burning slowly behind us, we lay near the edge of the water on a soft bed of rusty pine needles and watched the sun slip down behind the trees.

Matt lay on his side, propped up on one elbow, facing me. "My mom said Alec was out late mowing your lawn a few nights ago. You know, I would have done that for you. . . ."

"I didn't ask him to do it."

Matt looked away, shaking his head.

"He was just being nice, Matt. I mean, do you really know him?"

"I know enough."

"Like what?"

"Like the way he struts around school," Matt said. "The way

he talks about girls he goes out with. You should hear the things he says about Marcy."

"Marcy's crazy."

"Maybe so. But why go out with her if he doesn't even *like* her?"

"What could he say about me?" I said. "Nothing's even happened. Besides, maybe he's changed."

"Since baseball season? Don't be naive. And what actually happens has nothing to do with what he says."

How could I respond? I knew Alec's reputation. But the things I'd heard didn't match the person I'd been getting to know.

"I just want you to see what's going on, Katie. Alec is a guy who's used to getting what he wants when he wants it. Right now, he wants *you*."

Water lapped gently at the shore near my feet, a soft rhythm.

"Why?" I said quietly, more to myself than to Matt.

When I turned to him, his soft brown eyes searched my face. "You don't get it, do you?" he said.

I had no answer. It was true; I didn't.

"Why *wouldn't* he?"

I had no answer for that, either. I *didn't* understand why he was after me—if that's what it was. I was nothing like the girls he usually hooked up with. And why, if he had so many damn options, would he pick *me*?

I could look in the mirror and see that I was pretty—tall, slim, strong. Everyone said I had a beautiful smile. Cassie said

I looked like a young Courteney Cox. But to me, I was nothing special. I was the opposite of special. Sometimes I even wondered why Matt and Cassie put up with me.

My eyes met Matt's, and for a moment we just looked at each other. We were so familiar to each other, yet so different, too.

Matt had a big, close family. He complained sometimes that he couldn't get one minute alone without someone barging into his room. He didn't know what it was like to be so lonely you thought the hole in your gut would swallow you alive. He didn't understand desperation: how I just wanted to feel good, to feel *right*, for even a few minutes when I was off the playing field; how I hadn't felt right for a single day since my father left. He didn't understand how one drink could calm me down, how two could make the world seem okay, how three could make anything seem possible—or how easy the fourth and fifth and sixth went down until I lost count.

Matt was still looking at me; I could see his face in the fading light.

"You deserve way better than Alec," he said softly, and reached out for my hand.

A familiar lump lodged in my throat. Lying back on the smooth pine needles, my hand tight in his, Matt and I looked up and waited for the stars to emerge against the darkening sky.

Did I?

7

A few days after the camping trip, I got a phone call that changed everything.

It was the coach of the University of Maine field hockey team, Carol Hollyhock. Coach Riley had called her up and talked to her in the spring about my potential for a scholarship—I knew that. But this was different. This time Coach Hollyhock was calling *me*.

"I've heard some great things about you, Katie," she said, "and I'd like to see you play. We have a lot of athletes to visit in the fall, and I can't guarantee I'll personally get to one of your games. But I've talked to your coach at the high school about making a video tape so that we can see you one way or the other. Have you thought about playing for Maine?"

"Yeah," I said. I was so excited, I could barely catch my breath. "I've thought about it a lot. I mean, I'd really like to."

"Well, that's great to hear. Like I said, I've heard some very good things about you—and read about you, too. I know you've made the Maine All-Star Team the last two years, and First Team All-Conference as a freshman."

I couldn't believe she knew that.

"Actually, I saw you play last summer when you were on the Maine Event Team. I was surprised I didn't see you this June."

"I couldn't afford to travel with them this summer—plus I have two jobs."

"Well, I hope we can help you afford to come to Maine. You have an exceptional record. We keep an eye out for the best players in the state, Katie, and you're one of them."

"Thank you."

"I'll be in touch, okay? We'll see if we can get you up here to visit the campus, meet some of the other players this fall. Would you like to do that?"

"I'd love it."

"Great. We'll be in touch."

I hung up the phone, my heart pounding in my chest. I'd wanted this since the day I picked up my first hockey stick. I couldn't wait to tell Coach Riley, Matt—*everybody.*

"Wow!" Matt said. "I always said you'd play in the Olympics someday. You know, other coaches are going to call, too."

"I'm wicked nervous."

"Don't be. You'll be great. How many people even get this chance? All you have to do is play like you always do."

"Yeah. I just don't want to blow it, you know? I've been slacking off this summer, eating too much ice cream at work. I need to get in better shape."

"Go for it," Matt said. "When you want to do something, you've got more willpower than anyone I know."

Matt was right: When I put my mind to something, I did it. I was the master of fresh starts, the queen of turning over new leaves. Sure, I'd get off course, slack off in my classes, party too much, stop doing my homework for a while, but I always made a comeback. *Always*.

"I'm doing it," I said. And I meant it.

My alarm rang at five thirty the next morning. By five fifty, I was on the road. The rubber soles of my sneakers hit the pavement in a steady rhythm, breaking the silence.

In front of Westland's general store, workers pulled up in their pickup trucks and headed inside to grab a quick coffee and a doughnut. BAILEY'S HEATING AND PLUMBING arched across the side of a red truck, and Ron Bailey stepped out, clad head to foot in green work clothes. He looked at his watch and then at me.

"What you training for at this hour, girl, a marathon?" he said with a slow smile. He was always so nice. I wished now my mother would go back to dating *him*.

"Olympics." I grinned and sped on by.

I was a bird moving effortlessly through the cool morning air, soaring, on top of my game. By September, I'd be in the best shape of my life.

The phone call from U. Maine had given me just what I needed: a purpose. For three years, Coach Riley had told me I could get recruited if I worked hard, and she had always helped me whenever I needed her, working with me on my flick until the ball and cage disappeared in the dark, teaching me how to keep my head during a breakaway.

Once, when I was a freshman and my mother didn't show up to drive me home from practice, Coach Riley brought me all the way out to Westland herself.

My mother's car had been parked in the driveway when we pulled in.

"Mind if I come in for a minute?" Coach Riley asked.

"Okay," I said. The truth was, I didn't want her to meet my mother. It was bad enough that my mom forgot me, leaving me at the gym like I didn't exist. But how could I say no to Coach Riley after she'd driven me a half hour home?

Coach Riley was perfect. When my mom said she'd gotten hung up at work, Coach Riley didn't say, *Then why are you here and not on your way to get Katie?* Or, *Then why didn't you just call?* No, she just looked from the jug of wine on the counter to my mother's face to the glass in her hand, taking it all in.

Then she smiled and said, "You really should come and see Katie play sometime. She's exceptionally talented."

Exceptionally talented.

I was fourteen years old, and it was the nicest thing a grown-up had ever said to me. Every time I thought about why my dad had taken off and never bothered to call us or tell us where he lived, why my mother was never home long enough to know what the hell was going on with her own kids, why my only brother had basically moved into his best friend's house, I'd think, *Coach Riley thinks I'm exceptionally talented.*

It was something to hang on to. Sometimes it felt like the only thing.

Alec hadn't shown up at the beach in the week since my camping trip with Matt. Each day as I dove in alone and felt the cool water rush around my body, relief washed through me. I'd felt connected to Alec, that was true, but it didn't matter anymore. Maybe Matt was right about him, or maybe I was, but there was one thing I wasn't confused about: I wanted a full scholarship to a Division I school.

Nothing and nobody would divert me from that.

It was time to start playing. I pulled some teammates together and we met at the field a couple times a week, hitting the ball around, practicing corners, scrimmaging if we had enough bodies.

The first time, practically the whole team showed up. Megan, Cheryl, some sophomores competing for starting positions—even Marcy Mattison.

Marcy was a skilled halfback, but she had an attitude problem, too, and I worried about her impact on the team this year. With long, white-blond hair, high color in her cheeks, and striking green eyes, Marcy looked angelic, but anyone who knew her knew that was far from the truth. She was the only member of our team who'd ever gotten cards for misconduct—one for foul language and one for mouthing off to a ref—in two separate games the year before.

And for some reason, Marcy had never liked me.

Cassie always said she was jealous.

"Of *what?*" I'd asked.

"Of *everything*," Cassie replied. "That's just Marcy."

Never subtle, Marcy stood across the field that first afternoon, glaring at me.

Before, it didn't make sense, but now she had an actual reason to hate me: Alec. They'd been off and on constantly since freshman year. Off on Alec's terms—and on on his terms, too. He called the shots. She'd take him back in a heartbeat whenever he said the word. It was truly pathetic. And if a girl so much as flirted with him—and there were plenty who did—that girl was on Marcy's shit list for *life*. Apparently, I was now in that category.

On my nights off, I made dinner for Will and we'd rent a movie or, if it was hot, go for an evening swim. Sometimes I'd fall asleep in the middle of watching something with him and Will would nudge my arm, wake me up, and tell me I needed to go up to bed.

"You need your rest," he'd whisper, something he'd heard me say to him a thousand times over the years. He was excited about his big sister getting recruited for an athletic scholarship.

My mother was more pragmatic. "Try for the full scholarship, Katie. Lord knows we're going to need it to get you through school."

I knew she had one goal: to get me through college. How I got there didn't matter. Coach Riley telling her I was exceptionally talented hadn't gotten her attention—but a scholarship? That was something she could understand.

In the following weeks, I got another call, this one from the coach at the University of New Hampshire, then one from Syracuse, a letter from Holy Cross, and a follow-up letter from Maine. There were times I thought I must be dreaming, that the post office and the phone company had the wrong Katie Martin. How did these people know about me? Coaches from places I'd never been to or seen? I had to look on a map to find out where in New York State Syracuse was. I called Coach Riley and told her what was happening.

"How do they know I'm a good player?" I asked. "Some of them have never even seen me."

"It's their job to know," she said. "I'll be in my office today before you go to work. Come by if you can. I want to show you something."

Spread open on her desk when I arrived was a three-ring binder with my name on it, filled with news clippings about me—awards I'd received, all the games I'd played in. Articles from the *Portland Press Herald*, the *Lewiston Sun Journal*, and the *Greater Deerfield Weekly* were all in there, chronologically, going back three years. Every article I'd ever wished my father had seen about me was there.

"I've been saving these since I first saw you play." She looked up and smiled. "I had a feeling we might need them someday.

I made copies this spring and sent them around. I've talked to three of the coaches, too. As you know, they're interested."

Stunned, I flipped through the articles. I picked up one from the *Portland Press Herald*, written my freshman year right after we lost the state championship.

A freshman, Katie Martin, was Deerfield's leading scorer in regular season play, and notched the only goal the Eagles scored in today's tense 2–1 loss in the Class B finals. Martin is one of those rare few who is blessed with the mix of physical and mental skill that makes an exceptional athlete.

Coach Riley had highlighted the passage in yellow.

"Wow. Thank you so much. I don't know what to say."

"You don't need to say anything. It's been my pleasure." She grinned. "This is exciting for me, too."

"Thanks, Coach Riley. You're the best."

Alec hadn't stopped by the beach or called since my camping trip, and I figured he wasn't interested anymore, which made everything simple. I wrote it off as a summer fling, a fluke that would never have happened during the school year.

Sometimes I caught myself thinking about him, though. Sometimes when swimming lessons ended, I'd sit in the sand and remember how he looked when he walked into the water, his broad shoulders turned brown by the sun, his blond hair falling in his face as he looked back at me, motioning me to follow. I'd miss seeing his truck pull in just as my classes ended, knowing he was there because he wanted to see *me*.

But those things weren't enough. I had to focus. I didn't think he'd show up again, anyway. Whatever it was, it was over.

It was several days later when the phone rang.

"Why didn't you tell me?" It was Alec, and he sounded excited.

"Tell you what?"

"Tell me *what*? I ran into Megan. I heard you got some big news, that's what."

I told him everything that had happened: the letters, the calls, Coach Riley's folder, my training routine. The truth was, I was so excited, I would have told the mailman if he'd asked. But Alec was so enthusiastic, it made it fun.

"That is so cool," he said. "And it definitely calls for a celebration. There's a big party on Friday in Bethel. What do you say we make it your night?"

The words were out of my mouth before I had time to think.

"Sounds great."

8

Alec was at my door at eight o'clock sharp.

"I brought you something." He pulled a large pink rose from behind his back.

"It's beautiful, thank you." My cheeks burned. The only time a guy had ever given me a flower was for the homecoming dance.

"I stole it from my stepmonster's garden," he said. "You'll know she noticed it was missing if you never hear from me again."

My mother had arrived home earlier that day. She'd filled the cupboards with groceries, washed her uniforms, packed herself some clean clothes, and then started cooking lasagna, macaroni and cheese, tuna casserole—anything she could label and put in the freezer for us. I'd been hoping she'd leave for her eleven o'clock shift before Alec arrived, but she was in no rush, and when she'd heard Alec was picking me up, she said she wanted to meet my "new boyfriend."

"He's not my boyfriend, Mom," I said. But she'd already decided in her head that he was.

When Alec walked in, she was in the kitchen wearing shorts and a T-shirt, her long dark hair falling loose past her shoulders, just like mine. These days, I was used to her running out the door in her nurse's uniform, hair pulled back and pinned up, her face stressed. But tonight, as she loaded up the refrigerator, her hair swung across her back like a teenager's.

"This is my mother. Mom, Alec."

My mom turned and looked up, smiling.

"Wow, you look too young to be Katie's mother. . . . Sorry, Mrs. Martin. It's nice to meet you." He reached out his hand.

My mother was blushing now and smiling, and I was about ready to die from embarrassment. "You could be sisters," he was saying.

"Well, I wasn't very old when I had Katie. Not that I encourage that." She caught his eye. *I'm only thirty-seven*, she liked to remind me. *I had you when I was still in nursing school*. As if I didn't already know that.

"We should get going, Mom."

"Let's at least put that lovely flower in some water before you go," she said, and took it from my hand, glancing at Alec as she moved across the room for a vase.

I couldn't wait to get out of there.

JUDD AND PEG OSBORNE the sign read in script; under the names were two small, painted chickadees.

Alec hadn't mentioned a trip to his house before heading to the party. "Did you forget something?" I asked.

He stopped his car, a vintage BMW he'd been working on over the summer.

"I thought we'd swing by here for a cocktail first. Peg and Judd are out for a few hours. I know tequila's your favorite, and margaritas are a bitch to mix in the car," he added.

"How do you even know that?"

Alec looked at me sideways. "That tequila's your favorite? I think everyone knows after Cheryl's party last April."

Oh God, I thought, color rushing to my cheeks. My friend Stan had been mixing margaritas that night and they'd tasted like heaven, but after a few of those, the night had been a blur. All I knew was that Cassie had taken me back to her house and helped me into bed.

I didn't want to think about that night. "You can make a margarita?" I asked.

"The best."

Inside their new house, a shiny oak bar stretched along one side of a room filled with overstuffed couches. French doors, through which I could see a patio and the large inground pool, lined the far wall. On top of the bar, in neat little rows, were the smallest bottles of alcohol I'd ever seen. They were like tiny toy soldiers with black tops and fancy labels, each filled with a shot or two of transparent or golden brown liquid. I picked one up and studied it.

"Where did you get these?"

"Those? They're from airplanes. My dad collects them when he flies, then refills them at home. They're great for traveling—

or school." He grinned. "Here, take one. My dad's taught me everything—which is why I know what to do with this." Alec reached under the bar and pulled out some full-size bottles.

"What's this?" I asked, pointing to a bright blue bottle shaped like a banjo.

"Blue curaçao," he said. "I'm going to make you a special margarita, one the color of that swimming pool."

"A *blue* margarita?"

"Exactly," he said, mixing. "See?" He finished and handed me the glass.

"It's beautiful."

"Taste it."

"Wow," I said, sipping. It was hard not to drink fast. "That's amazing."

"An amazing drink for an amazing girl." He lifted his own glass and clinked it against mine. "Here's to a free ride to the college of your choice."

The two margaritas at Alec's house had left me feeling giddy, unstoppable. Suddenly I was beautiful and brilliant, talented and funny. I looked great and I felt great and I was going to college on a hockey scholarship. I was as full of myself as I could get.

We pulled up to the party and Alec opened my car door, then put his arm around me as we walked up the long dirt driveway. He stopped once, wrapping his strong arms around me, pulling me in for a kiss. For a moment, everything around us disappeared.

"You like that," he whispered. "Later," he said, taking my hand. "Let's go to the party first."

Cars were parked everywhere: up the driveway, on the lawn, in front of the garage. I'd heard that somebody's twenty-something cousin owned the house and didn't care who came. The kids scattered across the lawn and deck ranged anywhere from fifteen to midtwenties, but one drunk guy looked about my mother's age. And he kept staring at me like he wanted something.

"Loser," I mumbled under my breath.

"Give it a rest, buddy—she's jailbait," Alec yelled to him. The guy put his arms up, palms out, as if to say *What did I do?* and stumbled away.

Inside, the sour stench of beer slopped on linoleum mixed with the sweat of bodies pushing toward the keg on the counter.

"I'll get us some beers," Alec said, and disappeared into the fray.

I looked around and didn't see any faces I recognized right away. Wait, that was the back of Megan's head, and Cheryl's, too, I was sure.

And there was Marcy, her unmistakable white-blond hair free from its braid and falling down her back like spun gold—walking proof, I thought, that beauty is only skin deep.

"Meg!" I hollered. "Cheryl!"

The bass vibrated the floorboards under my sandals. There was no way they would ever hear me. I pushed my way through the crowd, moving in their direction.

"Hey." I felt a tap on my shoulder. "Hey, you!"

I turned my head and found myself face-to-face with the drunk guy who'd been watching me before. A lank piece of greasy hair fell across his forehead; his breath reeked of alcohol and cigarettes. I couldn't believe he was at a party with kids half his age—and what was he following *me* around for?

"I know you," he said.

It was a lame line by anyone's standards. "No you don't." I turned and started pushing through the crowd again, but he grabbed my arm. Furious, I pulled it away. "What're you *doing*?"

"Sorry!" He pulled his hands back, palms toward me again. "I'm a friend of your father's." He smiled, revealing teeth stained a yellow brown. "Tommy Martin, right? I met you when you was this high." He held his hand about three feet in the air. "You haven't changed a bit, just taller. Remember me? Wade Dwyer. I been to your house, over to Westland."

I did remember him now—his name, anyway. As a kid, I'd thought his name was funny. *Wade*. It had made me think of the ocean.

"How's Sandra . . . I mean, your mother, doin'? She was always something." He shook his head, grinning. "We went to school together, your mom and me. What's your name again?"

"Katie. She's fine."

"Gosh, I haven't seen them two in years. How's your father?" His face clouded over slightly. "I heard they split up, your parents. Your dad lives up to Bangor now, somebody said." He looked at me expectantly.

My heart dropped. "Who said that?"

"I don't know. Why? Where's he livin' now?"

My mind went blank. I looked at him, then turned away and started moving through the crowd as fast as I could, not even looking where I was going. Wade called my name behind me. He was following me and I had to lose him.

I knocked into somebody's beer, sending a golden wave over the top of the cup.

"Hey, watch it!"

"Sorry," I mumbled.

Wade, I should have said, *you know more about it than I do.* But how could I say something like that? Shame welled up inside me, twisting my stomach in knots. My father obviously cared more about other people than he did about us—they knew where he lived, and it was right here in Maine all this time! I felt humiliated for ever thinking he was out there, in trouble, unable to reach us, maybe even dead. For ever thinking he loved us at all.

Outside, I ducked around the side of the chalet and then back into the basement, where there were fewer people. Finding a bathroom, I locked myself in and sat with my head in my hands. The margaritas weren't working anymore. I wanted to die.

A couple people rapped on the door, but I ignored them. Finally, after about twenty minutes, I looked in the mirror. The only thing worse than feeling this way was having it show. I smiled, then smiled again, trying to make it look more natural. Not bad. My eyes were a little red, but maybe people would just think I was high.

Actually, that sounded really good right now. Why not have

a good time? My father wasn't shedding any tears over us *three hours away* up in *Bangor*. Maybe I'd find Megan again. She was always good for a smoke.

Alec found me later, on the edge of the woods, passing a joint back to Cheryl. Megan had just said something moderately funny, and Cheryl and I were collapsing into giggles when I caught sight of him coming toward us, two big cups overflowing with beer in his hands.

"Jesus Christ. Where the hell have you been?" he said. "I go to get you a beer, and you disappear for two hours." He handed me a cup.

"She had a *need* for *weed*," Megan said, and Cheryl and I started giggling uncontrollably again. My stomach hurt from laughing so hard, but I didn't think I could stop. Everything that came out of Megan's mouth struck me as hilarious. My father may have ruined my life, but he was not ruining this party. "Lighten up, Alec," Megan added, and handed him the joint.

He inhaled deeply, then looked at me, "You ready to go?"

Go? We'd only been there a couple hours. It was barely eleven. "Go where?"

"Yeah, where?" Megan said. "We're just getting warmed up."

"Anywhere but here. This party sucks." He looked toward the chalet. "I saw your friend in there, *Wade*. He was asking for you."

"He's not my friend."

"Sure looked that way when I saw you talking to him."

"I thought you couldn't find me."

Alec looked away. "I'll be back. Don't go anywhere, okay," he said. It was more a command than a request, but I was too drunk and too high to care.

Across the yard, Marcy hung on her new boyfriend, Rob, but her eyes were searching the crowd for someone else. She saw me and scowled, then found who she'd been looking for—Alec—her eyes following him into the chalet.

"Hey, sweetheart," a voice boomed behind me.

"Hey, Stanfield!" I turned and looked up into my friend Stan's broad, smiling face.

He wrapped his arms around me in a bear hug, practically lifting me off the ground.

"I thought I saw you earlier," he said, "walking up the driveway with *Alec Osborne.*" He made a face and chuckled. "Then I thought, *not damn likely.*"

"What can I say? You caught me," I said, keeping it light. "I like to keep people guessing."

"You're kidding." Stan caught my eye, sure I was joking, but I nodded. "What are you doing hanging out with that character?"

"Nothing too serious," I said.

"Better not be," he answered.

"Hey, I got to run," he said finally. "We'll see you at Haley Pond in a couple weeks?"

Every August, as summer was winding down, there was a party a couple miles down a narrow, winding dirt road at Haley Pond. It was in the middle of nowhere, but that's why we went there: no cottages, no people. When it was hot, people jumped in the water with their clothes on; if they were drunk enough, with nothing on at all. Everyone would be there.

"Absolutely," I replied.

Alec came back, in a better mood now, and stuck close to me the rest of the night. Around midnight he pulled me away from the crowd and whispered in my ear. "There's a place I want to show you over near Westland where I had that painting job. The view is amazing. Let's go there and stargaze." He slipped his hand into mine. "What d'you say, gorgeous?"

Alec had this way of looking at me sometimes like I was the single most extraordinary person on the planet. I looked into his eyes, swaying slightly in my sandals. Suddenly, I was in an incredible mood.

"Let's go," I said.

I let things go too far, it's true. But girls get carried away, too. Don't let anyone tell you we don't. We lose control, do things we shouldn't, have to pull back. We'd gazed at the stars for about two minutes before we started kissing, the sky and his car and the party melting away. In the black heat, I closed my eyes and let myself slip away, too. The world disappeared and all I knew were his touch on my bare chest, his lips on my neck. He pulled off his T-shirt, his warm skin pressing against mine. My shorts lay on the car floor and his hand slid beneath my panties, trying to slip them off.

"Let's get in the backseat," he said.

But I wasn't ready for that—not yet.

"Stay here," I said. "Leave them on."

"Come on, Katie," he whispered. "We're almost there." He pushed his hand back under the cotton bikinis and started to pull.

"I mean it, Alec, I don't want to." I tried to move his hand away, and that's when he snapped.

"Jesus *Christ*," he said impatiently. He grabbed my underwear in his fist and pulled. A loud rip followed and then they were gone. He tossed what was left in his hand out the open window.

The world snapped back into place. The mood was more than gone—I was furious. Trembling, I pushed the car door open and jumped out into the dark before he could stop me, grabbing my shorts and cami as I went.

I threw on my top quickly. Shaking, hopping on one leg, I tried to get my shorts back on without losing my balance. I wanted to get home as fast as I could, be safe in my bedroom, but we were at least a mile away from the nearest house and there weren't any streetlights this far out.

Even with my shorts back on I felt naked. Exposed. I was relieved Alec didn't flip on the headlights, that he couldn't see me right now. My hands were on the ground, searching in the dirt and weeds for my torn underwear, but I was lost and confused in the dark. I grabbed something sharp and cried out; I felt a wet spot on my hand that grew sticky even as I wiped it on my cami. Shit. Broken glass. I was done looking.

"Get back in the car, Katie."

"Take me home," I said sharply, but my voice quavered.

"Come on, Katie. I'm sorry, okay?" he said. But he didn't sound at all sorry. "Get back in the car."

"Only if you'll drive me home."

"For Christ's sake . . ."

"Will you take me home?"

"Yeah. Just get in."

We pulled into my driveway after one o'clock. He didn't look at me, didn't walk me to the door, just stared straight ahead through the windshield. "I'll see you around," he said.

My body was still drunk but my mind was wide-awake as I stumbled toward the porch and let myself in, locking the door behind me. What had happened? The shorts had been a bad idea. If I'd worn jeans, things wouldn't have happened so quickly. Irrational thoughts. Crazy thoughts.

Under the kitchen light, I held out my hands, palms up. One was bleeding and throbbing, cut by what had no doubt been a broken beer bottle on the ground. My hands shook as I washed them. I watched the pink water swirl in the sink and disappear, then grabbed a paper towel and pressed it on the cut, hoping to stop the blood.

Swaying, I moved cautiously toward the cabinet where my mother always kept a couple big jugs of wine. I pulled out the red one, steadied myself, and poured as much as I could into a large glass. Purple liquid sloshed onto the counter; I wiped it up with my good hand. In the living room, I turned the television on loud and sat down to drink the wine.

An hour later I staggered up the stairs, pulling myself up by the banister. My only thought by the time I dropped onto my bed was how to keep it from spinning. I didn't make it to the bathroom before I threw up.

9

The only thing to be grateful for the next morning was that it was Saturday and there were no swimming lessons to teach. I threw up again and tried to push Alec out of my mind. Why had I agreed to go to that party with him? What happened to writing him off like a stupid summer fling? Why did I ever start making out with him like that? Why did I ever do *half* the things I did?

Yeah, I was a master of turning over new leaves, all right; my problem was sticking to them. After drinking margaritas at Cheryl's camp last spring, I'd been so sick, so hungover, that I'd sworn off the hard stuff for good. From then on, it was going to be beer only for me. But here I was, throwing up tequila again. Whatever happened to *that* great idea?

Shit. I took a sip, carefully, from a glass of tap water and looked in the bathroom mirror. Vomit from the night before, dried and crusty, held together several strands of dark hair. My skin was blotchy, my eyes puffy and red as if I'd been crying. *Had I been?* Not in front of Alec, I was sure of that. But after I'd gotten home and started in on the wine, everything had gotten a little fuzzy.

But Wade—I remembered him. More than I wanted to. He'd been in my dreams half the night, repeating himself again and again: *Your dad lives up to Bangor now. . . . Your dad lives up to Bangor now. . . .*

Shut up, Wade. I said to the mirror. Then another voice, my own: *Don't shoot the messenger.* True, it wasn't Wade's fault. He was just trying to be friendly. Wade didn't know I'd convinced myself—even now, five years after his disappearance—that my father would have been in touch with us if he possibly could. That something serious must have prevented him from calling. The idea that he lived just three hours away—and that other people knew it—was more than I could bear.

I needed to clean up the mess in the hall, then take a shower and get the smell of puke off me. I needed to sleep. After that, I had a phone call to make. Wade didn't know better, but there was another person who should have. I had a few questions for my mother.

By late afternoon, I'd slept a little. My hands had stopped shaking. I'd kept down a couple bites of toast. Next to the phone in the kitchen, scraps of paper covered with numbers my mother had left on the answering machine littered the counter. I shuffled through them, discarding the ones that looked old or with names that I never heard anymore, asking myself for the tenth time why she didn't get herself a damn cell phone like everybody else.

"It's too expensive," she always said. "And half the time there's no signal out here. I'm not paying for that."

Months ago, when I'd bitched to Cassie and Matt about how she wouldn't get herself a phone, Cassie had been furious. "It's the least your mother could do if she's just going to leave you here by yourself. You know you can always call my parents if you need anything, if you ever can't find her."

"I know."

"I wish we could just adopt you." Cassie was half-serious.

I smiled. "I'm used to it, Cass."

"That doesn't make it right," Matt said.

"I always find her," I'd said. The truth was, the whole thing made me feel like crap and I didn't like talking about it. I wished I'd never mentioned the cell phone to begin with.

Here's the one, I thought, holding up a bright blue sticky note with *Ken/Mom* and a phone number written on it in my mother's hand. My stomach churned. I was afraid of what my mother would say. Suddenly, my hands were shaking again. I punched in the numbers three times before getting them right.

A man's voice answered on the fourth ring.

"I'm looking for Sandra Martin. It's her daughter," I said. "Is she there?"

"Sandra," he called out. "I think it's your daughter."

"I just said I was, you moron," I muttered, but he was gone. The phone had clunked down on a hard surface and all I could hear was the sound of a baseball game on television.

"Hi, honey," my mother said. "What's up?"

I was not in the mood for small talk.

"Mom, where does Dad live?"

"What?"

"Where does he live? I want to know."

"Honey, we've been over this. I don't know where."

"I don't believe you."

"Well, it's the truth, darlin'."

"Yeah? Then why did I meet a guy last night who says he knows you and who says Dad lives in Bangor? *Wade* somebody."

"Wade . . .Wade *Dwyer*?"

"Why didn't you tell us?"

Silence.

"Mom, why didn't you *tell* us?"

My mother cleared her throat.

"You okay, Sandra?" the man's voice said.

My mother's hand slapped over the receiver, muffling her voice.

"Katie," she said into the phone, whispering now. "Can we talk about this when I get home?"

"Right, whenever *that* is!" My face flushed and my whole body trembled. She had never made me so mad. "This is important, Mom. I want to know *now*."

She must have heard the craziness in my voice because finally she answered me.

"Yes, your father lives near Bangor. He doesn't want to see us," she said. "That's why I never told you."

A flash of heat ripped through me. My heart stopped for an

instant, then pounded forward, faster than ever before. I was yelling now.

"Maybe the one he doesn't want to see is *you!*"

I hung up the phone and sobbed like I was twelve all over again.

A week had passed and the morning was sweltering. An unrelenting sun beat down from a hazy blue sky. For four days it had been boiling hot and humid, over ninety-five degrees. I stood up to my waist in the water while I taught, dunking under between classes to wet my face and hair, but the water was warm now, and the effect was fleeting.

Around ten o'clock, something shifted. The air changed. Clouds started rolling in, dark and ominous, and the wind picked up, straining the leaves on their branches and turning them back. Then the sun disappeared and the sky turned an eerie gray green, a color that I'd seen only once before, when a small tornado came through town in July three years ago, leaving behind a twenty-foot-wide swath of destruction. A chill ran through me; it had all happened so quickly then, and it was happening quickly now.

I blew my whistle. "Everybody out!" I yelled. There was no lifeguard at our beach; I'd have to do.

No one needed convincing. The beach grew quiet quickly as mothers pulled their kids out of the water, put them into cars, and drove out of the dirt parking lot across the road, their wheels sending swarms of dust into the hot air. Lightning lit the sky, then vanished. The wind stopped as quickly as it had started, and now everything was dead calm: silent, still. I needed to get out of there, too. I looked around. Everyone was out of the water. I ran for my backpack, then sprinted toward my bike. Large drops of rain started down from the sky, pelting my face, my head, my back. I wondered if it would hail. *Better that than another tornado*, I thought. I grabbed my bike from under a tree and ran.

Then I saw his truck.

Alec stopped quickly in the road next to me and jumped out. "Get in," he said. I started to lift up my bike but he grabbed it, throwing it in the back of the truck. "Get in!"

Inside the cab, I took out my towel and dried my face. Goose bumps rose on my skin. The temperature had dropped quickly. "Thanks," I said, not looking at him.

"Don't you listen to the weather reports?" His tone was nearly parental. I felt scolded, like a child.

"Well, I guess nobody did, because everyone showed up for class today," I shot back.

What are you doing here, anyway, I thought, *if you assumed everyone would have heard the weather and stayed home?*

Large pieces of hail began striking his windshield, ice the size of golf balls that made it hard to see. It would have been nearly impossible to get home on my bike in this.

"Thanks for the ride," I said, and passed him my towel. He wiped his dripping face and hair.

"You're welcome."

Neither of us looked at the other; neither of us spoke. Minutes later, I was home.

We were in my driveway, truck idling, wipers sweeping rhythmically across the glass. The hail had stopped as suddenly as it started, and now it was just pouring rain.

"I have to get back to work," he said.

"In *this*?"

"I'm painting a bathroom."

"Oh." I shoved my towel in my backpack and reached for the door handle. Alec jumped out of the truck, retrieved my bike, and ran it into the garage while I sprinted toward the porch.

A moment later, Alec ran back to his truck. He lifted one hand to wave as he pulled out of the driveway, and then he was gone.

That afternoon, I turned the scene over in my mind: Alec appearing, lifting my bike into his truck, driving me home in the storm. *Maybe he just happened to be driving by at the right moment,* I thought, but that made no sense. The beach road was a dead end. Had he been working when the storm struck and come from wherever he was to check on me, to make sure I was okay? He'd heard the weather reports—he'd made that clear. He often listened to the radio when he worked.

Whatever had happened, he'd been there, helping me out. After the party in Bethel, it was the last thing I expected.

I was just beginning to understand how unpredictable he could be.

10

Megan and Cheryl and I were going to the party at Haley Pond together; we'd planned it weeks ago. It was our annual last-act-of-the-summer ritual. When Megan called at four o'clock the day of the party with some lame excuse and said she couldn't give me a ride after all, I was furious. The beat-up Escort my mother let me drive was in the shop for a couple days—Megan knew this. I had no car of my own. And who wants to show up at a party alone, anyway? There was no way I was going by myself.

"You'll find another ride," Megan said. "We'll catch you there."

"Probably not," I said, but she'd hung up already.

From the table next to the phone, I picked up a postcard from England that had arrived a couple days before. It was a photograph of a guy with a Mohawk and about twenty piercings leaning against a bright red phone booth. On the back, Cassie's scrawl:

Hey Girlfriend,
I think I'm in love. His name is Simon. (This is NOT him).
More soon—
Love, Cass

If Cassie were here right now, no other plans would be necessary. She was my partner for all nights out. Not to mention someone I desperately needed to talk to. *God*, I couldn't wait until she got home.

I dropped the postcard and dialed Stan. Whoever he was going with, he'd haul them out to Westland to pick me up. That's the way Stan was—generous, easygoing, always willing to help out. To him, no favor was too big for a friend. But Stan didn't pick up his phone. *Damn it.* I slammed the receiver down. I was getting desperate.

When the phone rang at six thirty, I jumped off the couch. Maybe Stan had finally picked up my message.

"Katie." There was no mistaking Alec's voice. "Katie? It's Alec."

"I know who it is."

"Listen, I heard you need a ride tonight. I can give you one."

Megan and Alec had been friends for a long time; they'd talked.

"No, thanks."

"Come on, Katie. I'm sorry about what happened after the other party, okay? Things definitely got out of hand." His tone was sweet, conciliatory. "What do you say?"

What I said was nothing. I knew only one thing: I wanted to go to that party.

"Let me give you a lift. Let me make up to you for last time. I was a jerk, okay? And Megan told me you need a ride. I know you want to go."

He sounded truly sorry. The image of him lifting my bike into his truck during the hailstorm flashed through my mind. I supposed that had been his way of trying to make it up to me, too.

"Okay," I said at last. "But this isn't—I mean . . . we're just *friends*, Alec."

"I'll pick you up at eight."

It started like every other party I'd been to at Haley Pond, cars and pickup trucks pulled in close to the small beach where Stan and some other guys had built a bonfire, despite the heat. The flames curled upward, casting an eerie, flickering light on the nearby trees. I hopped out of Alec's old BMW as soon as it stopped and ditched him, beer in hand, searching the crowd for my friends.

"Kay—tee!" Stan's voice echoed across the pond. "Come on in—the water's *great!*"

All I could make out were the shadows of four or five heads bobbing in the water. I flipped off my sandals and waded in up to my thighs, then stopped, scanning the pond for Stan. A sturdy figure emerged, making its way toward me. "Come on in. It feels *awe*some."

"This is it for me tonight, Stan. I didn't bring a bathing suit."

"No suit required, darlin'."

"*Stan.*"

"Kidding!" he called back. "I'll be out in a few. Don't go too far." He dove back into the shallow water and disappeared.

"Katie. Try this." His voice was behind me.

I turned and took a cup from Alec's extended hand.

"That's excellent," I said. He knew my weakness; it was a margarita. It tasted like the one he'd made me at his house the night of the Bethel party.

"There's plenty in the car when you're ready for a refill." He took the empty beer bottle from my other hand and walked away through the shallow water, back toward the fire where I'd spotted Cheryl, Megan, and some other field hockey players when I'd first arrived.

I watched Alec toss my beer bottle into a garbage bag and wander into the crowd. *Maybe hitching a ride with him was no big deal after all*, I thought, and headed toward my friends.

I couldn't have been more wrong.

"People get crazy when the moon's full," my mother always said, though I'd never really believed her. "They say commitments up to the state hospital double. From what I've seen coming through the emergency room, it wouldn't surprise me. It happens every month," she said.

Later, long after it was over, I would swear to myself that the moon had been full that night. I'd swear I watched it rise over Haley Pond, a pale lantern in the sky, guiding my trips to Alec's car, which was parked far from the light of the dying bonfire.

Could it have made me crazy, too?

Could I just plead the moon?

Temporary insanity. *Full moon* insanity.

I do remember this: rumbling gray clouds moving in around midnight, shifting the dead heat that had been sitting on us for days, bringing in rain that broke through the thick, stifling air. That same rain had driven me back into Alec's car, seeking shelter from the downpour on the beach. And Alec had been right behind me. He climbed in, slammed the door shut, and shook his head like a cat, sending sharp pellets of water spewing off his hair and around the interior. We were soaked.

"Give me the keys," I said.

His charm, I'd noticed, had disappeared about an hour earlier, when he'd pushed me up against a car, tried to kiss me for the *second* time, and I'd again had to explain the concept of *just friends*. The message wasn't getting through. Alec's auditory skills were selective: He heard only what he wanted to hear.

I'd made a beeline for the driver's side for a reason, and I was relieved when Alec pulled the keys from his pocket and tossed them onto my lap. I switched on the ignition and cranked the AC, flipping the fans to high. Our breath mixed with the cool air pumping from the vents. Foggy windows sealed us off from the scene outside the car. I could hear voices, drunken yells, engines starting, the thump of what sounded like someone slipping in the mud and hitting the ground near our front tire, and then swearing. A shriek of laughter.

I rubbed the wet sleeve of my T-shirt across my face and looked over at Alec. He had the tequila bottle to his lips, head back. We'd ditched the margarita mix hours ago. He swallowed and handed the bottle to me. I slid the driver's seat back as far as I could to stretch out my legs, then lifted the bottle to my mouth. The taste gagged me, but I liked the burning path it made down my throat and the explosion of warmth in my belly.

"Jesus, Martini. You drink like a dying man in the desert. Save some of that for me, will ya?"

I pulled the bottle from my lips and handed it to Alec without looking at him. It was his, after all. He'd just offered to share. He wanted something in return for his generosity—he'd made that clear—but that wasn't my problem. We were in his car, but I was in the driver's seat. I was feeling invincible in the tequila high, like nothing could touch me.

Outside the car, sounds were dying down. Only a few engines hummed and the rain splattered on the windshield and the roof of the car—big drops of water hammering an uneven tune. I shut off the fan and rubbed my fingers across the glass to see who was left. I saw Stanfield's green pickup truck and the headlights of a second car I didn't recognize. Most everyone had disappeared, headed for home. Fluorescent green numbers on the dashboard clock beamed out the time: 1:29.

Alec dropped the tequila bottle on the car floor. The rain had started to let up, and I opened the window to get some fresh air. I was starting to feel queasy and tired, depressed. The party was over and the high feeling was slipping away. I gazed into the darkness outside the car and pretended not to notice when Alec put his hand on my bare leg.

The keys jingled and the car engine died. I turned my head toward Alec.

"We don't want to run out of gas," he said. He squeezed my leg slightly and circled his torso in front of me, moving in for another kiss. His breath carried the musty stench of the beer he'd been drinking earlier.

"Excuse me," I said, pushing him away. The car door swung open and I stumbled out onto the uneven ground next to the car.

"What are you doing?"

"I'll be right back."

Our headlights were off and the sky was black. Clouds hid the moon and stars from view. My whole body felt heavy, like I was moving in slow motion. I was drunker than I wanted to be, but it was too late to take that back.

I veered into the woods, tripping on the root of a tall pine tree, then walked farther until I could barely make out the car back in the clearing. Wet pine needles dug into my flesh as I sank down to my bare knees. Palms down in front to steady myself, I gagged, my body convulsing forward. Bitter liquid filled my mouth and I spit it out quickly, just in time for the next wave of nausea to rock me again. *Shit.* I hated puking more than anything. Drinking on an empty stomach was always a mistake. I spit again and again, trying to get the taste out of my mouth, then sat still, hunched over and breathing carefully, hoping it was over.

Hands fixed on a slender tree trunk, I managed to pull myself up. I brushed off the needles stuck to my knees and made my way back to the car, groping for trees in the dark to keep myself from falling.

The rain had stopped, but fog had risen off the pond next to the clearing and it was hard to see. The car was running again, and Alec was outside leaning against it, his arms folded in front of his chest.

"Did you boot, Martini?" He was slurring slightly. "I thought you could drink like an Irishman. You disappoint me." He handed me the tequila bottle. "Here, there's a little left. Mouthwash."

I ignored his words and grabbed the bottle, rinsed my mouth with what was left of the alcohol, then spit it out before reaching for the driver's side door.

"Hey." He put his hand on my shoulder and spun me around. "What are you doing?"

"I'm wet, I . . ." My tongue felt thick in my mouth. Suddenly I was so tired. Alec looked pissed off. And for the first time, it hit me that we were all alone at Haley Pond. Everyone had gone.

His arms were around me before I could stop him, his tongue pressing into my mouth. I pushed my arms against him and tried to twist my face away from his, but he followed my moves with his own. When he finally pulled his mouth off of mine, it was when *he* was ready. I had to get myself together and get out of there.

"Let's get in the car," he said, reaching for the back door handle.

"Let's go back to my house, dry off, hang out where it's comfortable." My words tripped together in a hurry to get out. Alec eyed me with suspicion. Staying calm was the only thing that would get me out of this. I fixed my eyes on his. "What do you say? You know how my mom is. She won't care—she won't be there. She's working tonight." I tried to smile.

Alec stared down at me for a moment without blinking. "Getting comfortable sounds good."

"Great," I said. "It's a mud pit here. Mind if I drive?" I got in the driver's side again without waiting for his reply. I was starting to feel better just knowing in fifteen minutes I'd be home and in my own bed, with Alec and this night far behind me. I'd figure out a way to get rid of him once we got to my house.

Another wave of nausea hit me as I wiped my hand across the foggy windshield. "Any beers left back there?"

Alec reached behind the seat, pulled out a brown bottle, and handed it to me. I twisted off the top and took a sip, just enough to get the lingering taste of bile out of my mouth. I took a few gulps and handed it back to Alec. "You can finish it."

He killed it and tossed the bottle out the window as our wheels spun on the dirt and we took off into the night.

11

It is a dream with no end—a deep, painful sleep.

There is nothing outside it, nothing beyond it. It is all there is in the world: darkness.

Struggling to get out of the black, I will my eyelids to open. All they do is flutter and snap shut. It hurts too hard to try.

A quick vision—a dream beyond the darkness: my body on pavement, at the base of a brick wall. There I am now, lying flat—so still, so far away. How can I be here and there? And where is here? My memory is in pieces: a jigsaw puzzle broken and scattered across the floor. There is no gathering up the pieces or fitting them together.

For an instant, my eyes open. A thin ridge of pink light spreads across a night sky. Morning.

Then everything is gone.

A pale morning sun lights the scene. In front of me, a dashboard, a steering wheel. A large pine tree fixed against a car's hood.

The tree trunk has jammed in the metal and folded it up like an accordion. Part of the windshield is broken; shattered crystal spreads outward like a spider's web.

My shirt is bloody, my shoulder wet. Fresh red liquid oozes out from under layers of dark blood that have already dried. I don't connect it to me. It is like a picture on television when you first click it on and you don't know what the program is or what's going on.

Nothing is real. I can't touch it, can't feel it.

I sleep.

A jolt of fear wakes me.

The car is sunk deep in the trees. Alec's car. And I am in it.

An image of Haley Pond flashes by. Then more images—but they are quick snapshots, not a story: Alec kissing me. Puking on my knees in the woods. Rain.

The memories explode then; the fragments burst into place. The party, the tequila, driving away from the pond. My pulse begins to race. My head pounds. I am seeing it—really seeing it—for the first time. We are in the woods, the car rammed into a tree trunk—totaled, wrecked, destroyed. Branches, leaves, twigs, and bushes are shoved up against the side windows. My shoulder is badly cut, and a sharp pain in my breast jabs with every breath. Carefully, I move my hand to touch it. Have I been stabbed by a piece of broken glass? But there is nothing there; the wound in my chest is inside.

Then I see him.

Alec, in the passenger seat next to me.

His eyes are closed, his jaw slack. Dried blood covers his mouth and chin like cracked paint. For the first time, I realize that he is there, and that he could be dead.

And if he is, I have killed him.

I shake Alec's shoulder hard, but he doesn't respond. The pain in my chest screams. The sound of my own breath, heavy, labored, fills the car. Even the slightest move I make feels like a knife thrust between my ribs.

"Alec. Alec, wake up!"

I put my hand on his head. He is hot. That means he can't be dead, right? Dead people are cold. Rigor mortis sets in. I pick up his hand and move his fingers. He isn't stiff. He is alive, I can tell, but his face and head are bleeding.

I call his name again. I have to do something. Where is his cell phone? Does he have it? I can't remember. A thick tangle of brush and branches have swallowed his side of the car and poked in his window, but my side looks clear. I push with my left elbow. Miraculously, the door opens.

"Katieisatyou?" His voice is soft and low and his words tumble together. He sounds younger, like a little kid. Like my brother when he was three years old.

"Alec?" I whisper. "Are you okay?"

"I'm okay," he slurs. "R'you okay?" He turns his head slowly toward me, resting his bloody cheek on the seat back. "Don' worry 'bout me."

"I'm going to find someone."

His eyes are shut. "Okay. I'm okay," he mumbles.

The ground outside the car is uneven; I stumble, lose my balance, spin toward the earth. The world melts and blurs, the ground rushing to meet me. I lie in the wet leaves. Time slips away.

Somehow I get up, gripping the wrecked car until the world stands still. Each arm, each leg conspires to pull me back to the ground. My tongue, thick and dry, sticks to the roof of my mouth. A can of beer lies on the floor, driver's side. I open it and take several long, deep pulls.

Slowly I begin, counting my steps, watching my feet: one, two, three . . .

The empty beer can slips from my hand. My mouth and throat are desert dry, cracked like parched earth. I see visions: fountains; rivers; lakes; glasses of lemonade, pink, with ice.

Mosquitoes emerge from the thick wet forest and land on my head, legs, arms—any bit of flesh. Tiny black flies swarm around the blood on my shoulder. Little bites of pain, a frantic urge to scratch, but moving—reaching, twisting, slapping—is too hard. The pain is too sharp in my chest. The insects devour me.

I walk forever.

The sun is higher in the sky now, edging above the trees. On a stretch of Route 117, just outside town, the dirt road meets the pavement. I stumble toward an abandoned Sunoco station. An ancient public telephone booth stands near the locked-up restrooms. The glass is dirty and scratched, the folding door broken. I try to remember Matt's telephone number, which I've known by heart since I was twelve—then everything goes black.

Ron Bailey finds me on the ground covered with cuts, bug bites, and blood and reeking of beer and vomit.

I try hard to drink the Coke Ron has put in my hand and not throw up as we drive fast down the bumpy dirt road toward Alec.

"Jesus," Ron says under his breath when he sees the car. "Jesus *H.* Christ."

When we arrive, Alec is conscious. He has slid into the driver's seat of his wrecked car, toward the door I'd left open—the only door not pinned shut by trees, the only way out.

"Jesus Christ, boy! What in hell were you thinking?" Ron says. "Can you move?"

Alec nods and pushes himself out of the car. Ron holds Alec steady and helps him into the truck. "We need to get you to a hospital. Buckle up, boy."

Alec is shoulder to shoulder with me in the cab, his head resting on the back window. There is a long gash on his face, caked in blood. He looks stunned, exhausted, vulnerable. It is like looking at a stranger. It terrifies me.

Ron is captain of the Westland Volunteer Fire Department; he flips on the flashing red light on his dashboard, steps heavy on the gas, and we hurtle toward the hospital.

"Your mother know where you are? She even know you were out with this character?" he says.

"Working," I mumble. My throat hurts. I gulp the Coke, then offer it to Alec, but he doesn't even see me. I close my eyes.

"Jesus Christ, Katie," Ron's voice says. "You could've been killed."

That's the only thing I hear as we speed to the hospital.

Dr. Trumbull knows my mother from when she worked at this hospital. He is talking, his face stern: You have a concussion. You're dehydrated. The pain in your chest is a bruised lung. He gives me six tight stitches in my shoulder. He gives me a speech about drinking, a speech about riding with someone who has been drinking, a speech about drinking so much it can poison you. He has never looked at me like this before—horror, revulsion, fear. He finishes and sends me away.

I wake on a couch in the waiting room, stumble toward the bathroom, vomit.

In the hallway, voices rise. Dr. Trumbull is reaming out Ron for not calling an ambulance.

"I got 'em here in fifteen minutes," Ron says. "Would've taken an ambulance longer than that just to find 'em."

"Alec could have had a back or neck injury," Dr. Trumbull says.

Their argument fades away.

I am alone now, except for Ron. Alec needs stitches and his parents are in Bermuda. I don't know what they need me to know: a cell phone number, a hotel name—something. They are bringing in a special surgeon to put his cheek back together. They need permission to treat. Why won't Ron stop talking? I want to curl up in a ball in the corner. I want to sleep.

Ron is calling Portland again, talking to my mother. He is handing me juice, telling me to drink. He is bringing me soda from the vending machine. He folds up his cell phone, sits down next to me, waits. I pretend to drink what he hands me. I have nothing to say.

"You mind telling me what happened?" he says. He doesn't say it mean. "There were bottles from here to kingdom come in that kid's car, and they weren't for Coca-Cola."

I stare straight ahead, stare at nothing. He tries again.

"What were you thinking, gettin' in a car with a drunk kid like that? Couldn't you find someone else to drive you home?"

His question hits like a fist in the stomach. I press my back into the vinyl couch, willing myself not to cry.

"It wasn't like that, Ron," I whisper.

"You tryin' to tell me you two weren't drinking? I wasn't born yesterday, Katie," he says softly and catches my eye, shaking his head. Even then his face looks kind. "I've known you since you was born and this is the first time I've ever seen you smellin' like the inside of a barroom after hours. You have any idea how many laws you broke just *being* in that car with all them bottles? You got any idea the trouble you're in?"

Trouble. I can hear Ron talking still, saying words I don't want to hear: *possession, transporting alcohol, minors, open containers . . .*

Thoughts dart through my mind, hit walls, and recede. There is no way out of this, no way to take it back. The realization drops on me like a bomb. Everything I might lose tears through my mind—field hockey, Coach Riley, a scholarship, Matt. Even Ron, with his kind eyes and offers to help, will disappear when he learns the truth: Alec was not driving that car. *I* was.

Ron is looking at me, waiting.

"I know I'm in trouble." My voice is barely audible. Tears flood my eyes, run down my cheeks. I hide my face, burying it in my knees. How can I tell him?

Ron looks around the waiting room, brow furrowed. His thoughts are somewhere else.

"You tell your mother when she gets here that I'll be right back. Don't you move." He points at me. "You drink that soda. And don't talk to anybody, you understand me?"

He pushes open the lobby door with one hand and is gone.

My mother arrives. After Dr. Trumbull assures her that I am okay, she starts grilling me about "how Alec drove the car off the road."

I curl up in a ball, my head in my knees, and refuse to talk to her.

They can find out the truth when they talk to Alec. I just want a few more minutes before the rug is jerked out from under me and my life as I know it is gone.

Ron is back forty minutes later with Harlan Reed in tow. Harlan is the constable in Westland, the law, the only thing resembling a police officer in our tiny village. If there is a complaint, an unexplained noise, a missing animal, a domestic quarrel, he takes care of it. Now he is here to take care of me.

They are talking, heads down, voices low. They find my mother, then disappear.

I have dozed off on the couch in the waiting room when I wake to familiar voices. I stay perfectly still, opening my eyes a slit.

"If the state police get called in she'll end up in court, and God knows what will happen to her." Ron's voice is rising. He looks in my direction and checks himself.

I listen carefully, don't move.

"I'd say she and the young man are in serious trouble, regardless," Dr. Trumbull says. "Do you realize they were both still legally drunk when they arrived here this morning? And this was a good five or six hours *after* the accident. I think a visit to court might do your daughter some good." He is looking at my mother.

"You listen to me, Fred," my mother says fiercely. "I worked here with you for fifteen years and you've known Katie since I carried her. She's a good kid. Never been in any kind of trouble. The state police come in and she can forget that hockey scholarship, and unless you want to pay her way through four years of college or have a better idea, I'm asking for you to be reasonable."

Ron interrupts. "Fact is, this happened out in Westland and that's Harlan's jurisdiction. You can consider the police notified, Doc. You do your job and let Harlan do his."

"I'll take care of it from here, Doctor," Harlan says.

"I'm not talking about *police*." Dr. Trumbull's voice is raised now. "I'm talking about getting that child some *help*."

Outnumbered, the doctor wheels around and faces my mother again. "Sandra, I'll go along with your wishes," he says in a voice so low I can barely hear. "But don't kid yourself. Your daughter's in trouble, and I don't mean with the law. First time or not, Katie needs some help. And you know damn well it's my responsibility to make sure she gets it. Remember fifteen years of friendship when you think about that." He turns and strides down the corridor.

My mother stares at the tile on the floor for a minute. When she finally lifts her head, her face is defiant but her eyes fill with tears.

"My daughter's not in trouble, damn it," she says to Ron, who guides her back to a couch, one hand on the small of her back. "She's just a kid." She rubs away the tears angrily.

"It's gonna be okay, Sandra," Ron says softly. "Katie's going to be okay."

Finally, Alec is released. A friend of Alec's parents waits to take him home. His left cheek is covered by puffy gauze, the dressing bordered by a shiny, deep purple bruise. At the top, the filmy tape securing the bandage covers the soft hollow beneath his eye. A vision from the car—Alec's cheek mangled and bloody—flits through my mind and is gone. He doesn't look at me as he walks by and I'm too terrified to speak.

Crazy as it is, I am afraid of what he might do to me.

At home, I hide in my room. Lying on my bed, I pull the blankets up tight around my neck and try to stop shivering. I will my brain to shut off, to forget what I know: nothing will ever be the same again. Today was bad; tomorrow will be worse. The truth will be all over Westland—all over Deerfield—in an instant, as soon as Alec is well enough to pick up a phone or walk out the door of his house.

My eyes land on a spot on the wall next to my bed. For years, there had been a picture of my father and me hanging there. The paint is still slightly darker in that spot, a small square shadow on the lavender wall. After my father left, I'd put the picture in a little frame myself, staring at it every night before I fell asleep.

Then, sometime freshman year, after a bad day at school or at practice or something, I'd taken a swing at it. Just swiped at it with one arm and watched it fly across the room where it landed, its frame broken. It had lain there for days before I'd stuffed it into my desk. Out of sight, out of mind.

On November third it will be five years since my father left. I'd circled the day in red Magic Marker on my calendar that year, back in seventh grade. As each day passed, I'd crossed it off with a big *X*, watching the red circle around the three get farther and farther away. Each day I thought, *this has to be the day he comes back. He can't stay away any longer.* Each day, I was wrong.

I jump up suddenly. Pain shoots through my chest. Across the room, I whip open the top left drawer of my desk and dig around, throwing stuff on the floor. There it is, finally, under some postcards from Cassie and an English paper with an A at the top. The frame is gone and the edges of the photo curl up slightly.

I stare at the picture of us together. We are on the lawn in front of our house and it is summertime. My father is kneeling on the ground next to me, smiling, his eyes focused on the camera. He looks younger than I remember him. Would I even know him if I saw him now? Would he know *me*?

I wonder what he would do if he knew about the accident. Would he even care? Care that I could have *died*?

I want him to know about it. Not the part about the drinking, or Alec's stitches, or the trouble I'm in, but the part about how close I came to death. I want him to know that I might not be around forever just *waiting* for him.

I might disappear, too.

12

The first night lasts forever. I'm in and out of sleep, in and out of dreams. Awake, my heart hammers in my chest, cutting short my breath. Panic mounts until I fear my lungs will burst. But asleep, it is no better. I'm hurtling through the forest. Branches scratch the windshield and it shatters. Blood splatters my face and hands. Alec lies dead beside me. I wake with a start and the cycle begins again.

Now, before dawn, I stare into space. Sheets lay twisted around my legs, blankets bunched up on the floor. My face is wet, as if I've been crying, damp hair plastered to my forehead. My body aches and the slightest movement brings a rush of pain. Bruises—deep purple, lavender, yellow—have appeared on my arms and legs like grotesque tattoos. Bug bites, red and raw from scratching, cover me like a rash.

Outside, a thin band of light appears on the horizon. I reach for the glass of water on my nightstand, but my trembling hand knocks it to the floor. Shards of glass now lie there in tiny pools. The day has barely begun.

How will I survive it?

My stomach heaves and I run to the bathroom. I've eaten nothing and nothing comes up. Sprawled on the bathroom floor, I wish, for a fleeting moment, that I had died in that car.

I feel a crazy urge to see Alec, to see if he's okay. But it's more than that. Waiting here is unbearable. I've got to *do* something.

Ripping through my desk drawer again, I search for my bankbook, the account where I keep all the money I've saved. I flip it open. Just over two thousand dollars. It's certainly not enough for a new car, but it's something. It's got to be: it's everything I have.

I stare out the window and wait for the clock to strike nine.

Nothing could prepare me for what I see.

When Alec swings his front door open, the gauze bandage is gone. His eye is black, his cheek purple. Exposed, a long row of stitches curves down his face from his cheekbone to his jaw. The wound is nearly four inches in all: red, swollen, held tenuously together by slender black thread. I hear the sharp intake of my breath. The ground is no longer solid beneath my feet. I can't take my eyes off it.

Alec doesn't speak. He simply waits, expecting me to enter. Hand gripping the door frame, I step inside.

In the living room, I offer him everything—all the money in my account—to pay for his car, his medical bills, whatever he needs. I even offer him the beat-up Escort.

He just turns his head away, and the black stitches on his bruised cheek stare back at me. "I don't want your old shit box," he says. "Or your money."

Beyond the couch where he lays stretched out, I can see rain falling on the pool, sending tiny rings rippling outward in the unnatural cerulean blue. I haven't been in this room since the night we went to the party in Bethel and we'd come here first to mix margaritas at his father's bar. Margaritas the color of that pool.

Alec shifts slowly on the couch and winces, as if it hurts to move. My body is tense, perched on the edge of a nearby chair, hand clenching the rejected bankbook. He looks horrible.

"So your redneck friend was here last night, the one who has the hots for your mother."

"Redneck guy . . . ?"

"The one who drove us to the hospital."

"Ron Bailey." I have no right to be mad at Alec now, but he has no right to talk about Ron that way, either. "He's a nice man, Alec."

"Whatever. He was here."

I swallow, hold my breath, wait. It's as if hearing Alec say it will finally make it real. Ron knows, I think. He's already been here. He knows now that I was driving.

"You wouldn't believe what he said." Alec looks at me as if he can see through me, inside me; his eyes accuse. Stitches like miniature railroad tracks carve through the purple mess where his cheek used to be.

"He told me not to go around bragging about the accident

to my friends or I could have a DUI on my head. Imagine my surprise." He pauses. "I didn't even know I was driving."

"What did he say?" My words are a whisper.

"He said this thing will just blow over if I keep it to myself, don't make a big deal out of it. Told me if I pulled a stunt like that again, it would be different." Alec's eyes never leave me. He is taking in every ounce of my reaction.

"So you told him . . ."

"So I told him, 'Thank you, sir. I appreciate that,'" Alec says in mock politeness. "And he says, 'I'm not doing it for you.'" There's a faint smirk on Alec's face. He looks straight into my eyes. "Maybe it's *you* he has the hots for."

I bristle, but I don't want him to see my reaction. He's baiting me, but I can't bite. I have no right. I lost my rights when I drove his car into that tree.

"Why didn't you tell him I was driving?" The words tumble out but they are low, barely audible. I am shaking again. Can he see that?

"Alec?" I repeat.

He lets me wait; it seems like days before he replies.

"Why didn't *you*?" he says.

"He—he—" I'm stammering now and I hate myself for it. "He didn't ask me."

"Right." Alec's eyes leave my face at last, drifting toward the French doors and the pool beyond. I cannot imagine what he is thinking, but it is clear that he is. It's as if he's no longer here in the room with me. He's gone.

"I'll tell him now . . ." I move toward the phone but Alec's hand reaches it first, clamping the receiver down.

"Don't be an idiot." His voice is firm, like a father admonishing a small child.

I pull back my hand, searching his face for a clue. I have no idea what to do.

Neither of us speaks.

"I need a nap," he says finally.

"Okay." I hesitate. *We can't just leave things like this, can we?* I think. But I am no longer in charge.

"I'll see you around," he says. That's my cue to leave.

I'm at the door when his voice reaches across the room like a hand and stops me.

"Don't worry, Katie." His tone is quiet, measured. His eyes are on something beyond the French doors, on something far away. All I can see is the back of his blond head resting on the couch. "Your secret is safe with me."

13

Back at my house, Alec's words run through my head.

Your secret is safe with me.

Trembling, I pace my bedroom, unable to sit still. Can I do this? Can I let Alec take the blame for something I've done? Can I live in a lie this big? Can I actually fool people? Pull this off? Do I *want* to?

People have called while I am at Alec's. Word is out across Westland and Deerfield. Alec Osborne crashed his car with me in it. That's the story.

I have to pull it off. There is no other choice left.

The panic I've been feeling over losing my scholarship is replaced by the dread of being found out.

"Katie!" my mother calls up the stairs. "Matt's here!"

I freeze. I've been so caught up in my thoughts, I didn't even see him walking across the yard.

"I don't want to see anyone, Mom!"

But it is too late. I recognize his footsteps on the stairs.

He is hugging me before I have time to think, his long, lanky arms squeezing me tight.

I pull away and sit down on the bed. "I was going to call you. . . ." My voice trails off.

"I'd gone to work," he says. "I started hearing stories. . . . I told them I couldn't stay. I just left."

I grip the crumpled sheet on the bed, clench a ball of it in my fingers, and look out the window. I don't want to cry again, but my voice is shaking now. I can feel the tears coming.

"You didn't have to do that."

"I had to," he says simply. "I had to see you for myself."

"Thanks for being here."

He nods and looks into my eyes, then sits down on the bed beside me.

"It scared the hell out of me," he says.

I wipe a forearm across my nose and face like a five-year-old. My head hurts. Matt crosses the room and brings back a box of tissues.

"So what happened? You look like an army of mosquitoes got you."

Small red bumps cover my arms and face. I've been scratching them nervously and some are raw, bleeding. I've dabbed each bite with calamine lotion, but the pale pink blotches make me look like I've been splattered with Pepto-Bismol.

"I had to walk down Haley Pond Road to get help. The bugs were awful."

Matt nods, but that isn't what he meant. "So what happened?"

I explain how I'd ended up going to the party with Alec after Megan bailed on me, how I'd ended up in his car. "It was pouring out. The road was a mess. A real mud pit—and we were . . . we were just going way too fast." I shake my head and gaze out the window. I can't meet his eyes.

Matt doesn't say a word, but I can feel him looking at me. It's the way he looks when he knows I'm not being straight with him. The look he gave me when I turned fourteen and swore to him that I didn't think about my dad at all anymore, especially on my birthday, and why did he even have to bring it up?

"We were going way too fast," I say again.

"Were you guys drunk?" he asks.

I freeze inside. I need sympathy, not an inquisition. Up until now, I thought that's what I was getting.

"No," I say.

"Come on, Katie. People know."

It is the wrong thing for him to say. If he'd just shut up, I might have given in, told him the truth. Maybe even the whole truth. But it is a matter of pride now; I won't admit anything.

"They weren't there. I was."

Matt stands up and walks slowly across the room. "Lots of people were there—at the party."

I don't say anything. He stands by the window, looking at me, waiting for me to say something. Waiting for me to tell him the truth. The low evening light shines through the window, illuminating half his face.

"A deer jumped out in front of the car, Matt. It was slippery and late. That's it." It is a colossal lie, a stupid fake lie, but it is too late now. It is out. And I am not backing down.

Silence stretches out between us like the widest part of the lake, deep and blue.

"Sometimes I feel like I don't know you," he says softly.

It isn't an accusation and it isn't a threat. It's just Matt trying to put into words how he feels. But that doesn't matter to me. He might as well have launched a missile at my heart.

"Then maybe you should just stay out of my *goddamn* life." I spit the words out, my whole body trembling. I want to snatch them back that very instant, but I can't. It's like hitting the tree; it's done, over. There is nothing I can do to take them back.

The hit is hard. Matt stares at me, mouth half-open, but no words come out. It is as if I am Scott and I've just pushed his head into that snowbank all those years ago. He blinks, lets out a quick breath, and turns on his heel.

Then he is gone.

"Matt!" I call after him.

But he doesn't come back.

I stare at Matt's house, at the kitchen door, hoping it will swing open and he'll come back out, come back and say he knows I didn't mean it. It has been an hour since he left and disappeared into his house.

The phone rings. I jump and run to the top of the stairs, but my mother calls out that it is Stan; he wants to see if I'm all right.

"Tell him I'm fine," I say. "Tell him I'm asleep."

I go back to my vigil. Soon it will grow dark, and Matt's light will shine in his room. Maybe I'll catch a glimpse of him. See if he is okay.

Below, in the driveway, is Ron Bailey's truck. I can hear my mother talking to him downstairs, their voices muffled. Alec told the lie—or let it stand, anyway. But if I see Ron now, I have to let him believe it. Keep believing it. Can I play my part? Will he see the guilt in my eyes? "Please don't make me face him," I whisper, and curl up on my bed, eyes still glued to Matt's house through the open window.

Footsteps come up the stairs, then down the hall, and pause at my door. A knock. I sit up. "Come in," I say, my voice weak.

Ron stands at my door and looks at me with his gentle eyes. "How you doing, sweetheart?"

"I'm okay."

He nods, his eyes still on me. It is clear that I am not.

"Listen, if you need anything—anything at all—you just give me a holler, okay?"

He won't leave until I nod my head in agreement. "Okay, Ron."

"Okay then, take care of yourself."

I stare out the window into the dark. The lie is fixed now; it is fact. The truth? I feel like I don't know myself anymore, either.

fall

14

A week passed and I'd barely moved. I ate in my room, I slept there, I went nowhere. A cluster of maple leaves tipped with orange hung outside my window. Fall had arrived.

Cassie came to see me the minute her plane landed, before she'd even slept, insisting her parents drop her off at my house before she went home. She burst into my bedroom, tripping over a pile of dirty dishes. But it was the sight of me that stopped her cold. "Oh my God, Kay," she said, her face grave. Her red hair had been cut short around her ears. "I'm sorry I wasn't here for you."

That was the first thing out of her mouth. It was so Cassie to apologize for something that wasn't her fault. As if she should have *known* I'd be crashing a car so she could cut her trip to England short.

"You didn't know . . ."

"I just mean . . ." She shook her head, her face pale under her freckles, her words tumbling out. "My mom said you both could

*117

have been killed, that you're lucky you're not dead. Is it true you had to walk a mile to get help?"

I sat up, nodded. "The mosquitoes didn't mind." I held out one arm. The red bumps had faded to small pink spots, tiny scabs where I'd scratched them raw.

Cassie's eyes landed on a bruise, now a sickly yellow and lavender blotch that covered the soft underside of my forearm. "Jesus," she said, her voice quiet, almost a whisper. She came and sat next to me and rested her hand on my arm. "Is it sore?"

"A little. Not so much now."

She nodded and we sat there, silent.

"Kay," she said finally. "Why . . . I mean, what . . ."

It was weird watching her pick her words—like I'd break if she said the wrong thing. We'd never held back before, always told each other everything.

"Alec," she said. "We used to . . ."

"Laugh about what a jerk he was?"

"Yeah." She seemed relieved I'd said it. "I was pretty surprised you were in his car."

"It's a long story."

She waited, but that's all I said. I didn't want to talk about Alec right now, didn't want to explain anything. It was too hard, too complicated.

"Was he drunk?"

"We both were." It was my stab at the truth, my attempt to come clean, for whatever it was worth. I'd screwed up with Matt; I wasn't going to do that again.

Cassie nodded, her lips pressed tight.

"Cassie, you can't tell anyone."

"Of course not," she said, and she meant it.

"I need that scholarship."

"I know." She got up and walked across the room, randomly picking things up off my desk, looking at them without seeing, and putting them back down.

"You look thin," she said, her eyes on me again. She sat on the edge of the bed. "Have you been eating?"

"A little," I said. "You know how I get when I'm stressed out."

"I know."

My room was quiet. The evening sun was peering through the window now, catching dust in shafts of light.

"I like your piercing," I said. I was so sick of the accident. Sick of talking about it, sick of thinking about it.

"What?"

"Your hoop, at the top of your ear. I like it."

"Oh, thanks." She smiled and reached up and touched it with her fingers. "Simon gave it to me." Color rose on her cheeks.

It was my turn to study her. "Oh my God," I said finally.

"What?" She looked sheepish.

"You did it, didn't you?"

Cassie turned bright red. She blushed so easily; she could never hide a thing.

"How did you know?" She was smiling now, beaming.

"I could tell. I *knew* there was something different about you!

You said you were going to wait for the right guy. So Simon, he's it?"

"Yeah, I guess he is."

"Oh. My. God. That's big." I hugged her and, for the first time in more than a week, I forgot about myself and my own stupid problems. "I'm really, really happy for you."

"Thanks," she said, still smiling. Her shoulders relaxed and she looked around my room. "This place is trashed," she said, flicking a pair of shorts with her toe, tossing them onto a chair.

"Hey, no changing the subject. I want to hear about Simon."

She laughed. "You will. But I'm hungry. Can we get a pizza or something? You need to get your strength back, girl. We're captains. We're taking this team to the state championship."

We *were* captains—elected at the end of last season. I had to get my shit together and get out of this house. I hadn't been running, eating—nothing. Practice began in two days.

"And Kay . . ."

"What?"

"Simon . . . You're the only one I'm telling. You know that, right?"

"Are you kidding? Of course, I'd never—"

Cassie shook her head. "Sorry," she said. "I didn't even need to ask."

15

Swarms of students rushed up the granite steps leading to the main school building. Hoping for invisibility, I pushed through them, head down. It was impossible: If the school had published its own version of *Star* magazine, Alec and I would've been the celebrities on its front cover. Right now, no news in Deerfield was more interesting than the after-party accident that could have killed the school's two top jocks.

I heard my name called several times—familiar voices, people I considered friends. Head down, I pretended not to hear.

"Hey, Katie, what's the rush?" It was Stanfield, coming up behind me just as I'd reached the main hall. "We've got ten minutes before class."

He took my shoulders, one in each big hand, spun me around, and studied my face. "Did that bastard hurt you?"

My chest tightened. I looked up and made my best attempt at a conspiratorial smile, one that said, *Yeah, that bastard Alec could have killed me when he drove the car off the road.* My lips turned up awkwardly.

"I'm okay, Stan." I was a fraud. Surely, Stan could see through me. Good and honest Stan.

He didn't. Stan didn't notice a thing.

"Coach has been having a field day with Alec, if it makes you feel any better," Stan said. "He's been making him come early and stay late every day for extra calisthenics, beating on him in practice, basically making the team hero the team scapegoat." Stan grinned.

"Because of . . . ?" *Shit.*

"There you are, girl." Cassie's voice rose above the crowd. "Hey, Stan! Long time . . ."

Stan swept her into a big bear hug. I watched as they chattered on about the summer, but their words meant nothing. My lie hung between us, splitting me apart from them like a great glass wall.

"Come on, we're going to be late." Cassie tugged my arm. "See you, Stan!"

I followed Cassie, her red hair bobbing just below the surface of the crowd, her grip tight on my wrist. My best friend. So why hadn't I told *her* the whole truth?

Cassie and I turned a corner and headed down a dead-end passage toward our first class. The crowd thinned out and Cassie let go of my arm. Ahead, Alec leaned against a wall, deep in conversation with Scott.

I hadn't seen Alec or talked to him since the day after the

accident at his house, and seeing him now made it come flooding back, everything I'd spent the last three weeks trying to forget. Panic crawled like fingers through my belly, gripping my chest.

"Jesus," Cassie said. She had stopped suddenly, her eyes riveted to Alec's face—to the bright purple scar that curved in a nearly perfect arch down the left side of his face. It was a large new moon. A smiley face slapped on crooked. A purple-red tattoo branded on his movie-star face. It was the first time she'd seen what had happened to him.

"He could have killed you both. . . ." She said it so softly, I almost didn't hear.

My heart skipped wildly. She was right, but he wasn't the one who had almost killed us both—it was *me*.

Scott glanced at me, then back at Alec, and left, slipping into the classroom.

"Can I talk to you?" Alec said to me. "*Alone.*"

Cassie's eyes widened, appalled that he'd even have the nerve to ask. My would-be murderer—that's what he was to her.

"It's okay," I whispered.

For a moment, she looked at me like I'd completely lost my mind. I nodded to her. "It's okay."

She looked at Alec, then back at me, an unasked question knit tightly in her brow. Then she walked away.

"What's up, Alec?" I wiped a damp strand of hair off my forehead. I badly wanted to sound normal, but my voice was quavering.

"Long time no see," he said. His blue eyes bored through me.

"I . . . yeah." What could I say? I'd spent the last three weeks convincing myself that Alec wanted nothing to do with me after what I'd done to him, after what he'd done *for me*. And it had worked: I'd believed it. I'd believed we'd just slide through our senior year, basically ignoring each other. A stupid, naive thought.

"I figured you didn't . . . ," I tried again.

"Didn't what?" There was a sharpness to his voice.

". . . didn't want to see me." I couldn't meet his eyes.

"Why would you think that?" he asked, but his voice was cold.

He's punishing me, I thought. *That's what this is about.*

And another thought: *I deserve it.*

For a moment, neither of us spoke.

"Listen, Stanfield's party is on Saturday," Alec said finally. "Scott and Alyssa are coming with us." With *us*?

"What?" He was confusing me now, completely shifting gears.

"We'll pick you up at eight," he said brusquely.

"Alec, I—"

The final bell rang; the hall was empty now except for us.

"I'm going with Cassie."

"Tell her there's been a change of plans," he said, his voice quiet, firm. "You're going with me."

He slipped into the classroom and was gone.

16

The field was deserted, practice over, the other girls gone. My sweaty T-shirt fluttered on my back, drying in the cool wind. Stick down, I took aim from just inside the shooting circle. A strong, high flick sailed straight into the upper left corner of the cage. It was my best shot, the one I was known for.

Perfect, I thought. *Unlike my life.* I ran to retrieve the ball.

How was I supposed to tell Cassie I was going to Stan's party with Alec? The look on her face when I'd spoken to him, *when I'd let him speak to me,* had said it all. She thought he was a criminal—and she assumed I'd want nothing to do with him.

"Katie, can you give me a hand with these cones?" Coach Riley came up behind me. "Then come to my office. I need to talk to you."

Coach Riley stepped into her dark, windowless office and shut the door.

"Sit down."

A wave of nausea swept through me. Something was seriously wrong; I could see it on her face. Behind her desk, she folded and unfolded her hands before she spoke. I sat in the single straight-backed chair, my hands tucked under my thighs, and waited.

"You're officially a captain of this team, Katie," she said finally. "Last year, when the girls elected you, I wasn't surprised. You've been a leader of this team for a long time. Actually, I predicted it when you were a freshman." A hint of pride flickered across her face, then disappeared.

I cleared my throat. "Thank you."

"But I need to talk to you about what happened this summer. I need to talk to you about the accident you got in with Alec Osborne."

I froze. My hands went numb under my thighs. What else did she know? That I'd been driving?

"Katie, I'll be frank. I'd heard things about you in the past. Some teachers said you were a partier—a drinker. I never knew what was true and what wasn't. I just heard things. Teachers hear more than you think."

I closed my eyes and pushed her words away. My ears hummed; I didn't want to know what she knew.

"Honestly," she was saying, "it was hard for me to believe. You were always so great to have on the team. You've got a heck of a lot of talent, a terrific attitude. You work hard and you play fair. Truthfully, I've enjoyed working with you as much as—maybe more than—any player I've had in twenty years. And I think I've let you down, Katie."

My head snapped up, eyes open. What did she just say? She'd let *me* down?

"I should have paid attention to what I'd heard and found out what was really going on. I should have spoken to you a long time ago."

"Nothing was going on," I said lamely, but relief flowed through me. She didn't know. She had no idea I'd been driving Alec's car. But I barely had time for this to sink in; Coach Riley hadn't stopped talking.

"I want you to get that scholarship. I think you know that. But this drinking, this accident . . ."

She paused and shook her head, then spoke with more determination. "The other girls look up to you, Katie." She cleared her throat. "And I'm just not sure that that's a good thing anymore."

In the split second that she paused, my stomach heaved and then dropped like a bomb inside me. "What do you mean?"

"I'm not sure if you should be in a leadership role on the team this year. I don't know if you're the right co-captain for the team."

Shame fluttered in my chest, then disappeared. A hot tide of anger swept through me. Suddenly I felt defiant. For three years, I'd had a clean record, except for a few bullshit rumors, and she'd supported me all the way. Now one thing happened—I did *one* thing wrong—and she was ready to take captain away from me? She didn't even know I was driving the *car*.

It was too much. A vision flashed through my mind of Coach Riley announcing to the whole team that there'd be a second election for captain because I had been found unworthy, and everyone staring at me to see my reaction. I could see Marcy Mattison's smirk now—that was one vote I'd never gotten. The whole school would know what had happened within days.

"But why?" I burst out. "What does this summer have to do with *now*, with this fall?"

It was the wrong thing to say. She bristled.

"It has quite a bit to do with it, in my view. You were drinking underage, Katie, in a car with a driver who was drunk. You're lucky you're not going to court. You could have ruined your chances for a scholarship completely."

The silence stretched out forever before she spoke again.

"I can't imagine what you were thinking. You both could've been killed." There was a slight tremor in her voice. "You almost were."

I pursed my lips and focused my eyes on the new cleats on my feet; already scratches and streaks of dirt covered the black and white leather after just two days of practice. My cheeks were on fire.

"The car was totaled, is that right?"

I nodded.

"And you weren't discovered out there in the woods until morning?"

"I—I woke up . . . I went for help."

"Your mother must have been frantic by then."

She wasn't home, I thought. But I didn't say it.

"Alec couldn't walk?"

"He wasn't awake," I murmured so low I could barely hear my own words.

"So Alec was unconscious. And I've seen his face. What about you?"

"I'm fine." The six stitches in my shoulder seemed like nothing next to Alec. They didn't even count. But she was looking at me, waiting.

"Three cracked ribs and a bruised lung," I said. These still hurt at practice after wind sprints. Pain in my chest from breathing hard.

"And stitches in your shoulder."

How did she even know that?

"Whatever," I muttered.

I couldn't believe she was forcing me to answer questions. It was obvious she knew the answers already.

"This whole thing . . ." She shook her head. "It's not like you, Katie."

Yes it is. I thought. *I did it, didn't I?* But suddenly I felt hollow and sad.

"I don't know," I whispered lamely.

"Well, I hope it scared you." Her voice was low. "It sure as heck scared me."

I nodded, eyes back on my cleats. I could feel tears welling up. *Don't let me cry in front of Coach Riley,* I prayed.

"Now listen, you have an excellent chance of getting at least a partial scholarship next year—maybe a full ride. I know that's what you want and I know it's what you *need*—and I'd hate to see you blow that chance. But the decision is entirely yours. You've got to know where I stand. The school has its rules and I have mine. If you drink, you don't play. It's as simple as that. And if you don't play, the whole team is affected. I know that means something to you."

It did. She paused, letting her words sink in.

"So what do you think? Do you think you can be a good leader this year? Be a good example for the underclassmen? Can you sign the drug and alcohol abstinence contract and stick to it?"

She looked me in the eye and nodded as if we were making a silent agreement that I would behave and play by the rules.

"Yes," I said quietly.

"Good." She smiled. "I need to lock up now."

I made for the door quickly. I had to get out. I knew I was going to start crying, and that made me madder than she did.

17

Later, sitting on my front porch, I watched as the sun faded behind Pitcher Mountain. Across the road, lights flicked on in Matt's house. I wanted desperately to talk to him. To have him hug me and say everything would be okay. But even if we were speaking—and we weren't; we hadn't since the day he'd left my house after the accident—even if he did say those words, could they be true? It felt like the ground had cracked open and any minute I would disappear into a gapping black hole.

The phone rang in the kitchen and I jumped to get it, praying it would be Matt. I'd been doing this for weeks, hoping against hope he'd call me. Every day—every minute—I wondered what he'd say if I called him or just walked over and knocked on his door. Would he hang up? Shut the door in my face? I didn't think I could take that. In the new twilight zone that had become my life, silence was a step above outright rejection. I'd stick with the sure thing.

Cassie's name blinked on the caller ID. Cassie McPherson:

best friend, other captain—*good* captain. Captain who didn't get dragged into Coach Riley's office and nearly get fired today. I couldn't talk to her right now. What would I say? That Coach Riley basically thinks I'm a drunk, irresponsible loser and that the other girls shouldn't look up to me anymore?

Yeah, that was a speech I wanted to share with my perfect best friend. Then, to top it off, I could tell her that, despite Coach Riley's lecture and threats, I would *still* be going to Stanfield's party Saturday night, but just not with her—I'd be going with *Alec*. It was a conversation I couldn't have.

The phone rang again, then stopped. Cassie's name disappeared. She'd wonder where I was, why I hadn't answered. She'd ask me later and I'd tell her I was in the shower. Another lie.

At practice earlier that day, Cassie told me that Matt had asked about me.

"Call him, Kay," she'd said. "He really misses you."

I picked up the phone and went back out to the porch, my eyes on Matt's house. He was close enough that if I called his name loud and his bedroom window was open—and it was, I could see—he would hear me. But I was afraid. We had always fought about alcohol—or, more specifically, about me drinking it. Fought, yes. Ended our friendship, no. But what if this time was different?

The air cooled. I put the phone down. A light glimmered on the second floor, then sharpened in the dusk: Matt was in his room. Downstairs, his parents' television glowed. I stared at his house, replaying our last conversation in my head. *Maybe you should just stay out of my goddamn life.* Why had I ever said that?

I'd blurted it out without thinking, that's why, and I regretted it as much as anything I'd ever said. But would Matt understand that? And could he ever understand doing something as insanely stupid as getting in a car accident, drunk, with Alec Osborne? Matt wasn't impulsive like me. He didn't understand how you could sometimes do or say things and then wish you could take them back, and how sometimes you couldn't even explain why you did them in the first place. He thought things through, then made a decision based on the facts. For him, life was like deciding which camera was the better buy when you only had money for one. But it wasn't that simple for me.

I thought about the way he was on the soccer field—all grace and quiet energy. He surprised his opponents with his quick, subtle movements and his skill handling the ball. Moving down the field, he was patient, unassuming; there was nothing that made him stand out from the crowd. But just when a defensive player thought Matt was dribbling into a trap, he'd surprise him by executing a flawless pass without even blinking. His teammates said that Matt had great vision, that he could "see the whole field," and that made him a brilliant player.

Right now I just wished he could see things my way.

18

The next day after school, the locker room buzzed. In a few minutes, we'd take the field for our first scrimmage, and even though it wasn't an official game, we were fired up, ready to go. The year before, we'd finished second in the state in our division. This year we had to be first. For seniors, it was our last chance to be champions.

"Let's kick some butt today!" Megan hollered. She turned and high-fived me as I made my way to my locker. "Seniors rule!"

Shouts of agreement rang out. Locker doors slammed. The buzz was about the scrimmage but also about Stan's party, the one that marked the start of the school year. The same group of us always went; the rest couldn't or weren't interested. My friends assumed I'd be there with them.

"Better hurry up," Cassie said. "I hear Coach Riley coming." I threw my kilt on and fumbled with the buttons.

"Listen up, girls!" Coach Riley pulled her wire-rimmed glasses down off the bridge of her nose. "I got your drug and alcohol contracts from the athletic director today." She waved a stack of white papers as she spoke. "I want you to sign them now. Quickly. Get out a pen."

There were low murmurs of conversation as girls shuffled through backpacks. Megan glanced at me and rolled her eyes.

"Let me draw your attention to the line about zero tolerance," Coach Riley said as she passed them out. "That means if you drink or drug, you *do not play.*"

The room fell silent. The JV coach, Ms. Pingree, nodded in agreement, her solemn face aimed at her freshmen and sopho-mores.

"We've got a winning team here this year, but any one of you could blow it for the whole team if you don't keep your priori-ties straight for the next eight weeks. Coach Pingree and I take these very seriously."

My face was on fire. This was the first time she'd ever given us a speech like this. Ever. Her eyes were moving around the room, but it felt like she was talking straight to me.

"It's simple," she repeated. "You drink, you don't play. You drug, you don't play."

She collected the signed contracts, but she didn't move— she wasn't done with us yet.

"One more thing." Her eyes scanned our faces. "I don't want to hear any talk about parties at practice, on the bus, in the locker room, or anywhere else coming out of your mouths—not about Stan's party this Saturday night, or any other. Don't think we aren't paying attention."

There was a stunned silence. No one had ever heard a coach refer to a specific party like that.

Marcy Mattison smirked and actually laughed—a short, surprised *ha!* A sharp look from Coach Riley shut her down quickly. She turned toward her locker, hiding her face from sight.

Megan and Cheryl exchanged a look. A couple girls glanced at me, their eyes darting away again when I looked their way. They were gauging my reaction. I stared down at the gray cement floor beneath my feet.

When Coach Riley left, no one said a word.

Then Marcy broke the silence. "Good going, Martini. Way to ruin things for everybody."

My face burned. *Martini.*

Bobbi Crow came to my rescue, breaking the awkward silence. "Hey Katie, thanks for lending me this. It was awesome." She pulled a DVD, *The Four Fundamental Attack Skills for Successful Field Hockey*, out of her locker and handed it to me.

Relieved by the distraction, people started talking again, ignoring Marcy's outburst.

A minute later, Coach Riley was back. "Let's go, girls! Get out there and get warmed up. Cassie and Katie, stretch out everybody. Hustle now!" She clapped her hands a couple times as we paraded by her. "Let's start this year off right!"

I looked around at my teammates' flushed, dripping faces, then tipped up a bottle and squeezed; a shot of cold water hit the back of my throat. We'd only gone through warm-up drills and we looked like we'd played a whole game. I tossed the water bottle to Megan, who had thrown off her chest pad in a futile effort to cool down before the game began.

The refs called for the captains from each team. Cassie and I grinned at each other as we walked across the field toward them. It was our first game as seniors and as captains.

"Hey, Captain Kate," Cassie said, "how does it feel?"

"It feels good, Captain Cass."

We reported back to our team, and Coach Riley began reading the starting lineup.

"Megan in the goal; Cheryl Cooper at sweep . . ." I tuned her out and thought about the game. I wanted to play my best today. Start the season off right. Scrimmage or not, to me, a game was a game. I always played to win.

"Cassie, left wing; Sue Tapley, left inner . . ."

What? My head jerked up. Left inner was *my* position. I looked around, confused. Had I missed something? No. Sue Tapley looked confused, too. So did my other teammates. Cassie shot me a shocked, questioning look. Coach Riley finished reading the lineup.

"Sally Foster, right inner; Sarah Miles, right wing." *I wasn't on it.*

It felt like a swift kick in the stomach. I looked at Coach Riley for a clue, but her eyes stayed focused on the field. For a moment, no one moved.

"Hustle out there! Let's go!" Coach Riley said.

I stood on the sideline, watching my teammates jog onto the

field. Frozen in place, I didn't know who to look at or where to stand.

The whistle blew. Cassie's red hair bobbed in the distance. Beyond her, Sue Tapley, running parallel, waited for a cross-pass that should have been mine. The field blurred. No. I couldn't cry. I wouldn't.

A surge of anger ripped through me; my face grew hot. The only time a sub had gone in for me *ever* was when I'd twisted my ankle one game, and Riley'd let me go back in after twenty minutes when I insisted I was fine. *No one* else in Deerfield had made the Maine All-Star Team. No other freshman in the *state* had been named to the team. And I was watching from the *bench?*

Farther down the sideline, Coach Riley was doing her usual thing, pacing up and down, kneeling, then standing up again, jotting notes on her clipboard. I willed her to look at me, to call my name and put me in, but she was totally absorbed in the game.

Sue Tapley had a clear shot on goal and fired it away, missing the goal cage completely. Ten minutes later, the other team scored. My heart pounded. It was the perfect time for a substitute. Still, Riley never looked my way.

At halftime, Cassie and the others came off the field panting and dripping with sweat. They collapsed in a circle, sucking their water bottles. I stood behind them with the second-stringers as Coach Riley talked. She hadn't looked at me once since the game began.

She put in a couple substitutes at halftime. I wasn't one of them. I was beginning to hate her.

Five minutes into the second half, the other team scored again. It was 2–0 now.

"Katie!" Riley called in my direction. Her eyes stayed on the game. "Stretch out and take a lap—then go in for Sue. Pronto."

19

I hadn't done this before. It was tough going in in the middle of a game, barely warmed up, trying to find the rhythm of my team, nervous as hell that I would blow my chance to contribute—or, in this case, redeem myself—by missing a shot or making a bad pass. All my confidence had evaporated in the last forty minutes.

They intercepted our pass-back and carried the ball toward their goal, shooting almost immediately. Megan deflected the shot and kicked the ball way out to the side, where one of our halfbacks fought for it and won, shooting it up to Cassie, who was waiting above the twenty-five yard line to pick up the pass and go. My anxiety slipped away as I sprinted forward, but Cassie lost the ball in a tackle.

The rest of the game was a tired series of scrambles. We managed to keep the ball on our end for the remaining fifteen minutes, and I even tapped one into the goal on a rebound, but with about three minutes left, we had no chance; we still needed a second goal to tie things up.

The lead ref blew her whistle and raised her arms. "Game!" she called.

For me, it felt like it was over before it began. We'd lost 2–1. There wasn't enough time to even things up no matter how hard I tried.

And I really did try.

I slammed my locker door and reached down to where my backpack lay on the cement floor. I was in no hurry to go back outside and run into anyone. If my complete humiliation had been Coach Riley's goal today, she'd achieved it.

Behind me, footsteps. "I need to lock up now, Katie," Coach Riley said.

This was my only chance to ask. She was going to leave if I didn't.

"Why didn't I play the whole game?" I said, my back to her.

"You know why, Katie."

"I *don't* know. If I knew why, I wouldn't be asking." I turned and looked at her.

Coach Riley's eyebrows shot up in surprise, but her expression remained calm. "Think about it."

"I don't know."

"I told you when I handed out the contracts. You drink, you don't play."

"But I *haven't* . . ."

"Not since the accident. I know. And I don't want to hear again that you have."

"This was for the *summer*?" My face was burning. I nearly spit the words out.

"This was for the summer. You have to understand what it will be like if I hear anything about you drinking at *any* time during the next two months. It was only a scrimmage today, Katie. I did it so that it won't have to happen during the real season. The team needs to know that captains aren't above this policy. It applies equally to everyone."

My head was spinning. Imagine if she knew the *truth*.

"Can I go now?" I said. I picked up my bag and left without looking back.

Cassie had waited for me outside. "*What* is going on?" she asked, her face incredulous. "Why did she bench you?"

I kicked at some gravel with my cleat, sending pebbles bouncing across the blacktop. "She heard Alec and I were drinking before the accident this summer, and if you drink, you don't play." I gazed across the empty field, my voice monotone.

Cassie looked confused. "Well, that came out of nowhere."

"No, it didn't."

"What are you talking about?"

I finally looked at her. "She talked to me about it yesterday." I told Cassie what Coach Riley had said—how she didn't want me to blow my chance at a scholarship, how worried she'd been, how she threatened to take captain away from me.

"Why didn't you tell me? You still are, right? I mean, you were captain today," Cassie said.

"Yeah."

"Because I would have resigned in protest if she'd booted you." She really would have; I knew that.

For a moment, neither of us spoke.

"Look," Cassie said finally, "Coach Riley just wants you to have a great season your last year. Wants you to stay out of trouble so you can score goals for her. You'll be starting again Saturday. She couldn't even keep you on the bench the whole game today."

"She kept me there long enough."

"You're telling me. I had to deal with Sue Tapley. That girl needs a compass to know what direction she's running in."

I smiled, despite myself.

"Don't worry," she said. "There's nothing you can do about any of this now. It's over."

But Alec's words about Stan's party rang in my head: *You're going with me.* I thought about the accident. His face. The lie.

No, Cassie, I thought, *it isn't.*

20

Outside my bedroom window, a loud *whoosh* startled me out of my sleep.

The rapid clunking of wood tumbling on wood followed, like a hundred building blocks dropped in a heap: The winter's wood had arrived.

A large truck growled and whined as it moved forward and then back again at a different angle. With another enormous clatter, it deposited the rest of its load. I groaned and rolled over, pulling the covers with me. I'd barely slept. Coach Riley's words had circled through my head long after midnight. *It's simple. You drink, you don't play.* Clearly, I couldn't go to Stan's party on Saturday. But what would I say to Alec? He had not asked me to go. He had *told* me I was going. With *him.*

I peered out the window, trying to clear my head. Ron Bailey looked up and lifted a hand in greeting. The pile looked gargantuan. The pile meant work.

Ron shut off the engine and stepped down from the cab of the truck when I appeared outside.

"Looks like I got you out of bed." His face was broad and gentle, his smile kind.

I looked down. Bare feet and flannel pajama bottoms: a dead giveaway.

"So how you doin'?" He walked around, surveying the pile. "That Alec character isn't giving you any problems, is he?"

My cheeks flushed. "No—no," I stammered. "He's fine."

"Don't know if I'd agree about that." Ron scowled. "Scared the life out of me when I found you that day. He's damn lucky you're standing here walking around."

He was looking at me now, waiting for me to speak, but how could I?

"Well," he said. "You'd better be gettin' ready for school. If you need a hand with this, you just give a call. You know where to find me."

I mustered a smile. "Thanks, Ron."

The sharp scent of cut wood filled the cold morning air. Panic rushed through me as Ron pulled out of our yard. What was I going to do? Every year since my dad left, Matt and his father had helped me split and stack three cords. There was no way I could do it alone. But how could I call Matt now and ask him for help? I couldn't.

I'll split it myself, damn it, I thought. *I'll do it by hand. I don't need any help.*

I blinked and looked up. There, out of nowhere, was Matt,

standing by our tallest pine tree, hands shoved in his pockets, shoulders high like he was shrugging.

"Hey, Katie," he said.

"Hey, Matt." I picked up a stray log and flung it onto the pile, where it landed with a solid *clunk*.

He raised his brows and lifted his chin in the direction of the pile. "That's a lot of wood."

I nodded.

Neither of us spoke for a moment. I shivered and rubbed my arms. The sun was shining through the trees now, burning away the mist, revealing sky as blue as a robin's egg.

"My dad said he could come over a couple weekends from now and give you a hand."

"That'd be great, Matt, thanks." My heart pounded.

"No problem. I heard it's getting cold early this year. Might snow before Thanksgiving."

"Really? That's cool. Good field hockey weather. The cold, I mean." I was babbling.

"Cassie told me U. Maine's coach is definitely coming to see you. Congratulations."

I nodded. Matt kicked at a stick on the ground in front of him, then tried to lift it with his toe and keep it airborne.

"How's soccer?"

"Good. We have our first game after school today."

"I'll come see it."

"I think it's during your practice."

"Oh," I said. "Right. Good luck."

"Thanks," he said. Silence.

"Well, see ya." He turned slowly and walked across the lawn toward his house, his flannel shirttails flapping behind him.

Miss you! I wanted to call after him, but I couldn't.

What if he ignored me? Just left my words to hang in the air, then fall flat on the ground? What if his father had made him come over and he was just as mad at me as ever?

I watched him cross the street and go into his house, then went inside and collapsed on the couch.

A loud knock startled me. I jumped up and headed for the door, glancing at the clock as I ran. I hadn't meant to fall asleep; it was time to leave for school.

I swung the door open. Matt.

"Hi," he said.

"Um, are we talking?"

"Yeah, we're talking. I talked to you an hour ago. I told you we'd help with the wood."

"I thought maybe your dad made you do that."

"No. He didn't make me do it."

A wave of relief rushed through me; behind it, tears.

Matt reached out for me. "Don't cry," he said gently. "It'll ruin your strength."

I laughed and squeezed my eyes tight. "I'm sorry."

"I've seen you cry before," he said, pulling me close.

"No, I'm *sorry*. About what I said to you." I buried my face in his chest. "I didn't mean it. I don't want you out of my life. I'd never want that."

"I know," he said.

"Don't ever forget that, no matter what I do."

Matt pushed me away so he could look at my face. "I won't, but don't go doing anything else crazy, okay?"

"I've got no plans for that."

"I heard Alec asked you to go to Stan's party with him."

"*What?* I don't need you checking up on me, Matt."

He didn't say anything, just kicked at the floor of the porch with one sneaker. "Well, you're staying away from Alec, right?"

"Yes. I am. It's just . . . things are complicated, Matt."

Matt looked into my eyes, searching for a clue.

"Believe me. I don't like Alec either," I said quietly.

"Okay," he said. "I believe you."

We stood there for a moment, taking each other in.

"Go get dressed, quick," he said. "I'll give you a ride to school."

21

Saturday morning a cool September breeze blew through the fan in my bedroom window. I put on my uniform and let the air flow over me. Finally, relief from the heat. *This* was field hockey weather. It had to be a good omen. Cassie had to be right: I'd paid my dues. My career on the bench was over.

Downstairs in the kitchen, my mother cradled the phone between her ear and shoulder. She covered the receiver and turned to me. "Do you have a game today?"

I nodded.

"Make sure you eat something."

Her back was to me again before I could reply. Her head, still attached to the phone, disappeared into the refrigerator.

"Okay, I'll see you at eleven thirty, then." She closed the door and hung up.

"Hot date tonight, Mom?" She was moving at a frenetic pace around the kitchen, grabbing a can of tuna out of the pantry, slicing a tomato, whipping her hair up into a bun and securing it with a clip she dug out of her pocket. *Maybe that's why she's so thin*, I thought, *because she never stops moving*.

"I'd hardly call it *a date*. We've been together three months." I recognized the smile on her face when she said it. She definitely liked this guy.

"Damn." She tried to sponge a coffee spill off her nurse's uniform. "Is your hockey uniform clean? I haven't done laundry . . ."

"I washed it, Mom. I'm wearing it."

She gave up on the coffee stain and headed back to the fridge, dodging me on her way. "Sorry, Kate, I'm late for work. I'm doing a double today. It means overtime this week. I'll be too exhausted to drive anywhere tonight. I'll be at the hospital until eleven, then at Ken's. Will's at Ben's again tonight."

"He should pay rent there," I said.

She ignored that and gathered her things to go. "I went shopping. There's plenty for dinner. And don't forget the wood. We need to get started on that. Cover it with the tarps in the garage if it looks like it's going to rain, will you, Kate?"

Moments later, I watched her back out of the driveway, relieved that she was gone. It was time to focus. Today was the start of a stellar season. Nothing was going to come between me and a perfect record, between me and a scholarship, between me and a *future*.

How many people even get this chance? That's what Matt said when the college letters started arriving. He was right. There was no way I was going to blow it. I knew what I had to do, and I'd do it: Say no to drinking. Say no to Stan's party.

How hard could it be?

*　*　*

When the whistle blew and the game began, I felt like I was flying. Any anxiety I'd felt was gone. The world around me slipped away. All that existed was my body in motion and the ball moving toward me. My movements were spontaneous reactions to what had happened the split second before. There was no time to ponder, or worry, or consider. I thought no more of how I moved and reacted than a person considers her own breathing. This was the freedom of sport, a freedom that eluded me off the field no matter how hard I tried to find it.

A pass from Cassie, timed perfectly, shot straight and hard across the field. I rushed it with my stick down and made the connection. One tap put it under my control and into the circle. Stick on ball, ball into cage. It happened so fast, their goalie didn't know what hit her. Neither did I. A rush of adrenaline zipped through me. It was perfect: a goal in the first five minutes.

I glanced toward Coach Riley as we jogged back to the fifty yard line. She was grinning. "Way to go, girls! Keep it up."

Matt, smiling, too, caught my eye as I ran by.

Everything's going to be all right, I thought as I took my position. *Everything's going to be just fine.*

Clouds were moving over the sun as we stepped out of the gym. My hair still damp from showering, I reached into my bag and pulled out my Windbreaker, happily throwing it on over my head. We'd won our first official game.

But from the corner of my eye I spotted Alec, standing near

the field with Rob, Scott, and some other football players. My stomach turned, the excitement of our 3–0 win slipping away. We hadn't spoken since that moment in the hall when Alec told me they'd pick me up at eight. I'd avoided him and he hadn't come near me. Now I had to tell him; the party was tonight. I had no choice.

"What's up?" Cassie asked.

I looked around the field for Coach Riley. She was near the bench still, talking to some parents. "It seems like everyone's going to Stanfield's," I said, "so I guess they're not worried about Riley finding out."

"Megan said they aren't taking their own cars, just in case she's patrolling the neighborhood or something," Cassie said. "She asked me to go in her brother's car."

"*Are* you?"

"Are you kidding? There's no way it's worth it. I can't believe they're going."

"Let them see how it feels to get caught," I said, kicking at the grass.

"You don't mean that," Cassie said. "I mean, we could forget going undefeated if they get benched."

"True." *But how fair will it be if they get away with it?* I thought. I was sick of being the team scapegoat.

"I'll bring the pizza and movies to your house?" Cassie asked.

"That sounds great," I said, but my eyes were back on Alec, who'd tossed the football to Scott and was heading straight for me. I did not want to talk to him in front of Cassie.

"I left something in my locker." I dropped my bag on the ground and walked quickly toward the gym.

Sneakers squeaked on the concrete floor outside the bathroom stall where I'd taken refuge.

"Kay?" Cassie's voice sounded hollow in the empty basement room. "Alec's out there, you know. He claims you're going to Stanfield's with him."

Despite the dread I was feeling, I had to keep this light. I didn't want Cassie thinking it was a big deal. *I* didn't want to think it was a big deal.

"How could I be going with him?" I said, emerging from the stall. "Before I wasn't going at all, I was going with you."

Her smile was fleeting. "Seriously. What's his problem?"

"He wants me to go." I shrugged. "I never said I would."

"I *really* don't like him, Kay." Cassie hit the button of a hand dryer—*bam*—with the palm of her hand and stuck her damp head beneath it. Hot air rushed out of the nozzle, the roar like a vacuum cleaner.

"It's no big deal, Cassie," I said when it stopped. "I'll get rid of him."

She picked up her bag and finally cracked a smile. "Please do."

Alec's loud laugh carried across the field and bounced off the gym as I emerged. In the distance, I could see Matt talking to Coach Riley, his head tilted to one side, a habit he'd developed from being so tall. Behind them, the oak trees on the hill swayed slightly in the wind. Most everyone else was gone.

But not Alec.

"Hey, good game, Katie," he said, approaching with Scott at his side.

"Congratulations."

Scott glanced at Alec, then walked away, football tucked under one arm.

"We'll pick you up at eight," Alec said to me.

"I can't go." My eyes darted uneasily in Coach Riley and Matt's direction.

"How come?" His words were a challenge. He looked at me as if he dared me to say it again.

"Katie. *How come?* Scott and Alyssa are counting on us."

"My mom won't let me."

"Bull."

"What?"

"I said *bull.*" He flashed a smile. "Your mother lets you go anywhere you want—when she's *home.* You've been to every party within fifty miles since freshman year."

"So? That was before I ended up drunk in an emergency room at six a.m. She's not so trusting anymore."

His smile vanished. "So your mother's home tonight?"

I didn't say anything, just looked past him toward the field. I didn't want him to know the truth. How scared I was of getting caught by Coach Riley, of blowing my future.

"I didn't think so," he said.

I barely heard him. Coach Riley had turned and stood still now, her eyes fastened on Alec and me. My stomach lurched; I had to get away.

"I have to stay in tonight, Alec. I *have* to."

His eyes fixed on mine and held. "Well, I'd give it some serious thought, Martini. I mean—if I were in your shoes."

Was that a threat? Something inside me snapped. What was he going to do, tell everyone I was driving? Accuse me of that *now*? Who would actually believe him?

"You know what?" I said, emboldened. "Do what you want. If I go, my hockey career is over, anyway."

"Well," he said, a slight smirk on his face. "Then we'll just have to work something else out."

22

The sun had slipped behind the mountains on the western side of the lake, turning them a dusky blue, then darker still—a black ridge against a clear, star-filled sky.

Inside my house, I paced the living room, restless. I flipped on the stereo and turned the volume up loud—loud enough that I could feel the music vibrating up through the floorboards and into my bare feet—then flopped onto the couch. The Fly: the best band in the world.

The phone rang behind me. I reached over my head and grabbed it. "Hello?" I said. "Hold on . . ." I ran to shut off the music; it was Stan.

"Tell me the vicious rumor isn't true."

My heart stopped. Had Alec freaked out on me and told people?

"What are you talking about, Stan?"

"That you're not coming to my party tonight, what else?"

"Oh, shit, *that.*"

"Hey, what's more important than my big event?"

I laughed, relieved. "Nothing, believe me."

"All right, then, that's what I like to hear. So we'll see you tonight?"

"No, no, you heard right. But believe me, staying home wasn't my idea." I filled him in on Coach Riley's lecture, what she'd said about contracts and parties, how she'd benched me at the scrimmage.

"Whoa. That's harsh. You weren't even driving the damn car."

"She's freaked out about the scholarship thing."

"Damn, that sucks. Maybe we could smuggle you in, hide you somewhere. My attic's pretty nice. A few bats, but they've never bitten anyone."

"It wouldn't matter. Riley might not find me, but *Alec* would."

"What's that supposed to mean?"

"Nothing," I said. "Alec's just . . ."

"Alec's just *what*?"

I'd said too much; I felt it right away. If Alec heard I was bad-mouthing him, even a little, he might feel like getting even. And what right did I have to say anything about him after what *I'd* done?

"He's just being a jerk. But what's new, right?" I said, lightly.

"Christ, he almost killed you. Isn't that enough?"

It was weird how used to hearing that I was—from Stan, from Cassie—used to hearing everyone talk about Alec crashing the car. "He just wanted me to go with him tonight. No big deal.

Alec doesn't get it. Why would he? Your coach is nothing like Riley. A few extra push-ups and it's over, right?"

"Word is Alec's dad took care of that. He's buddies with Coach Swenson."

"See? It figures. Listen, I was just kidding about Alec. He's fine. And I'm sorry I can't come tonight, Stan. I really am."

"Well, my sources tell me a bunch of your sworn-to-sobriety teammates are going to show up, but I won't give you a hard time."

"Thanks, Stan."

I hung up, walked through the kitchen, and stepped out onto the porch. A full moon had risen high over the tree line and hung suspended, shiny and pale. Its luminous glow backlit thin clouds, making them visible in the night sky. Cold air filled my lungs and goose bumps rose on the flesh of my bare arms.

Stan would have a fire burning in the big stone fireplace in his barn tonight. They'd be sitting around it, laughing and talking, playing quarters with mugs of beer on the wide wooden floorboards.

Let them, I thought. There'll be other parties. My friends, Coach Riley, a hockey scholarship: these things were more important than a night out. They had to be.

A door slammed across the street, the sound echoing up our lonely dead-end street. A moment later Matt appeared out of the shadows and waved as he stepped onto the silvery moonlit grass.

"Help me get some wood?" I asked.

He nodded and followed me out toward the barn.

By the time Cassie's father dropped her off, the wood stove was lit and the fire crackling. She put a large pizza and three DVDs on the kitchen table: a new horror movie and a couple of comedies. Since I was going to be home alone all night after they left, the scary one was going in first. A comedy would help me forget it.

"If we're going to watch this, I want you guys on either side of me," I hollered from the kitchen, where I was digging for cookies in the overflowing cupboards. My mother kept the place stocked with enough food to feed several professional basketball teams at all times. I think it made her feel like she was taking care of us.

"It's not like you haven't seen it before," Matt hollered back.

"I haven't."

"Well, one just like it," he said.

"It's not the same thing."

He snuck up behind me then and grabbed me suddenly with both hands, poking me in the ribs. I dropped the cookies I'd found and went after him, chasing him into the living room. "You're dead, buddy!"

"Break it up, you guys. I'm starting it." Cassie was on the couch with the remote aimed at the television screen like a gun.

I picked up a pillow and hurled it across the room at Matt. He ducked.

"Hey!" Cassie yelled, but Matt tackled me, tickling me.

"Cut it out! I can't breathe."

"Leave her alone," Cassie said.

"What're you, my mother?" Matt let go of me and whipped a pillow at Cassie.

"You're a bully," she said, and scowled at him.

Thoughts of Stan's party were gone. Snuggled between my two best friends on the couch, I felt safe. By the end of the first movie, I'd completely relaxed, my head on a pillow on Matt's shoulder.

Hours later, Cassie and I stood barefoot on the cold porch and watched Matt disappear into his house across the street.

"Why don't you come home with me?" Cassie said. "Spend the night?"

"Thanks, Cass, but that's okay."

"It's not healthy for you to be alone so much."

"Don't look at me like that," I said.

"Like what?" She cocked her head to one side.

"Like you feel sorry for me. If your parents had wanted another daughter, they would have had one. They don't need me hanging around all the time."

"Don't you like my parents?" Her question was genuine.

"You know I do. I'm just . . . I'm not a charity case."

"I know you're not."

"Anyway, I can't imagine they're too happy with me right now."

"They're fine with you."

"Come on, Cassie. If you'd been in that accident, you'd be

grounded for the rest of your life. I'm surprised they let you come over here tonight."

Cassie looked away.

"I wish you could stay overnight here for once," I said.

"You know I can't unless there's an adult here."

"Yeah, and *that* never happens."

"I'm sorry . . ."

"Don't be," I said. "At least you know they care."

23

Cassie and Matt were long gone.

From my bed, I could see the lone light that Matt's mother left on in their upstairs hallway each night. When I was a kid, my mother would leave my window shade half up so I could see their light anytime I woke up. It was like a distant night light that kept me company.

The moon had risen high over the dark silhouette of Matt's house. It looked calm sitting up there, spreading light across the cold September sky. I read a few pages of my book until the words began to run together. . . .

It was nearly two thirty a.m. when I woke up, suddenly, to the sounds of a car swinging into my dirt driveway, gravel crackling under its wheels, the engine humming loudly in the quiet night. My body was in full alert; my heart beat like crazy. Who would be in my driveway at this hour?

I peered out the window, frozen, unsure what to do. The headlights were bright and I couldn't tell the shape of the car attached to them. But I had to find out—or get to a phone. Slipping out from under the bedcovers, I made my way across the dark bedroom toward the hall.

Possibilities raced through my mind: Had my mother's schedule changed? It wouldn't matter—she never drove home this late. Had Matt's uncle Paul showed up drunk again and pulled into the wrong driveway? Not impossible, but not likely either, since Matt's mom had banished him from their house months ago. Fear crept through my belly. This was a dead-end street. The only people who came by here lived out here. There was no good explanation, and I knew it.

The car moved forward around the curve of the driveway as I tiptoed down the stairs, its high beams flashing through the windows and across the living room like a searchlight. I wondered if I should turn on the lights to let it be known I was there—awake, alert, ready to take on intruders. *No*, I thought. *See the car first.* Still as a statue, I waited.

It seemed like forever before the headlights clicked off and the driver cut the engine. A car door slammed; then the hollow *thunk* of footsteps crossed the old wood floorboards of the porch. Heart bursting from my chest, I ran for the phone, ready to push a button and call Ron Bailey or Harlan Reed, but someone was knocking loudly, persistently—urgently. *If someone's pounding on my door at two a.m., maybe they have a good reason*, I thought desperately. I took a deep breath, switched on the porch light, and peered out the window.

It was Alec, one muscular arm extended, hand on the doorframe, the other holding a six-pack by his side.

"Jesus Christ," I said loudly, fear turning to anger.

"Katie?" he called. "Open the damn door. It's cold out here." He rapped again impatiently. "I know you're in there."

I flung the door open. "How'd you know it wasn't my mother? Keep your voice down, will you?" I whispered.

"You can cut the act. Your mother wasn't here before and she's not here now. Her car's gone."

"Well, she could've been. And my brother is sleeping upstairs." There was no way he could know that wasn't true.

"Right," he replied, pushing past me into the kitchen. "Beer?" he asked. "I got Corona—your favorite. I even"—he reached into his jean pocket—"brought a lime." He held it out on his palm like he was presenting a golden egg.

"What are you doing here? It's two in the morning, in case you haven't noticed."

"You couldn't go to the party, so I'm bringing the party to you. This is the thanks I get? Shit, Martini, I expected some gratitude." He took a swig off a beer, then handed me a full one. "Have a seat," he said to me. "Make yourself at home."

I looked at the bottle in my hand, then put it on the table. Was Alec trying to get me in trouble? Give me beer, then make sure my coach heard about our after-hours party of two?

"Drink up. There's plenty more."

"I'm not thirsty."

"Right. Like that ever stopped you."

"Look, you can't stay here. You're going to wake up Will."

"You know, you're a little uptight lately. You need to loosen up, have some fun." He banged his beer down on the table loudly and fixed his eyes on me. "You're not getting out enough."

I looked back at him, then away, speechless. I still couldn't believe he was sitting at my kitchen table. Why had I opened the door? I'd known I had to break it off with Alec before we ever got into the stupid accident. Well, he was proving me right, but that wasn't helping me now. I'd let him in—now I had to get him out.

"How was Stanfield's?" I tried to sound casual.

"Great—you should've been there. Marcy caught Rob in the hall closet making out with Sue Tapley, so Marcy flings the door open and Sue jumps up, her shirt off—hanging free for all to see—and Marcy takes a swing at her. I couldn't believe it." He laughed. "It was a real cat fight."

"What did Rob do?"

"That's the best part. He just leaves them there and he's out in the barn mixing gin and tonics for your teammates."

"Nice guy."

Alec shrugged. "The guy knows how to take care of himself. Marcy's whacked. I should know."

"Who else was there from field hockey?" I asked. "Besides Sue and Marcy." I couldn't believe the sophomore who'd replaced me in that first scrimmage had the nerve to show up and drink.

"Megan, of course, and Cheryl. Basically your key defensive players and one half-assed sub. Wasn't the same without you, though. People were asking for you."

Alec opened another beer and drank, neither of us speaking

for a moment. I leaned against the refrigerator, arms folded across my chest.

"Well, thanks for stopping by," I said, taking a new tack. Maybe if I was nice he'd leave. "I'm going to go to bed."

"Want some company?"

"*What?*"

"Take it easy. Can't you take a joke anymore? You know, you used to be fun." He stood up then, and I hoped he was leaving, but he came and stood next to me.

"The guys on the team have been calling me Frank—you know, for Frankenstein. A highly creative group," he said, turning his cheek toward me, rubbing his scar. "But Scottie just calls me Scarface. I prefer that, don't you? Not original, but it's the Al Pacino thing. You know that old flick *Scarface*, right?" He fixed his blue eyes on mine.

"Yeah. But I don't think it's very nice," I said, looking away.

"It's true, though. You can't hide from the truth."

"Well, you don't have to rub it in, either."

"I don't mind. Scars add character to a guy's face. Don't you think?" He circled around me and we were chest to chest, my back pushed up against the refrigerator. His hands held my upper arms a little too firmly. There was nowhere to look but up at his face.

"Look, Alec. I'm sorry." My voice was barely audible. "I'm really, really sorry."

"What are you sorry for?" he whispered.

"I'm sorry . . . this happened to you. Sorry I totaled your car. Sorry you . . . got hurt."

"It's no big deal, Katie, I told you. All I want is to be friends again. I mean, why do you think I took the hit for you?" He looked me in the eye. "We both know what you've got on the line."

"We are friends, Alec."

"Friends are nice to each other. They spend time together. They welcome each other into their homes."

"You're welcome here. It's just a little too late is all."

"Too late for what?" He moved in to kiss me, and I realized how disgusting beer breath is when you don't have it yourself. I tried not to flinch and to kiss him back. *If I'm nice, maybe he'll leave*, I thought again. That was all I could think.

"See?" he said softly. "Isn't that better than fighting?"

"That's not friends, Alec."

"Don't start with that bullshit." He stepped back but didn't take his eyes off me. "You said that you wanted to be 'just friends' this summer, but you still went to Haley Pond with me. And you didn't exactly kiss me like I was your brother just now, did you?"

I didn't have a choice, I thought vaguely. But I did, didn't I? I shouldn't have tried to be nice.

He moved in and kissed me again, this time sliding his hands up under my loose T-shirt and onto my bare chest.

I pushed his hands away. "I don't want to do this."

"Bull*shit*, you don't." But he backed off then, and stepped away. "You know what your problem is? You say one thing and you do another. You oughta watch that." He paused, pointing an index finger at me. "It can get you into trouble."

He picked up the beer he was drinking. "I'm outta here," he said. "Thanks for the party."

And he left, the screen door slamming shut behind him. I closed the kitchen door, locked it, and listened to him peel out of the driveway.

Four beers and a lime sat on the kitchen table. I opened one, poured it into a tall glass, and sliced the fruit. "Don't mind if I do," I said to myself and sat down. My hands trembled.

I definitely needed a drink.

24

We won our second game and then our third and fourth. By the third week in September we were the team to beat in our league, and no one could do it—not yet. Coach Hollyhock from U. Maine contacted Coach Riley and made a date to come see me play. She was coming herself, not sending an assistant. Coach Riley said this was huge. It meant she was interested—very interested.

Cassie and I were mad at Megan and those guys for going to Stan's and to other parties, too, but they never got caught and I didn't care anymore. They could do what they wanted. My world revolved around field hockey, and I poured everything I had into the games we played twice a week. I showed up early at practice and was out on the field before anyone else, working on my flicks and driving at an empty goal cage. I worked my butt off during practice, leading our mile run each day, playing as if every scrimmage, every drill, was a tournament game.

My goal was singular. I would let nothing—no*body*—come between me and my future.

*   *   *

The hallway was deserted.

I dug through the books and papers at the bottom of my locker, searching for the text I needed to take back to study hall. Footsteps, rubber soles squeaking on the polished wood floor, rounded the corner. Alec appeared.

I slammed the locker door and headed toward my classroom. Alec and I saw each other every day—we had classes together— but we hadn't spoken since he'd showed up at my house that night weeks before. Our relationship had become what I'd wanted all along: silent coexistence.

"Hey," Alec called after me. "Katie?"

I spun around and faced him. What could he possibly want now?

"Listen," he said, walking up to me until we stood just two feet apart. "I owe you an apology—for barging into your house after Stanfield's. That was lame. I was drunk."

I hesitated, then looked at him. Could he actually mean it?

"Thanks," I said, turning to go.

"I just wanted to give you something."

My curiosity won. "What is it?"

He paused, eyes searching my face. "Here." He handed me an envelope. "The concert's already sold out and I know how much you love the Fly. I had an extra."

I opened the envelope and stared down at the single ticket. *The best band in the world* ran through my head involuntarily. The concert was just a few weeks away. Cassie and I tried to get tickets, but they had sold out in what seemed like seconds.

"A bunch of us are going if you want to come . . ." He faltered. " . . . Or not."

Everything in me wanted to go to that concert. But that would be a mistake. Going with Alec would be a huge mistake.

"No," I said finally. "Thanks anyway." I held it back out to him.

Alec pursed his lips. "Keep it," he said. "It's yours."

I looked down at my extended hand. He didn't reach out to take it.

A moment later, he was gone.

I stood in the empty hallway, staring at the ticket. All I wanted was to be rid of Alec. One minute he was ordering me to go to Stan's with him and swaggering around my kitchen drunk; the next he was—what? Ignoring me completely? Apologizing? Making it up to me with a free concert ticket? Who *was* he? He made no sense. Whatever game he was playing, I couldn't afford to get sucked back in. It was too easy for that to happen; I'd learned that over the summer.

I had to trust him with our secret—I had no choice—but beyond that, forget it. I had to remember that. I *had* to.

I didn't tell anyone about the concert ticket, especially Matt. What would I say? That I'd won it on the radio? Who wins *one* concert ticket? No, I also didn't want to lie to him again. The one lie hanging out there already was killing me. I didn't need any others.

But I couldn't keep it from Cassie forever, and as the concert date got closer, I still didn't know what to do. I needed her advice. On a warm Saturday afternoon, as chain saws wailed across the lake, I wheeled my bike out of the barn and headed toward her house.

I sped along the shore of the lake, breathing in the brilliant foliage; whole trees had changed color and lost their leaves, bright reds and yellows twirling down into pools of water where they lay just beneath the surface, shimmering like gems. I hopped off my bike and stood in the shadow of a towering maple tree covered with fiery orange leaves, waiting for Cassie to come out.

"You have a *what*?" she shrieked, her voice echoing across the water. "How did you get it?" She loved the Fly as much as I did—maybe more, if that was even possible.

"Don't freak out when I tell you. . . ."

She was practically levitating. "Oh my God. Oh my *God*! You're going to see them *live*?"

"No, no, listen. I don't know if I'm going . . ."

"What? Are you insane?" She was barely paying attention.

"Cassie." I grabbed her arm. "*Alec* gave it to me."

She stopped. Suddenly she was back, fully present. Sensible Cassie.

"Alec." Her voice was flat.

I told her the story.

"So he thought he could get you to go to the concert with him." She couldn't hide her disdain; she didn't even try. "What a loser. For someone who's supposed to be so popular, why act so desperate? I mean, Kay, I'm your biggest fan—but why is he so obsessed with you? Why doesn't the guy just move on to someone who actually *likes* him?"

"I don't know what to do. Should I go?"

"With *Alec?*"

I hesitated. "No . . . by myself. You know, just use the ticket."

Cassie paced across her yard. "I thought he was with Sue Tapley now. She's got terrible taste—she's perfect for him." She glanced at me, "No offense—but he wasn't your best pick."

"Sue *Tapley?*" Something like jealousy flickered through me and was gone. "He's with Sue Tapley? Since *when?*"

"You can't go. Shit." She picked up the ticket and stared at it. "But how can you *waste* it? The Fly," she whispered reverently.

"The Fly," I said back.

25

It was early, very early, but that's how we'd planned it.

Cassie and I had agreed I couldn't go with Alec. But wasting the ticket would have been sacrilegious. She refused to take it— *Alec owes you this,* she'd said—and there was just no other way I could part with it. Who knew if I'd ever have this chance again? So there I was, driving to Portland alone, early enough, I hoped, to get a front-row standing position on the floor of the Civic Center.

I'd heard that Scott's father, who was a big lawyer in Portland, had pulled some strings to get the tickets. For some reason that made me feel better. It wasn't like Alec had done anything special for them; the tickets had just dropped into his lap. Probably *free.*

Alec never asked me if I was going, and I never told him. He was going with Scott, Megan, Cheryl—the usual—and they'd never arrive five hours before the concert. They weren't that organized, plus, no matter how much they liked the band, they were in it for the party—and that was best achieved in a dark parking garage right before the show.

* * *

The plan worked. I arrived with the real die-hards, the ones there for the sheer love of the music. They knew if you were lining up outside the doors with them at three in the afternoon, then you were a die-hard, too, so it was less weird and lonely. We drank bottled water and shared food we'd stuffed in our pockets. Hours later, when the security guards finally opened the doors, we ran together down the stairs of the deserted Civic Center, streaming onto the wide empty floor like kids set free on a playground.

We whooped and hollered as we raced, grinning, right up to the rope in front of the stage. Breathless, I took in the scene in front of me—speakers, instruments, wires, microphones. I wasn't just going to hear the band live—I was going to *see* the band. Up close. I was ten feet away. I couldn't believe the Fly was going to be right *there*—or that I'd ever hesitated to come.

I was lost in the music: swaying, moving, singing. Every song was familiar. Every lyric I knew by heart. The band was sweating under the lights, their wet hair sticking to their faces—faces I'd only seen on television and in magazines and online. They were real. They were wonderful.

Heavy, sweet smoke filled the air. Bodies pushed against me, pulsing to the beat. Behind me on the floor and all around the stadium cell phones glowed, tiny torches of light, a salute to the ballad they had just begun playing—a favorite that everyone knew, even the kids who'd only heard the singles in rotation on the radio. I raised my arms over my head, my body moving like one with the people around me. We were united, all of us. The world outside was gone. The pinpricks of light that filled the arena were like stars in our own parallel universe.

A pair of hands gently touched down on my shoulders and stayed there. I turned my head and there was Alec, smiling a genuine smile.

His lips touched my ear. "I'm glad you came."

He'd found me in the crowd, among hundreds of people—*how*? I was so sure he'd be far away, up in the stands, drinking from tiny bottles he'd smuggled past security. But I was too happy to care, too absorbed in the music, in the moment, to let anything ruin it. I was here *because* of Alec—he'd given me this. He slid his hands down over my bare arms and took my hands, moving with me to the music, his chin on my shoulder, his face beaming. At that moment, it felt like the most natural thing in the world.

We threw ourselves into the encores, all of us, determined to get the band back onstage. They were ours, and they were holding us all together. We didn't want to let them go. I was dizzy with the heat, exhausted from yelling. My head felt light, barely attached to my shoulders, my body weightless, floating inches off the floor. The smoke had filled my lungs for hours and left my eyes stinging. A contact high? Probably. But that wasn't my fault. It felt good. Almost like tripping.

After coming back three times, the band was really gone. Kids on the outskirts of the arena had already bolted, hoping to escape before the traffic jammed. The cries of the die-hards around me and the sound of my own voice faded and then died as the auditorium lights came on. The spell had been broken.

Alec grabbed my hand and pulled me through the crowd, careful not to let me go. It felt right to be with him, like we'd been restored to what we should have been all along, to where we'd been months before. We were moving quickly together, pushing our way around slow movers and the clusters of kids who lingered, passing joints. On the stadium stairs, we dodged drunks—some barely alert, some fully gone—who slouched on the steps or lay prone, completely blocking our path.

"Watch your step," Alec said, and guided me to one side to bypass a pool of vomit.

It was easier to move through the lobby. We raced by the concession stands, cut through the long line of tired girls that snaked outside the women's bathroom, and reached the doors to the outside quickly.

The cold night air was a slap in the face, a wake-up call. I was holding Alec's hand. Was this what I wanted to do?

"Where're you parked?" Alec said.

"First floor." I pointed toward the parking garage next to the Holiday Inn.

"Nice," he said, and took off again, me in tow.

We wove through the cars that stood idling, bumper-to-bumper. Up the sidewalk and just ten feet inside the garage's main entrance was my car. He dropped my hand and I pulled the keys from my pocket. He took them and unlocked the door.

"I'll drive," he said. "If you want. You look beat."

"I'm okay," I said, confused. "Where's *your* car?"

"I came with Scott. He said he'd swing by your house and pick me up—"

"He doesn't have to do that. I can drive myself."

"It's no problem."

I glanced at my watch. "It's one o'clock. We won't get to Westland until after two, and I can't bring you into my house. My mom *is* home tonight. She really is." I looked toward the cars backed up on the street. "There's no knowing when Scott's going to get out of this mess."

Alec fixed his eyes on my face, and for a moment I stood accused—and not just by him, either. By my*self.* Could I just dump him after he'd given me this ticket—given me this whole amazing night? Did I even *want* to?

Alec blinked and the moment was gone. He put his hands on my shoulders, nodded, and kissed my forehead. His breath smelled sweet—no beer.

"I'll see you in school Monday," he said, and walked off through the parking garage to find his friends.

"Thanks for the ticket," I called after him.

He raised his hand to wave without turning back.

26

All the way home, the car racing down dark country roads, the Fly's latest CD blasting out the windows, images of Alec and the concert spun through my head. I wanted to be there still, in that moment, with the music swallowing me up, in a time and place where nothing mattered, where Alec's hands slipping down my arms felt wonderful—not risky, or dangerous, or criminal. I replayed that moment in my mind over and over until it hurt.

How could one person confuse me so much? How could I be so convinced one moment that he was threatening me— threatening to reveal our secret—and the next feel so . . . *what*? Like there was some real connection between us? What did I really feel? What did I really want?

What I wanted was the old Alec, the one from our early days on the beach. The one who listened to me talk about my father and who told me about his mom dying. The one who knew all about my field hockey team and our opponents and our chances at winning the States. I wanted the Alec who mowed my lawn and weeded the garden just to help me out, and who left work to pick me up at the beach during a hailstorm even though we hadn't spoken in a week. I wanted the Alec who had handed me a concert ticket, no questions asked, and who looked at me like I was the most beautiful girl he'd ever seen.

I wanted Alec to *be* the wonderful guy he'd been all those times.

But he wasn't, and I knew it. He'd been trouble, nearly from the start. Or maybe it wasn't even him. Maybe it was me. Or the two of us together. Maybe we were like a potent cocktail, a mixed drink whose single ingredients were harmless enough but when put together knocked you out flat. Maybe we were just a bad combination.

All the way home that night as my car bumped down the back roads from Portland to Westland, I reminded myself of what I knew was true—that he wasn't the guy from the beach or the guy at the concert. At least, he wasn't *only* that guy.

No matter how much I wanted him to be.

Nearly a week passed since the concert and Alec hadn't approached me at school, hadn't called me. Sometimes I thought about the way he'd kissed me on the forehead in the parking lot after the concert, then walked off to find Scott. When I said I'd drive myself home, I'd braced myself for a scene, but then off he'd gone, so easily. He must have realized it, too: The spark, the attraction that had pulled us together, didn't matter. It wasn't enough.

We caught each other's eye in English class one day and exchanged small smiles. We'd shared an incredible night at that concert and it had changed everything. We'd struck a truce, I was sure of it, reached an unspoken understanding. We weren't back together, but he wasn't going to try to force that anymore. Maybe he'd even forgiven me for the accident. Could I dare to hope it? He was certainly acting that way. It seemed like he'd let go of everything that had happened between us. We were in a new place, a place I could live with. It was a place from which I could finally move on.

Night was closing in quickly around the gym. I'd stayed late with Coach Riley and watched some video footage of myself playing. She'd wanted me to see it before she sent it out to a few colleges. I heaved my heavy backpack into the backseat of my car and reached for the driver's side handle.

"Katie." Alec's voice emerged from the shadows alongside the gym.

"Oh. Hi. I thought I was the only one left around here." I gestured aimlessly at the deserted parking lot.

"Amazing concert, huh?"

I couldn't help grinning. "Yeah."

"I'm glad you made it."

"Me too." I smiled. "Thanks again."

"No problem." Alec leaned against my car, his gym bag at his feet. "So what are you up to this weekend?" he asked.

"Not much," I said. "Hanging out with Matt and Cassie probably."

"Cheryl's parents are out of town, did you hear? She's having a little gathering at her house Saturday night. Nothing big—invitation only."

"She should watch it. Coach Riley's laid down the law with the whole team this year. It'll screw up everything if she gets caught."

"Riley doesn't have a clue," Alec scoffed. "This isn't exactly the first party of the year."

It was late and I didn't feel like arguing about it. Cheryl would do what she wanted to do. I opened my car door and started to climb in, but Alec reached out and touched my arm.

"Can I take you?"

"What?" My heart began to race.

"To Cheryl's."

"Alec . . . No, I'm not going. I'm not going to parties right now."

Impatience flickered in his eyes. "Okay, how about a movie? Just us."

My heart thumped. *Not again. Please, not this again.*

"What do you say?" There it was, just like before—that tone when he spoke to me. It was barely a question; it was a command, a given. His voice said I would go with him.

"Listen, I had a great time at the concert, but I think we should just—"

"Just *what?*" He kicked at some loose gravel and it skittered across the parking lot in the dark.

"I just don't think we should hang out together." There. I'd said it.

"Christ, Katie. What's the big deal?" His voice was loud now, carrying across the empty parking lot. I looked around furtively. No, no one was there.

"I just don't think we should."

"*Fuck.*" He clenched one hand and banged his fist once, hard, on the hood of my car, then turned to look at me.

"I took a fucking bullet for you. What else do you want?"

"I didn't . . ." My eyes were riveted to the hood of my car, to the dent the size of a softball he'd just made on it, my heart banging in my chest. It didn't matter that I hadn't asked him to take that bullet for me; I'd let him do it.

"What the *fuck* is the matter with you?"

"Nothing's the matter with me." My voice was trembling. I climbed into my car and shut the door quickly.

"That's where you're wrong, Martini," he said, practically jamming his head in the open window. "That's where you're *fucking wrong.*"

Hands shaking, I started the car. I needed to get away from him; I needed to get away fast.

I glanced in the rearview mirror just in time to see him pick up a rock and hurl it into the dark after me.

This time, at least, he missed.

27

No one knew how scared I was of Alec now. No one knew about the imprint his fist had made on the hood of my car. To anyone who asked, I said a tree branch fell on my already-battered Escort. All I'd told Cassie was that he'd asked me to go to the movies and got angry when I'd said no—nothing more. Bound to Alec in a tangled knot of guilt and fear and remorse, I couldn't escape what had happened between us. I threw myself in to the only thing that made sense: field hockey, a place where the rules were clear.

Our winning streak was still unbroken. By the end of September, we were 7–0 with just five games left in the regular season. If we kept it up, it would be the hockey team's first undefeated season in seven years; getting there was our first goal. It was something we could accomplish before the play-offs and would guarantee us the perfect seed going in.

Coach Hollyhock came to our eighth game to see me play. I took to the field, my heart pounding. Cassie smiled and nodded her assurance to me from her place at wing, but my thoughts raced out of control: *What if I had a bad game? What if she decided she was wrong, that I wasn't Division I material after all? Could my dream be destroyed in a single afternoon?* The thoughts terrified me.

The whistle blew and the first pass came to me; I botched it, my stick missing the ball completely. Luckily Sally was there and covered for me, carrying the ball toward our goal while I tried to shake off my first mistake of the day in front of Coach Hollyhock. The opposing goalie kicked Sally's shot right out of the circle, where one of their links grabbed it and took off. Ten minutes later, the other team had scored.

I glanced at the sideline. Coach Riley gripped her clipboard. She was nervous today, too, wanting me to do well. She nodded at me now. "You know what to do, Katie!" she called.

She's right, I thought. *I* do *know what to do.* I'd been in a daze, a jumble of nerves the whole first fifteen minutes of the game. It was time to snap out of it. Something in me clicked. The other team had scored! We were behind and a team with a 4–3 season record was threatening our winning streak. This was *not* going to happen. Especially on the day a university coach had driven three hours to see me play.

Sally took the center pass so that I could receive it. I passed it immediately to Cassie in a play we'd rehearsed a hundred times. "Switch!" I called to her, and she swept in toward the center of the field just outside the circle. I'd moved out to the left, where she'd come from, and received her pass back to me—something the other team never expected. As their attention switched to me, I sent the ball back across, smack into the circle where Cassie, Sally, and Sarah were all ready. Cassie's stick touched it first, and Sally finished it off. It was beautiful. The whole thing depended on quick, precise passes. Any hesitation, or a ball shot off course, and their defense would have been all over us.

Coach Riley threw her arm around me at halftime.

"You're doing great," she said in my ear. My confidence—and the whole team's—back in place, we rolled over our opponents in the second half and won the game 4–1.

Coach Riley, my mother, and Mr. Tenney, our athletic director, stood talking to Coach Hollyhock at the edge of the field. Coach Hollyhock looked young and fit, muscular and strong. She was tall, like me, maybe even taller. Coach Riley had told me that she'd been an All-American at the University of Connecticut ten years ago. A quick smile lit up her face when she saw me coming.

"Nice game today, Katie," she said, and stuck out her hand. "It's great to finally meet you."

"It's nice to meet you, Coach Hollyhock." I shook her hand.

"Coach Riley and Mr. Tenney have been telling me all about you," she said. "They speak very highly of you."

"Thank you," I said, my cheeks flushed.

Coach Hollyhock, my mother, and I left soon after, going downtown to get a bite to eat. All I had to do now was make a decent impression at dinner and hope my mother did, too. But she was recruiting me, not my mom—that's what Cassie had said. It would be okay.

*   *   *

"Katie's father is not in the picture," my mother was saying. "It's just me, and it'll be a struggle to get her to school next year at all." She put her fork down, cleared her throat, and paused. "Anything you can do to help her would be appreciated very much."

My mother wiped her hands with her napkin and tried to look Coach Hollyhock in the eye, but I could see it was a struggle. *She's a Yankee*, I thought. Raised to be self-sufficient, she'd rather drown than ask someone on the shore for help. She was putting aside her pride to ask Coach Hollyhock to help get me to college. Field hockey she didn't understand, but getting out of Deerfield—*that* she understood. And she knew I needed to go to school to do it.

"Katie works two jobs in the summer, and I've put aside some money, of course, but it's a lot." She cleared her throat again. "What with books, and room and board, and all."

"Well, I can tell you I think there's an excellent chance that I can work Katie into at least a partial scholarship—maybe more. I'd really like to see you at Maine," Coach Hollyhock said, looking at me. "I'll know more, and be able to tell you more, in December. But I can definitely do something. Do you think you want to go to Maine, Katie?"

"Maine or maybe the University of New Hampshire. Syracuse is too expensive unless they give me a full scholarship, but Coach Riley doesn't think they can do that for me."

"Whatever money you get, it'll go farther in-state than anywhere else."

I nodded. "I'd really like to play for you."

Coach Hollyhock smiled. "Let's get you scheduled for an official school visit to Orono soon, okay? That will give you a chance to meet the women on the team, see the school, get a feel for things, all right?"

"That would be great," I said, suddenly hungry. Before we left, I'd cleaned my plate.

28

The ride to the University of Maine was long. Winding back roads for an hour just to reach the highway, then I-95 north—straight, flat, and tedious—for two more hours, a monotonous stretch to Bangor. Exit at Orono, and it was another fifteen minutes to the school. One thing I dreaded about going to U. Maine was that I'd have to make this trip several times a year.

There was another thing I dreaded, but I'd been pushing it far out of my mind for as long as I could: Orono is next to Bangor.

Wade was just an overage drunk guy I'd met at a party over the summer, but his face was still vivid in my mind, and his words still haunted me.

Your dad lives up to Bangor now. . . .

Forget it, I said to myself. Concentrate on Coach Hollyhock's words, the only ones that matter:

I'd really like to see you at Maine.

I repeated those words over and over as I sped along in

Cassie's car. Cassie had lent me her little green Beetle for the occasion, the one her parents had given her for her birthday just weeks ago. When she handed me the keys the day before I left, I almost didn't accept—but she'd insisted.

"First of all," she said, "I don't need to be worrying about that beat-up car of yours dying on a desolate stretch of road and you without a cell phone."

"I bet there's no signal up there even if I did have one."

"That's what I figured. It's why I'm lending you my car instead of my phone." She grinned. "Plus, you deserve it."

I doubted that. But Cassie loved giving presents, so I said okay. And it would be fun pulling into the gym lot at the university in her shiny lime-green car rather than in my old beater.

The colors of the leaves faded from bright red and yellow to burnt orange and brown as I drove north. Fewer hung on the trees; more were scattered on the ground. Winter would come just a little earlier up here, spring a little later. That seemed impossible. Winter in Deerfield lasted six months, or so it seemed.

The gas gauge hit empty. I'd passed by the Augusta exits, and Waterville, too. Could I make it all the way to the school without stopping? A few miles outside Bangor, the gas light flashed on. *Damn.* I couldn't. There was an exit just ahead. I got off the highway and pulled into a convenience store.

I didn't move.

Staring out the window, I took in the scene: the gas pump next to my car; the store, its windows covered entirely with huge paper advertisements; a few small cars and pickup trucks scattered around the parking lot; people moving in and out of them with six-packs and junk food. But my eyes lingered on one particular pickup, one exactly like the truck my father had driven the day he left our house and never came back: My dad's old truck.

There are plenty of trucks like that one, I thought, *and his probably died years ago.* Still, my heart tapped furiously in my chest.

What if he's here?

It was an insane thought. A ridiculous idea. Bangor was no metropolis, but it wasn't tiny Westland either. What were the odds of a coincidence like that? Of my father driving the same exact truck he'd been driving when I was in seventh grade? Of his going into this one of a hundred convenience stores on the outskirts of Bangor, during the precise five minutes that his estranged daughter stopped to buy gas? I had a better shot of winning the Powerball on a Saturday night.

But it didn't matter. My body was shaking now. All day I'd pushed thoughts about my father out of my head, but they were winning now, these thoughts.

Would I recognize him?

Would he recognize me? *His very own* daughter?

I stared through the windshield until the storefront dissolved into a blur, then closed my eyes, sending tears tumbling down my cheeks. My shoulders shaking, I sank down deep into the seat where no one could see me.

A few moments later, I opened my eyes and saw a girl with a

U. Maine sweatshirt exit the store, walk over to the truck, climb in the driver's seat, and head for the highway.

I pushed away the tears, got out of Cassie's car, and pumped gas.

The weekend was a whirlwind, the excitement blowing away all thoughts of my father. There were two other prospective recruits visiting, one from Maine and another from Massachusetts. Coach Hollyhock matched each of us with one of her current players— mine was a sophomore from a small Maine school like Deerfield— and we basically did everything they did. On Friday we went to classes with them, Saturday morning we went to team study hall, and all our meals were with them in the dining hall. When they went out Saturday night, we did, too. But whatever they did or didn't do when we weren't around, they kept the fun clean during our visit. We went to a small Mexican restaurant down-town and then hung out at the student center and met some of their other friends. Nobody picked up a drink—not while I was looking, anyway.

But the highlight for me was their game Saturday after-noon. It was like watching professionals after years of playing in an amateur league. There were about half as many whistles interrupting the game. The ball wasn't sent out of bounds by accident or kicked by a forward trying to intercept a pass. It was faster, more intense. Drives arrived at their destinations, plays were called, shots on goal were consistently long and hard and on-target. The goalie came boldly out of her cage for saves. We tried to do some of that stuff in Deerfield, but we just weren't playing the same game.

I wanted so badly to get in there and play with these women. *Women*: that's what Coach Hollyhock called them—not girls. And she treated them like adults, too. I just knew that my game could reach its potential here—and what's more, so could *I*. I'd be different here. I'd be grown-up, too.

Before I left, Coach Hollyhock offered me a partial scholarship, one that would cover over half my tuition. All I had to do was get accepted by the school—not too hard for an in-state kid with grades like mine.

"What do you say? Would you like to play for Maine?" she asked, her smile luminous.

"Are you kidding? I'd love to," I said, and we shook on it.

Back in Deerfield on Monday, I left study hall on a bathroom pass, my mind still buzzing with excitement. As I walked down the wide corridor to the girls' room, long streaks of light passed through the tall windows, glimmering on the polished wood floor. Millions of dust particles swirled in the afternoon sunshine.

My lone footsteps echoed in the hallway, then were joined by another's, someone who had just exited a classroom behind me. I didn't think much of it until I reached the bathroom, glanced back, and saw Scott not more than fifteen feet behind me.

"Nice visit up to Maine this weekend, Katie? Got your future all sewn up?"

I looked at him blankly. How could I answer a question like

that—a question fired out not like a question at all, but an accusation?

He lifted his chin. "That's all that matters, isn't it?"

He strode past me without waiting for an answer, then paused, one arm on the swinging door he was about to push open, glaring back at me. Scott was tall, like Alec, his brown hair cut close to his head. His face was familiar, but his mouth twisted with contempt—not contempt for a meaningless assignment or a boring book we had to read for school, but for *me*.

"You hurt Alec a lot, you know."

We stood in the empty hall staring at each other. I opened my mouth, but nothing came out.

"Got nothing to say for yourself? Well, you know what?" He held up one palm like he was directing traffic. "Don't bother. You've caused enough trouble." He pushed through the door and was gone.

Inside the last stall in the bathroom, I leaned against a wall. My whole body shook like a small engine. Puking had not been on my agenda for study hall, but it was too late. I leaned over and gagged.

At the sink, I splashed cold water over my face and looked in the mirror.

You hurt Alec a lot, you know.

Scott couldn't know that I'd been driving Alec's car, could he? He was just messing with my head, trying to make me feel bad about breaking up with Alec. That had to be it. Didn't it?

Your secret is safe with me, Alec had said back in August.

Was it?

29

I sat in Matt's front yard on Saturday, cross-legged, holding a slender blade of grass between my fingers, examining it in the sun. The weather had turned unseasonably hot, and we were lolling on his front lawn like it was June, soaking in every ounce of sunshine.

"It's nice to see you smile," Matt said. His chin rested on his knees, his long arms wrapped around his legs.

I pulled the grass apart into two strips, then tossed them on the ground and looked up. "Why?"

"I don't know. . . . Don't get mad, okay? I'm not criticizing you. You seem, like—not yourself lately."

"Really?" I glanced at him quickly, then away. All week I'd been thinking about Scott's words, about what they might mean. About who knew what and who might still find out.

"Yeah, you seem pretty stressed out."

I lay back on the grass and stared up at the sky. Was "stressed" the right word when you were afraid your whole life could fall apart at any moment? But I couldn't say that.

"Wouldn't *you* be?" I said instead. "This whole thing with the scholarship . . . It's intense, you know? I won't feel better until it's over."

"You're going to get one," Matt said. "I mean, that trip to U. Maine went great, right? Didn't that seal the deal? I guess I thought you'd be excited."

"Nothing is absolutely official until you sign—and they can't sign you until the first Wednesday in *February*."

"I guess it's nerve-racking, waiting."

I rolled over, staring into the grass. "Yeah, it is."

"But there's no reason it won't happen, right?" Matt's eyes were on me, I could feel it. "I mean, if the coach thinks you're great now, she'll still think you're great in February."

Tears welled up in my eyes and the grass blurred, blending like watercolors. Why couldn't he just drop it? "It isn't just the scholarship, Matt. . . ."

"What is it, then? Tell me."

There was a sharp ache in the back of my throat. Matt had no idea that I was carrying a secret. No idea how badly I wanted to tell him what it was. *Don't you see?* I wanted to say. *Alec could destroy me.*

Matt was looking at me the same way he'd looked at me all those years ago when I'd told him the truth about my dad—that I really didn't know where he was, or if he was coming back—his eyes so kind, so understanding. I wanted to tell Matt about Alec and have him still look at me that way.

But it wasn't the same thing, was it? I wasn't an innocent

kid anymore. How sympathetic is a drunk driver who nearly kills two people and then lies about it so she can get money for college?

No, I had to remember where Matt stood. I had to remember the look on his face when all he knew was that I'd been *in* Alec's car. When he'd known I'd been drunk and I wouldn't even own up to *that*.

Sometimes I feel like I don't know you, he'd said.

I couldn't bear to lose him.

Matt searched my face. "Katie, what is it?"

Suddenly, his words felt like an interrogation. I didn't need him questioning me. Not now, not ever. This thing was between Alec and me. It was nobody's business but ours. Alec wanted to take the blame, and he took it. It wasn't even my idea.

I wiped angrily at my cheeks. *Great*, I thought, glancing across the lawn to where Matt's sisters played. *I've made a spectacle of myself in front of a couple little kids.*

"I need to go home," I said. I pushed myself up quickly and started walking toward my house.

A cloud moved over the sun, throwing a shadow across the lawn.

"Katie?" Matt called after me. "I didn't mean to—"

"I know, I'm fine—just tired," I lied without looking back. "See you tomorrow." I could hear my voice shaking, but I would admit to nothing. No one could make me admit anything: not that I was drunk, not that I was upset or angry, not that I was driving that goddamn car.

* * *

Later that night, alone in my living room, I thought about the two gallons of wine my mother kept in the low cabinet near the kitchen sink. I closed my eyes, and for a moment I could taste it, sharp and warm on my tongue. I could feel the familiar warmth as it slid down my throat and spread through every limb in my body. I could feel the relief that followed: the edge that melted away, the calm drowsiness that helped me to sleep.

I needed—badly—to sleep.

What harm could one glass of wine do? Especially if I could wake up, just one morning, rested? It wouldn't be doing any harm: That was my answer. It would be doing *good*.

I took a tall water glass out of the cupboard, filled it, and drank quickly, flipping through channels on the TV, pausing on one of those political shows where people sit in a semicircle and yell at each other. A large man with a red face made a comment and a woman retorted, "That's a fabrication—entirely untrue."

"Maybe so," the big man shot back, "but if you repeat anything three times in Washington, it becomes fact. The fact is, people *believe* it."

I shoved a piece of wood into the stove, clanged the door shut, and took another gulp of wine. *Repeat anything three times and it becomes fact.*

Alec was driving the car.

Alec was driving the car.

Alec was driving the *car*.

I'd never said the words out loud. I never had to. When

people called after the accident, they'd already heard the news: Alec had crashed his car with me in it. They took it as fact. The fact was, I'd never had to lie. Not directly, not straight out. Not once.

Alec was driving the car.

Maybe if I repeated it enough times to myself it would become the truth. Not just to everyone else, but to *me*.

30

The wind blew cold across the hockey field. The opposing team had just been awarded their third short corner in a row against us, and Coach Riley was getting antsy on the sideline, pacing, yelling, muttering stuff I couldn't hear.

Our forward line sprinted back behind the fifty yard line again, stuck there until the ball was hit, counting on one of our defenders to send it out of the circle where we could snag it and carry it upfield. It was the last game of the season and we had planned to be undefeated. It was what we were counting on. But things had become tense on the field.

"Get it out of there!" Cassie yelled. And *bang*, the ball was hit.

It struck the stick of one of the other team's forwards and popped ahead, just beyond her control. Marcy rushed in and tried to snatch and clear it. But they'd sensed we were off our game and they all went after Marcy at once. There was a scramble, and the ball disappeared into a crowd of players all desperately trying to score—or stop a goal—at the same time.

This scene was a goalie's worst nightmare, as Megan tried to keep her eye on the ball through the sticks and legs of eight or ten players.

Above the sound of sticks clacking, I heard Marcy swear loudly. I cringed. The ball was in the cage a second later, and the long whistle that followed signaled the goal. Green was ahead 1–0.

But that wasn't all. The head official lifted a green card over her head and pointed her other arm straight at Marcy. "Warning! Blue Number Seven. Language," she said to the scorekeeper's table. Then she turned to Marcy. "If I hear one more comment or inappropriate language, you'll be on the bench."

Great, I thought, and caught Cassie's eye.

"It doesn't matter anyway," Marcy muttered, and scowled.

"That's a yellow," the official said, flipping out a yellow card and pointing to Marcy again. "Five-minute suspension."

The official had clearly had enough of her. Though Marcy had managed to keep her mouth shut during the game up until now, the faces she'd been making at the referees' calls had invited trouble. And it wasn't the first time this season. Coach Riley had sent her home from practice early one day because of her foul mouth and then didn't start her the next game. But none of it changed her attitude. If we were winning, she was usually fine. We'd just been lucky this year that most of the time, we were.

We'd have to play short a defender for five minutes now, and there were only twelve minutes left. Marcy sulked on the far end of the bench while Coach Riley focused on the rest of us.

"Bobbi, you're going to have to work double-time now. Katie, come back into the circle on defense. You're shorthanded, but you're not finished. Let's score, girls!"

The whistle blew. Green intercepted the pass back and flew down toward their goal again, their strategy clearly to score again as quickly as possible, cement their lead, and shoot down what was left of our confidence. But Bobbi cut into a Green pass, snagged the ball, and shot it up to me for what should have been a clear breakaway.

I dodged the sweeper, hoping to get past the goalie with a high flick, but I tapped the ball too hard at the top of the circle trying to position it. The goalie saw her chance and came straight out at me; I panicked, shooting it right into her pads instead of diverting it to Sarah, who had appeared nearby. It was a rookie's mistake on my part and I was furious.

"Sorry, Sarah—I blew it," I said.

She shook her head. "That sweeper wouldn't have let it happen, anyway," she replied, referring to the defender who had circled back again to guard her. It was nice of her to say. She'd had a much clearer shot than I did.

Coach Riley put our only varsity freshman, Amy Wilson, in for Marcy when the five-minute penalty was up. Marcy would be fuming about not getting back in the game, but the rest of us were relieved. We had a couple more shots, but no goals. When the final whistle blew, we'd lost for the first time all season. Our perfect record was gone.

Coach Riley shook her head. "They deserved that one," she said.

Green was ecstatic—jumping, hugging, high-fiving sticks. Our heads were down as we slunk off the field, looking for our pullovers to protect us from the chilling wind. "Thank the officials and shake Greens' hands," Coach Riley said. "You too, Marcy."

Coach Riley talked to Marcy while the rest of us picked up our things and started toward the bus. Tight-lipped, Marcy folded her arms across her chest and looked straight ahead, over Coach Riley's shoulders.

The school bus was silent, most of us staring out the windows or off into space. Marcy climbed on board last and headed to the very back, where she stretched her legs and feet out across the seat, stone-faced, looking at no one.

For the first time all season, I wondered if our team really had what it would take to win the state championship.

31

Main Street was jammed with bumper-to-bumper traffic, the cars, trucks, RVs, and horse trailers all headed to the same destination: The Deerfield Fair had arrived.

"We'll follow you," I said, and Cassie led us through the thick Saturday crowd. Matt and I slid past the booth where they made fresh-squeezed lemonade with ice and pure cane sugar. Opposite that was a lone ATM with a line twelve people deep.

"I hope we all brought enough cash," I said, ducking around a family with three small children and a baby carriage. Matt nearly collided with a couple of seventh graders with pink hair and fake tattoos.

"Could you slow down, Cass?" I said. "We've got nine hours, you know."

"Sorry," she said. "I guess I'm hungry. Three large fries, please," she said to the woman in the booth she'd been leading us to.

"Just remember," Matt said, looking at the row of rides that lined the midway, "whatever you taste now, you will taste again later."

"That's gross, Matt," I said.

"I speak the truth," he declared with a laugh.

"It's almost too hot," I said, and took off my field hockey Windbreaker, tying it around my waist.

"I'm not so sure I want all these guys to know my first name, either," Cassie said, looking down at the embroidery on her sleeve. She pulled hers off, too. "Check this guy out." She nodded in the direction of a man who was urinating in an alley between two game booths filled with posters and stuffed-animal prizes. He zipped up and strolled casually back toward the Merry Mixer, where he apparently worked.

"Remind me not to go on that ride," I said.

"He's drunk," Matt said.

"You don't know that."

"You're the one who said you didn't want to go on his ride," Matt said, and aimed his camera at me.

"Don't even think about it," I said, and turned away as the shutter clicked.

Matt wanted pictures of everything. "This place is a photographer's dream," he said.

Hours later, when the sun went down, the midway lit up like Las Vegas: red, white, blue, and yellow lights filled the night sky. "Come on, I want to go on the Zipper!" I said.

"Thrill seeker," Matt said.

"Oh, you're just a baby about big, scary rides," I teased.

"I want to go to the farm museum."

"Hmmm, farm museum or *Zipper*," I said. "Tough call . . ."

"Ride junkie," Matt said, and elbowed me playfully, rocking me off balance.

I looked left and saw Megan coming through the crowd, followed, predictably, by Cheryl.

They asked us to go on the Gravitron, but Cassie put a single hand on her stomach and groaned. "Too many fries," she said. "I'll stay with Matt."

"Wimp," Megan said to Cassie, and Matt rolled his eyes. He'd always said Megan was obnoxious.

"You go," Cassie said to me. "We'll meet you after."

"Eleven fifteen at the main gate," Matt said to me. "Cassie has to be home at midnight."

"I know," I said. "I'll see you then."

I left Megan and Cheryl in line getting our ride tickets, cut through the crowd, and kept walking far from the midway, out near the animal barns, to where a low white building housed a set of men's and women's restrooms that never had long lines.

"I knew it would be dead out here," I said to myself, stepping into the fluorescent lights of the bathroom. Rows of wooden stalls, ten on either side, were mostly empty. A woman and a small child occupied one together, the child whining while her mother coaxed her to go. I finished quickly and went back outside. It was quiet there, too.

"Martini." A tall figure emerged from the men's room,

startling me. "What a pleasant surprise. Good to see you out of school, off the field. I didn't expect it."

I swore Alec had supernatural powers. One minute I was alone outside the deserted restrooms, the next he was there. *Bam*: Alec.

He'd stepped in front of me and was standing too close, his breath reeking of french fries and beer.

"Hey, Alec," I said, and moved around him. "I gotta go."

"Not so fast," he said coolly, and grabbed my arm, spinning me around. "We haven't had a chance to catch up."

"Hey!" I said. "Let go of me."

He released my arm and held his palms up in mock surrender. "I forgot myself, Martini. It's just . . . we used to be so close. I miss that."

"Right," I said. "Megan and Cheryl are waiting for me."

"Megan and Cheryl? Now I *am* hurt. I thought you'd given us all up. That's what I wanted to talk to you about."

"What I do is none of your business."

"You know, Martini," he said, "that's just not how I see it."

I tried to step around him but he stepped right along with me, blocking my way, his body inches from mine. Behind me was the wall of the restrooms. Where was that woman and her little girl? Had they gone out the other way? Didn't anybody else need to use the bathroom?

"Move, Alec." My heart was racing.

"You know what your problem is? You can't admit the truth. You may be hiding out lately, but that doesn't change the facts."

"What *facts?*"

I regretted asking right away, letting him pull me in to his stupid game.

"We're just alike, you and me. We're not pussies who play by the rules. We're not like your little friend Matt with his geeky cameras and his self-righteous horseshit."

"You don't know anything about Matt."

"I know enough," Alec said evenly. "He looks like he'd like to take me out—not that he'd ever dare try. You must have told him some pretty deep shit about me."

"Actually, you managed to alienate him without my help, Alec."

Alec smirked. "You're feisty, you know that? It's one of the things I like about you."

"I'm out of here," I said, and stepped to the left.

Alec stepped with me. His face was dead serious now, his eyes locked on mine, his voice low and intense. "Matt must be pretty mad at me for driving you around drunk, huh, Katie? That's a pretty serious offense. And Matt's a pretty serious guy."

The sound of the fair disappeared; there was nothing but Alec's eyes, his breath, my heart pounding furiously in my chest. I couldn't speak.

He held my gaze for an eternity, then abruptly stepped aside.

Legs unsteady, I moved past him, heading quickly for the crowded midway.

"Nice visiting with you, Martini," he said behind me. "Don't be a stranger now."

*　　*　　*

I was reeling, my whole body trembling as I stumbled back to the midway.

Megan, looking exasperated, held up the tickets. "Where the hell have you been?"

"Ask Alec. He cornered me by the bathroom. The *psycho*," I said, regretting it immediately. Even my voice was shaking.

"He's just not used to getting the heave, Martin," Megan said. "He liked you a little too much, that's all. Couldn't you *tell*?"

Couldn't I tell? What was that supposed to mean? By the way he ripped off my clothes after the Bethel party? By the way he lied about driving the car?

Jesus. What was he telling people?

Cheryl, predictably, said nothing.

I didn't feel like going on the Gravitron anymore. "You guys go," I said.

"I have a better idea anyway," Megan said. "Follow me."

Cheryl and I followed her, threading through the dense crowd. Beyond the midway, an area filled with kiddie rides sat silent, shut down for the night. I was relieved to be away from the crowd, away from everyone and anyone who might talk to me. Far away from Alec.

Beyond that, it was quiet, deserted. My heartbeat quickened again as Megan led Cheryl and me around some dark draft horse barns and then out farther still, across lumpy grass littered with beer cans. Finally we reached the woods that abutted the chain-link fence running around the entire perimeter of the fairgrounds. It was pitch black, the music and lights an island of life in the distance.

There was only one reason to come out here, but I was past caring what it was.

Megan leaned against the fence. "Katie, my friend, you have got to try this." She pulled a baggie out of her coat pocket and removed a single joint from what must have been six or seven. "It'll calm your nerves."

"No, thanks," I said.

"Lighten up," Megan said. "My sister brought this home from college. It's not your basic homegrown shit." She lit it up, inhaled deeply, and passed it to me.

I hadn't gotten high with these guys since that party over the summer, the one I'd gone to with Alec. I hadn't gotten high with anyone. But these two had been smoking their way through hockey season. Lightning hadn't struck them down.

I hesitated. The joint was burning between my fingers, a speck of orange in the night. The smoke was sweet, tempting.

"Jesus," Megan said, "just take a hit."

I put it to my lips and passed it to Cheryl before tilting my head back and releasing the smoke in a straight shot over my head.

A few rounds later Cheryl cracked a smile. She only did that when she was high.

"Riley could burn us for this," I said, and inhaled deeply. The space between Cheryl and Megan blurred every time I moved my eyes. "Here, you finish it."

"Riley's not burning anyone," Megan said, and took the glowing stub. "She doesn't have a clue."

Cheryl nodded unsteadily, tilted her head back, and tried to hit her eyes with some Visine. She kept missing, the drops running down her face like tears.

"You're losing your touch," Megan said, and took the bottle from her. She used it and handed it to me.

Back at the midway, we floated through the crowd. I moved my head quickly left, then right, the lights of the rides blurring together like a melting rainbow whizzing through the air. *Cool.* I brushed past people, but they were unreal, like characters on a television screen. My skin tingled. Even Megan and Cheryl seemed far, far away. I jerked my head side to side, marveling at the brilliant colors until I nearly fell over.

Megan looked back at me, eyes squinted, smile slow. "Good stuff, huh?"

I wondered vaguely what it had been laced with.

We boarded the Gravitron. A skinny guy with a goatee and long greasy hair took our tickets, then pushed back some younger kids behind us.

"It's full," he said, and slammed the door of the spaceship shut in their faces.

"It's been a long fucking day," he muttered, and, not looking at any of us, strode to his box and started the thing up. He had a gold stud through one cheek and another through his tongue that he stuck out and flicked against his teeth.

We were spinning fast now, and the goateed man, feet propped up on the side of his control box, threw his head back like a cowboy, pierced tongue flicking in the wind. The pressure flattened me back against the wall, the weight heavier than I remembered. Across the way a kid inched his feet slowly up and around on the wall until he was upside down, his head a foot off the floor.

I couldn't move my arm or a finger even. How had the kid managed to get upside down like that? I was pinned like a donkey to the wall of this capsule, the flesh on my face blown back, spread out like Silly Putty.

Suddenly it felt like I couldn't breathe at all, like the air was being sucked out of my lungs. My heart beat wildly in my chest. If the thing didn't stop, I would suffocate there against the wall, my face smeared like discarded bubble gum across its surface. I tried to catch my breath, but the harder I tried the more panicked I felt and the less air I got, and all I could see now was the goateed man at the controls in front of me, head flung back, looking like nothing would make him happier than ending his long fucking day by killing us all. . . .

We went in search of pizza. We were starving and I'd had a fantastic craving for pepperoni ever since, much to my surprise, I'd been set free from that space capsule alive.

Cheryl was spacey, her bloodshot eyes focused on nothing. "Is that your name on the intercom? I could've sworn I just heard your name. . . ." Her voice trailed off.

"What time is it?" I asked.

Megan shrugged.

A skinny woman turned to me, cigarette dangling from the corner of her mouth. "It's eleven forty-five, baby."

"*What?* I've gotta go."

It was nearly midnight by the time I made it to the main gate.

"Where have you been?" Cassie said. "Didn't you hear us paging you?"

"Sorry," I said. "We were on the Gravitron and the Zipper, and we kept running into people. . . ." Lies spilled out of my mouth. "I should've worn my watch."

I tried to focus on Cassie but I couldn't. The colors of the Ferris wheel lights behind her blended with the red of her hair like a trail of fire whenever I moved my head.

"You know I have to be home right now," Cassie said. "You know my curfew is nonnegotiable."

"Tell them it was my fault."

"That's not the point," Cassie said.

"Some people care what their parents think," Matt added.

"Yeah, and some people's parents *care*, Matt." I shot him a dirty look.

"It's not your *mother's* fault you blew off Cassie's curfew."

"Cut it out, you guys. I need to call my parents." Cassie pulled out her cell phone and turned her back to us. A minute later she turned around. "Let's go," she said.

She didn't look at me again.

32

Cassie leaned on her rake and looked back across the leaf-strewn lawn at her house. The day had turned gray, the temperature in the fifties.

"Of course I'm mad," she said. "I have to rake all day. Until I'm finished, anyway."

"Didn't you tell them it was my fault?" I was still straddling my bike, relieved I'd found her outside. I didn't want to see her parents.

"You know how they are. It doesn't matter. It was the situation I was in, I put myself in it, and I'm responsible. I'm not twelve, I've got a car, and I can get myself home when they ask."

She laid a bright blue tarp on the ground next to a large pile of leaves and began raking them onto it.

"You should have left me there. I could have gotten another ride."

"Like I'd leave my best friend stranded at the fair. And I kept thinking you'd be there any minute. Where were you guys, anyway?"

"Trapped on the Gravitron with a tattooed psychotic at the wheel. If he ran it any faster, I swear we would have lifted off. Megan loves that thing."

Cassie dropped her rake. "It figures," she said. "Megan's never on time for anything. Can you get the other end of this tarp?"

"Sure." I climbed off my bicycle and leaned it against the rail fence that bordered the front of their lawn. Each of us took two corners and carried it, like a picnic blanket, over the stone wall at the far back of their property, where we dumped the pile of dead leaves into the woods.

"You must have gone on a lot of rides," Cassie said, trailing the empty tarp behind her. "You were with them for three hours."

She looked at me, expecting me to fill her in. My stomach dropped. Was she waiting for a confession? Had she seen how high I was?

I wanted to tell her. I'd actually come over here thinking I'd tell her the whole thing—how I'd run into Alec, how Megan put the joint in my hand, my moment of weakness. I wanted to come clean—at least about this. But would she get it? She'd told me how she felt about them partying this season. *Everyone should care about not blowing the States,* she'd said. *We're a team.* No. Moment of weakness or not, she would not be impressed.

I looked at the ground and kicked at some leaves with the toe of my sneaker. I could still tell her part of the story.

"I ran into Alec last night," I said. "Or he ran into me is more like it."

"Where? What happened?"

"He cornered me by the bathrooms. There was no one around."

"What do you mean, cornered you? I can't believe you didn't tell me before." She looked relieved, like she could explain to herself now why I'd been acting so strange.

"He grabbed my arm and then . . . he wouldn't let me walk past him."

"He *what*? That's scary, Kay." Her face went dark. "You know, he's got a hell of a lot of nerve after what he did. That accident could have cost you your scholarship."

Heat rose in my cheeks and I looked away.

"What did he say?" she asked.

"Just bullshit." I kicked the ground. "He was picking on Matt. Said I must have told Matt some shit about him because Matt looks like he wants to fight him. Then he made some joke about that."

"I'd like to fight him," Cassie said. "I may be little but I'm mean."

"You're as far from mean as mean gets."

"Well, he brings it out in me," she said, serious again. "He's harassing you. You don't just *grab* someone and not let them walk past."

I picked up a loose rock and flung it into the woods, then began moving around the yard, gathering fallen twigs and branches that had dropped off a dying tree.

Cassie stood still, her eyes on me. "You should tell someone," she said.

"Tell who *what*?" I said. "That he's mad at me for not going to the movies with him?" For such a smart person, sometimes she was impossibly naive. "It's not against the law to be pissed off."

"Well, if he touches you again—he can't do that."

What Cassie didn't know was this: Alec could smash me over the head with a beer bottle and I wouldn't—I couldn't—tell anyone. He had too much on me. And he knew it.

"There's nothing I can do." I dropped a handful of twigs over the stone wall and looked up at her. "Just forget about it, okay?"

She stared at me then. Her blue eyes, for once, were baffled.

Sunday night was long and dark and lonely. Every time I started to doze, a floorboard creaked or a tree branch scratched the roof, jolting me awake. I hated this empty house, hated the emptiness I felt inside me. Sometimes, lying there at night, I felt like I'd explode if I couldn't go somewhere else, just *be* anywhere else other than this place—the place where my family had left me, one by one, to fend for myself.

I crawled out of bed and went downstairs, turning on every light I passed along the way. I threw a couple of thick logs onto the smoldering fire, then went into the kitchen, opening the low cabinet near the sink. I'd finished the red; now the white wine jug was nearly empty, too. I'd need to replace both—soon. Stan would get it for me; he could get anything.

With a tall, full glass in hand, I climbed into the overstuffed recliner where my father had liked to drink his beer and fall asleep in front of the heat of the fire. The wine felt warm against the back of my throat, the taste like an old friend. As the glass emptied, my anxiety floated away, too. The logs caught, the wine slid down my throat, and my feet—up high on the lip of the recliner—were bare but toasty. Finally, I nodded off to sleep.

In my dream, Cassie and Matt had hiked to the top of Pitcher Mountain and were waiting for me there. We were to meet at one o'clock. All night I tried to reach them, but I couldn't. First I lost my way, the trail dwindling off to nothing, my heart thumping as I searched for a way out of the woods. Then it rained and the leaves on the ground turned slick, and my feet slipped over and over, getting me nowhere. Finally the rain turned into a river and carried me away and I was falling—falling down the mountainside and into the lake, which was icy cold. . . .

When I woke up, the fire had burned out and I was shivering.

33

On Monday, I darted from class to class with my head down, avoiding everyone. One wiseass remark from Megan and everyone would know what we'd been up to at the fair. She might not care, but I did. In a week or two, play-offs would be over. Then, relief.

Matt finally caught up with me as school was clearing out for the day. He leaned back against the wall and locked his eyes into mine.

"What?" I looked away, pulling a sweatshirt out of my locker and putting it over my head. "Why are you looking at me like that?"

"Just trying to figure you out."

"Get to the point, Matt."

"Okay." He placed a stack of books on a window ledge. "You were so high Saturday night you'd have to be blind to miss it."

"Yeah, right." I leaned over and dug through my backpack. "Like you'd even know what *high* looks like."

"You weren't hiding much."

This was the last thing I wanted to talk about. I'd already kicked myself a million times for what I'd done at the fair. I didn't need Matt kicking me, too.

I shoved some books into my locker, hard. "Why are you my friend, Matt?"

"What's that supposed to mean?"

"Well, you don't seem to like me very much, so I'm just asking." I slammed the metal door, the clatter echoing down the hall. "Cassie didn't accuse me of being high."

"She'd never say anything even if she did think so."

"Why wouldn't she?"

"Because that's her idea of loyalty." He dropped his backpack on the floor by his feet.

"No, it's not. She was mad at me for being late and she said so. She's been pissed off at every hockey player who's partied this season for risking the States."

Matt shook his head and leaned against my locker door, arms folded across his chest. "You don't get it. She's blind when it comes to you. You're her *best friend*. To her, you can do no wrong. It's always been that way."

"You know, you've always been jealous of Cassie. Can I get back into my locker please? I forgot something."

He stepped aside. "Maybe I was, kind of, way back when she first moved here. But that has nothing to do with it."

"So what's your point? You see all the bad things about me but she can't?"

"Just forget it."

"I'd love to. You're the one who can't let anything go. I always end up feeling like I'm on trial with you." I slammed my locker door shut again. The hall was nearly empty now, and I was grateful.

"I didn't know I had to think you were perfect to be your friend."

"I didn't know I had to *be* perfect for you to *be* my friend."

"I just don't want you to blow it. I wish you could understand that. It's because I *am* your friend."

"Well, you know what? That's my business. If I blow it, it's my business."

"Forget I mentioned it," Matt said, but he wasn't over it.

Neither one of us spoke.

He stood there for a minute while I finished organizing my things.

"You're still coming over tonight, right?" he said finally. "To help me pick the final pictures for my portfolio?"

"Yeah, if you still want me to."

"I do," he said. "See you then." And he disappeared around the corner.

Matt had photographs spread out all over his bed when I arrived. "These are the ones I've made prints of," he said, not looking up at me. "The rest are still slides."

I glanced at a small cardboard box on the other bed. Inside it, in a thin plastic container, were several rows of slides we'd selected out of hundreds back in the summer.

I stood in the doorway, waiting, as Matt moved around the bed adjusting the photos, lining them up in perfect, neat rows.

Finally he stopped and looked over at me. "Are you coming in?"

I shrugged. "Do you want me to?"

He took a deep breath; his shoulders fell and relaxed. "I told you I did," he said quietly. "I *do* want your help."

He looked anxious—not just about the fight we'd had but about his portfolio. He wanted to study traditional photography, to take photos that were *art*, like Ansel Adams and Man Ray. He wanted to prove he could do that.

I stepped into his room. "Okay," I said. "What can I do?"

Matt threw himself into an armchair, head back. "I'm afraid I'll pick the wrong ones and they won't like them, you know?"

"That can't happen, Matt. There are so many good ones, it's hard to even narrow it down. They're *all* beautiful." I picked one up off the bed. "I like this one a lot." It was a close-up of a cow, taken with a telephoto lens by the side of a road. One narrow half of a cow's face, a single, soulful brown eye gazing into the camera, filled the frame.

"Me too," he said.

"Let's start a pile of our favorites."

"All right," he said. "Then we can start getting rid of the rest."

Matt liked abstract photographs the best, and working in black and white. First we went through the slides, placing them on the light box and viewing them through the loupe—a magnifying glass mounted on a clear plastic platform that made the picture larger and clearer to the eye. Then we considered the prints. We eliminated more than half as we went, and then put the rest into categories: personal favorites, different styles, color, and black and white. Finally we began choosing, agreeing and disagreeing, setting second and third choices to the side. We were almost finished when Matt went into a drawer and pulled out one last photo.

"I'd like to use this," he said. "It's one of my best portraits."

When Matt said "portraits" he didn't mean posed shots—he hated those. He meant photographs of people in their element, caught in real moments—candids. Honest shots, he called them. "There's nothing interesting about people smiling into a camera lens," he'd said many times. "Not to me, anyway."

I took the photo from his hand. It was one I'd never seen before. There I was, in black and white, on the bench next to the hockey field during that first scrimmage of the season, when Coach Riley had benched me. Around me were freshmen, JV players, second-string varsity, their eyes on the game. My arms were folded in front of me like I was shivering, even though it had been a very hot day. I was hunched over, my eyes cast down. Looking at it, I remembered that moment so clearly, the rocking motion of my body as I gazed at the grass, too humiliated to watch the game.

"I didn't know you took this."

"I know." Matt stood quietly in front of me. "I won't use it if you don't want me to."

I looked at it a moment longer. "That was a bad day."

"I know."

"You can use it," I said, and handed it back to him.

"Katie?"

"What?"

"I know you think I'm a jerk sometimes. That I'm always down on you or something," he said. "It's just . . ."

"What? Say it."

He held the picture in his hand, his lips pressed tightly together. "I just don't want you to feel this way."

"What way?"

"The way you did in this picture." His brown eyes shone.

"I'm okay, Matt," I said quietly. "Really, I am."

He nodded. But something in his face told me he wasn't so sure.

Later, outside, we crossed the road and walked across my lawn, dead leaves rustling like crumpled paper beneath our feet.

"I've got to rake these before it snows."

"I'll help you," Matt said.

We reached my porch and he hugged me. I didn't want to let him go.

34

Cassie told me everything that happened.

She'd caught up with Megan and Cheryl behind the field house as they were getting into Cheryl's car. Marcy was with them, too, her long blond braid swinging against her hockey jacket. She'd had a bad practice that day—she found out Sue Tapley was going to the homecoming dance with Alec, and Coach Riley had been on her about her attitude again.

Cassie shivered in the dimly lit parking lot. "Hey, can I talk to you guys for a minute?"

"What's up?" Megan said.

"You going to Scott's party this weekend?"

"Yeah, want to come?" Megan looked slightly surprised.

"No, I'm waiting until after the tournament. I figure we'll have a big party after we win the States."

"I'm having that one at my house," Megan said. "My parents are going to Florida for Thanksgiving."

Cassie nodded.

"So, what's up?"

"Well," she said slowly, "I was hoping you'd wait until then, too. Once the play-offs are over, it doesn't matter anymore if we party."

Cheryl rolled her eyes. "No offense, Cassie, but Riley hasn't exactly been on top of the situation this season. I don't think we've got anything to worry about." She rubbed her arms. "Damn, it's cold," she said, and climbed into the driver's seat. "You guys ready to go?"

"While you're on the lecture circuit, why don't you talk to your co-captain," Marcy said. "Wouldn't want Miss Scholarship to blow it."

"Shut up, Marcy. You're just jealous," Megan said, and Marcy got into the car, scowling. "I hear you, Cass, but don't worry. We're not going to do anything stupid. I'll guarantee you we'll all be playing in the quarterfinals on Monday."

"That'd be good, because we'd be sunk without you in the goal."

"Not to worry," Megan said. "See you tomorrow."

"I think she heard me," Cassie said now, backing her Beetle out of the parking lot. "I know they care about the play-offs as much as we do."

I was grateful to Megan: She hadn't blown my cover, and she'd put Marcy in her place. But Marcy was a real wild card—not someone you'd want on the other side playing against you. If she knew what I'd done, I could forget it.

Cassie stopped, looked both ways, and turned out of the lot.

If I reached over, I could touch her sitting there, her hands on the wheel. But I felt a million miles away. It had been that way ever since the accident, ever since the first lie. Then there'd been the concert, when I hadn't told her about dancing with Alec or holding his hand, and then that dent in the hood of my car. I thought about standing by the tall fence at the fair, blowing sweet smoke into the dark, relief coursing through my body as my mind slipped away. I could never explain that moment to her.

I stared out the window into the darkness. "Cassie . . ."

"What? You're nervous aren't you? You know, I shouldn't have made such a big deal out of the party. Everything's going to be fine."

"That's not it."

"What is it? You know, even if we lose the first game—which we *won't*, by the way—you've already got a scholarship. Coach Hollyhock promised you money."

"I know. The tournament won't change that."

"Listen, those guys can't ruin anything. Marcy's always a jerk—even Megan knows that—and Riley can handle her."

Her car sat idling in my driveway now. "We're kicking butt next week." She reached over and squeezed my shoulder. "Now get out of my car, or I'll be late getting home."

I was actually glad to have the house empty that night, to have it entirely to myself. I pulled the new jug of red wine Stan had gotten for me out of the cupboard and poured, filling my glass. I'd delivered the empty jugs to the recycling center in a brown paper bag earlier in the week. I'd wanted them gone the minute I took the last sip; once they were out of sight, it was like they'd never existed.

Sort of like how drinking alone could make it seem like you weren't drinking at all.

In the recliner in the living room, I considered the old riddle: *If a tree falls in the woods and there's no one there to hear it, does it still make a sound?*

A different version, my own, had been floating through my mind for weeks: *If you drink some wine and there's no one around to see it, does it still count against you?*

My theory was that it did not. What other choice did I have?

It was just one more thing I kept inside me, like a tightly wrapped package, ready to explode.

The following week we went into the quarterfinals ranked number one in Western Maine Class B and won the game 3–0. Marcy behaved perfectly, blank-faced and silent on the field, even when the ref made a clearly bad call in the second half and gave the other team a free hit into the circle on a ball that should have been ours.

"Nice job today," I said to her as we jogged off the field, and she actually smiled. I saw Coach Riley give her a thumbs-up, too.

Megan, Cheryl, and some others had partied over the weekend, but they were right. Nothing had happened. Nothing ever did. Coach Riley talked tough, but like most grown-ups, she didn't have a clue what was really going on.

35

It was Friday afternoon and it seemed like the entire school had gathered around the field. On Wednesday, we'd rolled over Jamaica 4–1 in the semifinals. If we won today, we'd be Western Maine champions, heading to what we hoped would be our final destination: the States.

Kids who had never been to a field hockey game in their lives were giddy—laughing, shivering, sipping soda. Cars paraded into the parking lot, filled with parents who had taken the afternoon off work to see their daughters play. Outside the locker room, I watched Bobbi Crow talk to her father, then hug him and go inside. *What would it be like to have a dad like that to support you at one of the most important moments of your life?* I wondered. A sharp ache jabbed at the back of my throat and I pushed the thought out of my mind. Sure, neither of my parents were going to be at the game, but I'd known that. I'd expected no different. I was here for myself and for my team.

Our nerves running high, we ran through our drills on the

field. We wanted to look strong, to psych the other team out. When Coach Riley gave us the signal, we jogged off the field in a line and gathered, sticks pounding the ground to the rhythm of our cheer.

It was time to play.

We dominate during the first half. They can't hang on to the ball. Their passes go nowhere. But we can't seem to score, either. We're within twenty-five yards of the goal most of the time, but their defense is tough, and their goalie is playing high, charging bravely out of the goal, which cuts off our angle. And she's got a sweeper backing her up who has dead-stopped two gorgeous line drives right in front of the cage. They're all defense. If they can't score, they'll keep us from doing the same. I catch a glimpse of Coach Riley on the sideline and meet her eye. She calls a time-out.

"Did they send that kid off to goalie boot camp since we last played them or what?" Marcy asks in the huddle.

"We'll just have to work around her," Coach Riley says. "Cassie, Sarah, go in deep and *wide*. You've got to watch the off sides, but her sweep is covering the goal when she comes out, so you can get in close without a violation. And she's vulnerable. Katie, Sarah, Bobbi, feed it out to them, then rush. We'll score, even if it's in a scramble. Ready?"

"Let's go!" we say together, and run back out onto the field.

The best way to score is not to think about it too much, just do it. Cassie goes in wide and waits. Bobbi receives the ball on a free hit and their goalie rushes her, but Bobbi's pass is fast and precise. Cassie picks it up and sends it. Their sweeper picks up Cassie's shot, but it bounces off her stick and Cassie grabs it again, taps it around her. Sarah dives for it and nudges it in over the line. We're screaming and jumping up and down as we help Sarah back to her feet.

"Now that's teamwork, girls! Way to go!" Coach Riley is beaming. Our crowd is on their feet.

They can't score, I think, and a chill zips up my spine. *They're all defense. We're really going to win this thing.*

But we've got to keep our heads, channel our adrenaline in the right direction. We're more determined than ever to notch a second goal and cement our lead. Within minutes, we're at our end of the field again. Inside the circle, I drive the ball toward the left corner of the goal before their defense can react; it speeds through every one of them. The goalie lunges and misses, and the ball flies into the net, making it inside the edge of the cage by an inch. We are 2–0.

Four minutes later the whistle blows and we are the Western Maine Class B champions.

36

The day of the States, the wind was gusting strong, picking up the dead leaves that skittered across the field, whipping them into mini cyclones that flew off into the crowd gathered on the University of Southern Maine's risers. The sun hit a tree with a lone cluster of bright orange foliage, lighting it up like fire against the cold blue sky.

I'd never seen so many people at a field hockey game before. It was like playing football in Deerfield on a Saturday afternoon. Will and Ben stood on the sideline with their friends, faces painted blue and white. Bobbi Crow's mother held a poster in one hand that read ALL THE WAY DEERFIELD! and a small blue-and-white pompom in the other. My mother stood apart from the crowd, hands pressed deep in her pockets, next to a man I assumed was her boyfriend, Ken. Our classmates pounded out a rhythm on the bleachers as we took our positions. "Here we go, Deerfield, here we go!" they chanted. A banner with all our names and numbers on it, strung across a nearby fence, flapped in the wind.

On our opponents' side, Clippers fans vied with ours, their voices carrying across the field. "You can't sink this ship! Hey! You can't sink this ship!"

As we warmed up, Cassie pointed out one especially fast girl who played my position on the other team. She was small and dark, with a beautiful, silky black braid down her back, almost to her hips. She stood out on the team from Eastern Maine, and I wondered for a moment if she was an exchange student. Did girls play field hockey in Latin America? Coach Riley told us that this girl was their leading scorer and that Marcy needed to mark her one-to-one at all times inside the circle.

We'd never played a team this strong.

I heard her with my own ears.

"Fucking Spic."

What? I was stunned. I'd heard a lot of foul things come out of Marcy's mouth over the years, but never anything like this. When she was mad, and you were her target, Marcy was never at a loss for words. But this was beyond an average violation. This was personal.

Bobbi Crow's jaw dropped and she looked at me. Had anyone else heard? The referee apparently hadn't, because rather than whip out a red card and suspend Marcy, she simply blew a loud, long whistle, indicating a goal had been scored. But the look on the other girl's face told me *she* had. Her moment of glory had been stolen. I'd scored a goal ten minutes before, and this girl with the long black braid had just tied up the game for her team, but her face was frozen in fury.

I was livid. I had to think fast. Marcy, it was clear from her face, was not over it. When she got that look, she was dangerous—she couldn't control her temper. She was a time bomb. We had to act fast or she would explode.

We've got to get her out of here, I thought as we sprinted back toward the fifty. We couldn't afford to play shorthanded, even for five minutes. The ref could go right for a red card and kick her out for the whole game. If that happened, we'd be outnumbered for good.

I needed to talk to Cassie. She'd been upfield when it happened; she hadn't heard a thing.

My concentration broken, I looked over at the sideline, searching Coach Riley's face for some sign that she knew what was going on. *Please know—please take her out of here.* But the crowd was loud, and Coach Riley didn't have ESP. Someone was going to have to tell her.

Coach Riley had told Cassie and me at the beginning of the season that as captains we could legally call a time-out, a privilege we should use carefully. We just had to wait until the referee made a call—any call—in our favor.

In field hockey, that doesn't take long, but I'd already wasted precious time. The Clippers had grabbed the ball on our center pass after the goal, and I was terrified Marcy was going to open her mouth again. But thirty seconds later they lost control and it went off the sideline. It was our ball. There was no time to confer with Cassie. I just had to do it.

I wanted to whisper, but I had to say it loud enough that she could hear me. "Time-out please," I said to the ref.

My teammates looked at me expectantly. Bobbi Crow nodded her head ever so slightly, feeding me courage. Cassie caught my eye questioningly, and we both sprinted to the sideline. We needed to get to Coach Riley before the rest of the team did.

Coach Riley was ripping mad at Marcy, but she tried to make the situation easy on me. She covered and gave us a generic pep talk, then, as if it were an afterthought, said, "Amy, go in for Marcy at center half." Amy's eyebrows shot up; she tried not to smile. She knew going in for Marcy meant trouble with her later, but she couldn't wait to play.

The Clippers were every bit our equal. We spent the rest of game wresting the ball from one another's control, only to get defeated by the opposing defensive players in the circle. Neither side could get off a decent shot. With five minutes left in the game, the score was 1–1. Five minutes later, when the horn blew, we were still tied.

We went into a ten-minute overtime, a "sudden death" period in which the first team to score wins the game, even if there is time left on the clock.

Ten minutes later, neither side had scored.

We took a five-minute break. The coaches and refs huddled, deciding our fate. The fans were getting edgy, irritable. A Clipper fan with a cowbell broke the silence with a series of deafening clanks.

"Give it a rest!" someone yelled, and the bell went silent.

It was getting late, getting dark. All of us were exhausted. The refs called for a series of penalty strokes to decide the game. It would be another sudden death situation: The first team to score more goals than their opponent after an equal number of strokes would win the game.

We won the coin toss and chose to go second, so that we'd have the last shot.

Up to five strokes would be taken by each team, by five different players. Cassie, Cheryl, and Sally Foster, our first three shooters, went up to the line one at a time. All three missed, their shots stopped by the goalie's feet or her glove. But the Clippers' first three shooters failed to score, too, and then their fourth.

The stadium was hushed. Overhead, a flock of birds, tiny black specks against the setting sun, headed toward a warmer clime. I was shooting fourth for our team, my whole body vibrating in anticipation. I had to stay calm.

I braced for the shot. Their goalie, too, was frozen still— mitt to one side, stick to the other, not allowed to move until the whistle blew and the split-second competition began and ended in a blink. Hovering low to the ground, my mind focused on the upper left corner, the goalie's stick side, the hardest place for my opponent to reach.

"Wheeeet!" As the whistle blew, I stepped, twisted my stick, and flicked the ball fast into the corner. The goalie lunged and missed it. The fans and my teammates erupted into a roaring cheer. Then they realized what the referee had already seen.

The ball had missed the net by an inch.

My heart dropped to my toes. We could lose and it would be my fault. I hit my stick on the ground, hard, and walked back behind the twenty-five yard line. I couldn't look at Coach Riley or at the stand full of Deerfield fans who had come so far to see this.

I knew the Clippers' next shooter well from the game. She was the halfback who'd made my life miserable every time I went anywhere near the circle, shadowing me like a Siamese twin. She was relentless. Would she flick it? That, I hadn't seen. I could only imagine what it must be like to be in Megan's shoes, anticipating what was next.

The girl placed her stick at an angle under the ball's curve. The whistle blew and she scooped it. It's a less forceful stroke by far, but it makes it easier to raise the ball high. It was heading in the right direction now, toward a top corner of the goal, but in slow motion. Its rainbow arc gave Megan enough time to gauge it. She threw her stick in front of it like she was bunting an out-of-control pitch. It dropped to the ground. Another roar erupted from our side of the bleachers. We were still in the game.

Bobbi Crow stepped up to the line. She was our last chance in this round. She looked calm, focused. The whistle blew. She lifted the ball and it flew. The goalie lunged, but the ball was moving too fast, and she was too late. It zoomed past her stick side and bounced into the net.

I'd never loved anyone more than I did Bobbi Crow in that instant.

The entire team sprinted onto the field. We threw ourselves

onto Bobbi, into each other, in the center of the field—laughing, crying, shouting. We'd won! We were state champions.

Coach Riley pulled me aside, away from the other players and Marcy, who was crying, as we waited to receive our awards in the post-game ceremony.

"You did the right thing today, Katie," Coach Riley assured me. "I'm very, *very* proud of you."

For the rest of the weekend, I relived the game over and over in my mind. It's true you can't remember every play, or exactly how it went down, but you remember the *feeling*: the moment when your stick hits the ball on the sweet spot and just sends it, the exhilaration when you reverse stick and pull the ball around the defender who's coming at you and you break away, the thrill of intercepting a cross-pass running at full speed and carrying it inside the circle for an open shot. The breakaway or penalty shot, when it's just you and the goalie and your shot misses the goal by inches—you remember that, too. But it's the high of getting it *just right*—that's the feeling you chase. That's what makes you go back for more and never want to stop playing. No matter how tired you are, how exhausted, how beat, it's that feeling of getting it right that makes you dread the long whistle ending the game, because you just want to keep playing forever.

37

At the annual Fall Sports Banquet, our school presented each of us with a trophy and our own beautiful varsity jacket. Big and warm, they had a round patch that said MAINE CLASS B STATE FIELD HOCKEY CHAMPIONS on one side and our name on the other. Only state champion teams got them, and since no other team at Deerfield High School had won the States in five years, we were the only kids in school with them.

Alec and a couple of his friends tried to ruin my moment at the banquet, calling out, "Martini, have another drink!" from behind cupped hands when it was time for me to receive my award. But Cassie, who stood beside me with our teammates at the front of the auditorium, squeezed my arm in solidarity. I focused my eyes on Coach Riley's proud face beaming at me from the podium as I stepped up, shook her hand, and hugged her.

The next day, all sixteen varsity hockey players wore their coats with pride. It was November now, and the heat rising from the school's antiquated radiators roasted us in some classrooms, but we didn't want to take the coats off, not even for a second. Finally, before going to art class, I gave in and hung mine in my locker. The last thing I wanted was to spill some paint on it or smudge it with a pastel or charcoal pencil. I locked the padlock, pulled to check it, and left.

I stayed a few minutes late in art class to finish up a project, then got a hall pass from the teacher to my next period, study hall. The corridor was quiet and empty when I went to my locker to retrieve my coat and a history book I needed.

Pulling out my jacket first, I paused to admire the patch and my name on the breast before slipping it back on. For four years I'd wanted one of these coats. Then, kneeling on the floor, I slid my history text into my backpack and put my hand into my jacket pocket, searching for a tube of Chapstick I'd left there.

The Chapstick was there, but I felt something else, too. It felt like a small cotton rag, one you would use to dust furniture. Puzzled, I pulled it out.

My face burned red the instant I saw it. Shoving the cloth back into my pocket, I leaned into my locker, trying to catch my breath. I scanned the hallway furtively, to make sure I was alone, then hunched over to look again. It was unmistakable: a pair of dirty, torn underwear—my own—retrieved from where Alec had thrown them out of his car window the night of that party in Bethel. I remembered crawling in the dark on my hands and knees trying to find them, just so that no one else would.

Apparently, someone had.

No one knew they'd been left there except Alec. Though for

all I knew, he'd told the whole football team the story, thinking it was some kind of joke. Maybe he'd even changed the ending, telling it so that, instead of jumping out of the car, I'd thrown the panties out the window myself in a fit of passion.

My heart hammered in my chest. The hallway was still deserted. I wanted to get rid of them, but nowhere felt safe. What if someone found them again? What if *Alec* did? No, I had to take them home myself, where I would burn them in the woodstove. In the meantime, the bottom of my backpack, hidden under heavy textbooks, would be the safest place.

I stumbled to the bathroom and locked myself in a stall. *Damn him*, I thought, emptying the contents of my pack onto the tiled floor. Why would he—why would *anyone*—do something like this? I ripped blank pages out of a notebook and folded the panties into them, hiding them under layers and layers of paper until the whole thing looked like some crazy Christmas package wrapped by a kid. Then I shoved them into the bottom of the pack, adding all my books on top. If anyone wanted to find them, they'd have to get through me and a lot of other shit first.

I glanced at my watch. Fifteen minutes had passed—almost twenty—since my art teacher had written my pass. Now the study hall teacher would be on my case, asking me where I'd been all this time. I'd have to tell her that I felt sick, that I'd been in the bathroom. Both were true.

I rounded the corner out of the bathroom and walked quickly down the hall.

"How you doing today, Martini? Nice *coat*." Alec stepped out of his math class, lavatory pass in hand. His eyes swept over me from head to toe and back again.

For a moment, I was too stunned to speak.

"What's the matter?" He smirked. "Cat got your tongue?"

"Get off my back, Alec," I hissed. My face was burning, but it was with fury now, not shame. I stepped around him, heading down the corridor toward my study hall.

"Now, Martini," he said innocently to my back. "Why would I want to do that?"

winter

38

Only a few dry leaves hung on the trees outside my window now, curled into fragile brown fists. Many trees were stripped entirely bare, their branches reaching into the sky like bony fingers on a slender silver hand. The days were short, the sun sinking in the sky by three thirty. Soon it would be winter solstice—the darkest night of the year.

It didn't matter. Every day felt dark to me. After hockey season ended and the excitement of winning had slipped away, there was nothing left holding me together. And it was as if Alec knew it. He haunted me like a spiteful ghost: I never knew when he'd appear, when he might pull something again that would knock the wind right out of me.

I wasn't going out now, even though I could. Why go to a party? It would be like putting a HARASS ME sign on my back for him and his friends. It wasn't worth it. At home, I had my own little parties, a glass of wine in one hand, the DVD remote in the other. My house had never felt so empty.

Will pestered me until I helped him string up Christmas lights on the porch. I didn't feel an ounce of Christmas cheer, but he wouldn't let up on me. He still got excited about Christmas, still hoped it would be magical, like on TV. I held one end of the lights while he climbed a stepladder with the other and secured them behind a hook, chattering about how he hoped to find a new snowboard under the tree Christmas Day. That was more than our mom could afford, but maybe I could chip in and the two of us could buy him one together.

Matt and his dad helped us pick out a Christmas tree at the Lion's Club sale and brought it home in their pickup truck, and Mom decorated it with us on her night off. When we hung ornaments up, one by one, she told us how old we were when we made this or that one, how she remembered one of us bringing it home from first or second or third grade.

Will persuaded me to bake some of his favorite Christmas cookies—the kind you make with cookie cutters and decorate with icing tinted with food coloring. He poked a hole in the top of each one before we baked them so we could push a slender string through after they'd cooled and hang them on the tree.

"I'll do the Santas!" he said as we pulled a tray out of the oven.

I smiled and handed him a bowl of red icing we'd prepared. How could I be grumpy when his face lit up like that?

Coach Hollyhock called every week to touch base, to see how I was doing. She promised she'd send the contract for me to sign on the first Wednesday in February, the first day rules permitted it. She'd offered me enough money that, after financial aid kicked in, my mom and I wouldn't have to pay a thing. That was a relief, a thrill—the best Christmas present I could ever have hoped for. In February, I'd have my paid ticket out of here—out of Westland, out of Deerfield High School, and away from Alec. Sometimes I didn't think I could wait that long. Other times I couldn't believe it would ever happen at all.

Alec had told me over the summer that he was applying to schools down south: Tulane, North Carolina, Emory.

"I plan to get as far away from this place as I can," he'd said.

It was a distance I was counting on.

Before Christmas a letter arrived at Cassie's house with the news—no surprise to me—that she'd gotten into Brown, early decision. Friday night, after school closed for winter break, her family threw their annual Christmas party, but with a twist. Though Cassie didn't know it, it was also a celebration of her good news.

The McPhersons' house glowed in the twilight. A single, perfect white light shone in each window. Fresh evergreen wreaths hung on the doors, decorated with deep red velvet bows. Matt and I left our boots at the door and stepped inside the warm house, which was already full of people. The wood floors gleamed, reflecting the fire that roared in the hearth. In the corner of the living room, a Christmas tree decorated with tiny white lights and more red bows towered over the guests. From the ceiling draped a banner: CONGRATULATIONS, CASSIE! BROWN, HERE SHE COMES!

Cassie moved around the room, glowing, accepting congratulations, talking about how excited she was about Brown. Her cheeks were on fire. All the attention embarrassed her, but she couldn't hide how happy she was. I watched her talk to one grown-up after another, so at ease with everyone, and I wished I could feel like that. Cassie always seemed to know how to act in any situation.

"I never know what to say to people," I said, gazing across the room. "Cassie's so good at that."

"Just ask people questions," Matt said. "That's what I do. Everybody likes to talk about themselves."

"I'd rather sit in the corner and eat cookies."

Matt smiled. "Who wouldn't?"

"Want anything else?" I asked him.

"Cookies," he said, and I walked back toward the food table.

Across the room, Cassie's father stood beside her now, his arm draped over her shoulders. He squeezed her and she looked up at him, beaming. They weren't just a normal family, the McPhersons, they were a *supernormal* family—like an ancient TV sitcom except her mother was the doctor in the family. Did they ever fight? Ever screw up? They'd welcomed me into their home, always, but I felt like an alien here. Cassie and I were from two different worlds.

At the buffet, my eyes scanned the food but lingered on the tall bottles of wine at the end of the table, one a dark burgundy, the other a pale white gold. Some wine—any color wine, it didn't matter—that's what I wanted, what I craved. For a moment I could taste it—the warmth of the red; the cool, sharp white. I could feel the wine flowing through my veins, the heat spreading through my limbs and reaching every part of me, soothing my mind. *Then* I would think of something to say to people. *Then* I would feel halfway normal. But how could I get any of that here?

"Can't decide?" an older man asked me cheerfully.

"What?" My face colored. He'd meant the food, of course. "Oh, it all looks so good," I said, and tried to smile. Reaching out for some cookies, I moved quickly back to where Matt was sitting.

Before we left, Cassie pulled me aside and handed me a tiny wrapped box. Inside was a necklace with a little charm—two crossed sterling silver field hockey sticks on a delicate silver chain.

"It's perfect," I said. "Thank you." And it was: perfect, just like Cassie.

We put on our jackets and boots while Cassie chattered about England. Her whole family was leaving the next day, going to visit the aunt Cassie had stayed with over the summer. They'd be gone for the whole winter break plus an extra week. Cassie glowed; she couldn't wait to see Simon.

"When's he coming over here so we can meet him, Cass?"

"Yeah," Matt said. "Approval is still pending."

"He's not kidding, you know," I said.

Cassie gave Matt a hug at the door. "Merry Christmas," she said. "Keep an eye on our girl while I'm gone." She glanced at me.

"I don't need anybody keeping tabs on me," I said sharply,

and all three of us, even me, were surprised at what had just flown out of my mouth.

"I know," Cassie said, but her eyes were hurt. "I was just kidding."

Matt pursed his lips and looked away.

Cassie looked at me, waiting, but something inside me had snapped, like a dead branch in the forest.

"Have a great trip" was all I said, and I was out the door.

My mother took three days in a row off at Christmas. Away more than ever now between shifts, she practically lived at her boyfriend's place in Portland. They'd been together five or six months, the longest I could remember her ever being with one guy. *Maybe it is serious*, I thought.

As we sat in front of the warm woodstove opening gifts on Christmas Day, I let myself hope for a fleeting moment that we could be a family again. Maybe if things worked out with this guy Ken, he'd come live with us here. Maybe my mother would take a job closer to home and she'd be here every night when we got home from school, maybe Will would stop spending four or five nights a week at Ben's house, maybe . . .

"When are we going to meet Ken, Mom?" Will asked.

She looked away and passed Will a wrapped box. "Soon," she said. "I promise."

"That's what you said last time I asked," Will said quietly. "And the time before that . . ."

A rush of anger swept through me. It was okay for me to

be disappointed; I could handle it. But not Will. He was barely twelve—and still so *little*.

"Why aren't you bringing him home, Mom?" I asked her later, when we were alone in the kitchen. "Can't you see Will's disappointed? It's not fair to him."

She opened a cupboard, hiding her face from view. "I'll bring him home when I'm ready," she said, and took out a coffee mug. "Now mind your business."

"I think it is my business when he's the reason you're never here anymore."

She looked at me sharply. "I'm not here because I'm making a living for this family."

"You're not here because you've moved in with your boyfriend, Mom—or you might as well have. Why can't you just admit it?" I strode out of the kitchen.

I walked past Will, who was on the floor, fiddling with a new gadget, a handheld game of some kind that he'd gotten from Ben's family. The snowboard my mother and I had bought for him leaned against a wall nearby. Did she really think she was fooling us with all her excuses about being too tired to drive home from work? She'd rather be with Ken than with us. That was the truth.

"Merry Christmas," I called out to the empty hallway, and headed for my room.

Later she came up and rapped on my bedroom door. She poked her head in when I didn't respond, waiting for me to look at her. Tucked under the covers in my pajamas, headphones on,

I kept my eyes on the book in my lap, but she didn't leave. She just stood there.

I sighed and pulled off the headphones. "What?" I said.

"I haven't brought Ken home to meet you because he wants to wait until his divorce is final," she said, like this explained everything. "It's important to him," she added.

"Whatever," I said, and picked up my headphones. *What about what's important to* us*?* I thought. *What about your own kids?*

"You know, Katie, I think you're old enough to understand this now. Ken is important to me. I wish you could be happy for me."

She waited for me to say something.

"You know," she said again, her voice rising now, "I think I deserve a little *happiness*."

I put my book down on my bedside table and put on my headphones.

"Sure, Mom. Whatever you say."

Music blaring in my ears, I reached over and shut off the light.

Winter break dragged along. Cassie was in England. Matt and I took Will and Ben snowboarding at the local ski area. Some days I'd spend the whole day in bed rereading *Twilight* or a fat Stephen King novel I'd borrowed from Matt.

Near the end of the week, New Year's Eve loomed. Like his first party of the year in September, Stan's New Year's Eve bash was a tradition. Cassie and I should have been going together like in other years. But Cassie wasn't here. I knew I could stay in with Matt, watch the ball drop in Times Square, but no matter how much I loved Matt, staying in on New Year's was a depressing thought.

Megan had called a couple times, trying to persuade me to go with her and Cheryl. Hockey was over; why not go out? she wanted to know. But she wasn't someone I could talk to about Alec, about not wanting to see him. Nobody was.

A couple of days after Christmas, Stan himself called.

"You're not going to blow off my party, are you, sweetheart?" he said. "It wouldn't be the same without you."

"I bet you're calling all the girls saying that, Stan," I said.

"Only my *best* girls . . ."

"You sure know how to make us *all* feel special, Stan."

He chuckled. "It's a date, then? I'll see you Friday?"

I paused.

"I'm not hanging up till you promise you'll be here."

Oh hell, I thought. Maybe it would be fun. It had to be better than watching the ball drop on TV.

"Okay, Stan, I'll see you then."

39

It started to snow around nine o'clock, and by the time Megan pulled out of my driveway it was coming down fast. She'd offered me a ride to Stan's, and I was grateful. I still avoided driving, especially at night, especially by myself. And there was no way I was showing up at this party alone.

Once we were on our way, though, I knew I'd made a mistake. Megan's headlights sliced through the dark, while thousands of tiny white snowflakes raced at us like stars in outer space, rapidly hitting the windshield and making me dizzy. It was like being on the Starship Enterprise—except there were things to crash into on either side of us that we couldn't see. It didn't appear to bother Megan that the road was covered and the lines marking both the middle and the edge of the road had disappeared under a slippery thin sheet of snow. She sipped the beer she held between her knees and drove fast.

Seat belt on, shoulders tense, I gripped the handle of the door with one hand, the seat with the other. I wanted out of this car. My heart banged in my chest, panic rising. I'd never told anyone how I felt in cars since the accident. No. Instead, for almost five months now, I'd done everything I could to hide it, to act like my old self, to pretend that nothing had changed. It was as if admitting the accident had hurt me would be admitting that it had happened. And that meant admitting it had hurt someone else, too.

But Megan was at the wheel now. I had no control over anything.

Cheryl lit up a bone in the backseat and passed it to me. I inhaled deeply and held. It would calm my nerves. It had to. I took another long hit and handed it back to her, but she passed it up to Megan. How drunk, how high would Megan be after midnight, when she was driving us home? I reached down and tugged at my seat belt, checking that it was there, holding fast. Then I reached for a beer, closed my eyes, and chugged it.

Stan lived in a grand old Federal-style house in a historic part of Deerfield, an area of five beautiful antique homes separated by acres of what used to be farmland.

"Have I ever shown you the whole house?" Stan asked after we'd arrived.

I brushed the snow off my parka and stepped inside the kitchen. "You sure haven't," I said.

"You already know the barn," he said, and waved toward a dark gray building, windows lit up. They'd insulated the barn years ago when Stan's older brothers and sisters needed a place to hang out with their friends. There, a massive stone fireplace generated enough heat to keep the whole space warm, even in the dead of winter. A small bathroom in a nearby shed kept nearly everyone out of the main house. Stan only had parties when his parents were away, and only out in the barn. We could go into the kitchen, but the rest of the house was supposed to be off-limits.

Downstairs, Stan took me through a living room, a family room, and a formal dining room furnished with antiques that had come down through both sides of the family. A center chimney meant fireplaces in nearly every room. The wide wood floorboards creaked and gleamed, and everything was in its place.

"It didn't look like this when I was little, when all six of us were here," Stan said. "I think my mom couldn't believe it when it started to stay neater and neater as each kid left. Now she's kind of compulsive about it. Making up for lost time, I guess."

"I can see why she doesn't want any of us in here."

Upstairs were four bedrooms. "The boys had one room, the girls had the other, and the oldest kid got his own—which meant I never did until Dave graduated six years ago." Stan laughed. "I know a few girls sneak over here when the line in the shed bathroom is long and use this one." He pointed to a door down the hallway. "I don't mind as long as they don't wander around the house. It's been okay so far."

"I have to admit, I've used it before."

"Listen, you're free to use it anytime, sweetheart. Just don't tell too many people. What I hate," he said, "is a few times I've found couples in the bedrooms—once even in my parents' room. No respect, you know?"

When we got back downstairs, the barn was full of people. Kids were crowded around the roaring fireplace at one end; at the other, a beer pong tournament was in full swing.

Scott slammed the tiny white ball. It landed in the mug on Marcy's side.

"Drink!" Megan hollered. If the ball hit the mug, you took a sip. If the ball landed *in* the mug, you chugged the whole thing. Marcy flung her head back and drank the entire beer.

"Damn, he's good," Marcy said, pointing at Scott. "Who's next?" she shouted, her words slurring. "Hey Meg, can I have a ride home? I forgot to ask you."

"Sure," Megan said. "I'm up!" Megan took the paddle from Marcy's hand.

"*Bitch*," Marcy said under her breath, and walked past me like I wasn't there.

Great, I thought. *Megan's already shit-faced* and *Marcy's riding with us.* Marcy hadn't looked me in the eye since the state championship game. When Cassie and I were together, she'd talk to Cassie and look through me like I wasn't there.

"I'll take you home." Stan appeared next to me and put his arm over my shoulders.

"You just read my mind. How'd you do that?"

"State secret, sweetheart. When do you have to be home?"

I smiled. I knew he'd be sober enough. Stan drank, but slowly, and not much. I'd never seen him drunk. His brother Dave, who was twenty-three, got Stan whatever we wanted: kegs, top shelf, special requests. But Stan always played the gracious host, caring for girls who had too much and threw up, taking car keys away from drunk drivers. Anyone who wanted to could crash in the barn, where there were plenty of old couches and blankets.

"Whenever," I said to Stan. "Whenever is good for you." Across the room, Alec had Sue Tapley against the wall, making out with her. *Get a room*, I thought, then turned back to Stan. "As soon after midnight as you can manage would be good."

"You got it, sweetheart."

If I wanted to drink, I could do that at home. I was beginning to wonder why I came at all.

At eleven thirty, the line for the bathroom in the barn was five deep—all girls—which meant the wait would be forever. I left the barn without my coat, shivering as I ran across the yard, my shoes sinking into the new snow. Inside the main house, the kitchen was empty. I ran up the stairs toward the bathroom, but the secret was clearly out: Four girls stood waiting there, too. *The guys must just pee outside*, I thought, and considered doing that myself. Midnight was only thirty minutes away; I wanted to be back downstairs for it. And squeezing my legs together was not helping my urge to go. I had a better idea. Down at the far end of the hall, a door led into Stan's parents' bedroom. Earlier, when Stan had given me the tour, I'd noticed they had a private bath off their room.

I knocked once quietly, then again, remembering what Stan

had said about couples sneaking up here. Back in the hall, there were now five girls in line. I waited until no one was looking, then slipped into the empty bedroom. Stan would not want half the school traipsing through his parents' private space. Quietly, I closed the door behind me.

Framed photographs of Stan and his older siblings covered his mother's bureau. I picked up one of Stan and studied it, then walked past the bed and into the bathroom, locking the door behind me.

When I stepped out of the bathroom, I jumped, jerking back. I hadn't heard a sound, but someone was there, waiting.

It was Alec, sitting on the edge of Stan's parents' bed, unfazed by my appearance. *Had he followed me here?*

"Where's Sue?" I asked, trying not to look startled.

"She's on the rag. She got all pissed off and left." Alec's eyes were bloodshot and unfocused. "That's what you get when you go out with a sophomore."

He looked around the room, then back at me, like he was noticing me there for the first time. I wondered if he was on something. I'd heard somebody in the barn talking about doing OxyContin.

"She'll be back—"

"She's a wench," he interrupted. "I can't wait to get out of here next year. Meet some *mature* women."

There was something not right with Alec. Something beyond the usual. He didn't seem like himself somehow—not like the cool, confident guy who had showed up at my house past midnight, demanding to be let in nearly four months before. There was something different tonight, simmering right below the surface.

Music blasted from the barn; even with the house shut up tight against the cold, I could hear it. You couldn't have a conversation out there over the music. I glanced at my watch.

"That's right," Alec said, "it's ten till midnight. Everyone's gone back to the barn to do the big countdown. We've got the whole house to ourselves, Martini."

I started for the door, but Alec reached out one long arm from where he sat on the bed and wrapped it around my thighs, tripping me and pulling me back.

"Alec!" Adrenaline rushed through me and I jerked away quickly, making for the door, but Alec stood up, jumped in front of me, and blocked my way. I was tall, but he was bigger. My forehead just touched the tip of his nose. His breath was musty and sour with beer. He reeked like a kitchen floor after a keg party.

"We could've had a great time, Martini. Why did you have to fuck it all up?"

He let me take a step backward. He still blocked my only exit, and he knew it. Except for the door to the bathroom. That was behind me. If he wouldn't let me by, I'd go in there and lock the door, and wait until Stan or someone came looking for me.

"I told you, Alec, I'm sorry about the accident. I really am. I wish it had never happened."

He shook his head and scoffed. "Not that, Martini. That's

over." He put his hand up to his face, feeling the ridge of the scar that was already not as strikingly purple as it had been four months ago. "I'll always have this to remind me of you, though. Wouldn't it be nice to have a better memory?"

My heart raced. Maybe Stan would come looking for me now. He'd been sticking close to me all night, joking with me, making me laugh. Talking about toasting in the new year with me. He must be wondering where I'd disappeared to.

"Stan's waiting for me . . ."

"*Stan!*" Alec's wide eyes mocked me. "So it's *Stan* now? What happened to your little friend Matt? Couldn't keep up with you?"

"Matt and I . . ." I stopped. Why explain myself to Alec? I put a hand out boldly to push him aside. I was damn sick of Alec. I was getting out of there. "I'll see you later."

"Whoa, Martini," he said, and grabbed my wrist, twisting my arm around and down to my side.

"Hey—!" I started, but I tried to stay calm. Alec had always been a bully, but he was all bluff. That's what Cassie had said once. But this time Cassie was wrong.

"Are we finished?" he whispered, twisting my wrist harder. "I don't think I said we're finished." The pressure on my arm was intense.

"Let go of me, Alec," I said quietly.

"I'd like to, Martini, but I can't, you know?"

"No, I don't know."

"You're over me, is that it? Forgotten all about your pal Alec who saved your *ass?*"

I wasn't looking at him now. My wrist was twisted, my arm pinned to my side, but he still couldn't make me look into those eyes.

"Remember how sweet it was over the summer? All the time we spent at the lake? You fell for me, Martini. You wanted me." He twisted my arm harder. "What was it, Martini? What was it about me you *liked*?"

His face pressed against my cheek, his breath rancid. He had to let go of me. My wrist was strong, but not as strong as he was. It was going to snap, I could feel it.

"You seemed like a nice guy," I whispered.

He released my arm and I let out a single cry as my wrist dropped to my side, limp, throbbing.

"*You seemed like a nice guy.*" He stepped away from me now, but he was still blocking the door. "I don't think so, Martini. You wanted to fuck me that night after the Bethel party. You were practically begging for it."

"You're disgusting, Alec."

"You know, you never thanked me for the gift I left in your jacket pocket." He shook his head. "And all I'd wanted was to remind you of the good times. There are a lot of things I like about you, but when it comes to gratitude—I gotta tell you, your attitude really *sucks.*"

My heart was pounding. His eyes burned into my face. "I don't know what you want me to say."

"Tell me how we can end this properly. Tell me that."

My palms were sweating, my left wrist still pulsing. I

had to get away from him. "I don't know." My voice cracked.

"I've got an idea," he said. His voice was low and even. "You owe me, Martini."

I made a break for it. Faking one way, then moving the other, I threw him off balance for a moment and ran for the bathroom, but he was behind me and as I tried to slam the door shut, he caught it and pushed harder on the other side.

"Open the door, Martini," he said, and heaved his body against it. "Open the fucking door." He shoved it against me, knocking me back.

"You shouldn't have done that, Martini. You know, you really have a way of taking the fun out of things."

There was no way I could get around him in this little bathroom. His whole body filled the door. What had I been thinking? I was trapped, cornered. Suddenly, I was enraged.

"Fuck you, Alec!"

He grabbed my throat with one large hand and shoved me against the wall. I felt my body slam into the floor, my head smash into the tile, a blast of pain. The bathroom was a blur of light and color. I could barely see his face, but I could feel him pushing me down with one arm, tugging at my jeans with the other. *Kick*, I thought, and I did, but he tackled me with his full weight, pressing me into the frigid floor. How had this happened? *You fucking bastard*, I thought, and I tried to say the words, but nothing came out. A hand gripped my throat; he was fumbling now, one knee shoved hard into my stomach, up under my ribs. I thrashed, tried to kick, tried to move so I could breathe, but trying to free myself made it worse. *There is no air*, I thought. *He is crushing me, crushing the life out of me.* Voices rose from the barn, counting down the new year in unison. No one was here. No one was near. He was going to kill me and no one would ever know. I struggled, but Alec gripped me harder, his movements growing more intense. He ground me into the floor, burying me.

I stopped moving then. *I'm dying*, I thought, and with this, a sense of relief fled through me. My eyes found the ceiling light above and focused. Such a white light, bright, piercing. Spots danced before me: gold, gray, fuchsia. Fuchsia. A funny word to think of at a time like this. But I was floating, my mind flowing like a river. My soul drifted away, severed itself from my physical body, and now I felt nothing and was nowhere but in this space with colored lights flashing before my eyes. Alec's weight, his nasty breath, his lunging body were gone, on some other girl in some other space far away while I floated on to a safer place where none of this was happening.

40

The house is quiet below.

Stan knocks on the bathroom door, turns the handle:

Katie?

I'm sick. (Is that my voice?)

You sound horrible. Are you okay?

Shut the door please. I'll be down soon.

I've been looking all over for you.

Sorry.

Sorry—as if I just hadn't been thinking, or had spent too much time fixing my hair. But Stan didn't know.

I've been sick—really sick, I say. The flu.

Somehow, my clothes are back on, nothing ripped, nothing askew. I find a brush, grip it in a shaking hand, pull it through my hair. A searing pain at the back of my head. I don't look in the mirror.

Stan looks me in the face when I come out. You're blotchy as hell.

I'm sick. I need to get home. Please take me home.

Stan warms up the truck. Drives me, slowly, on the slippery white road. Puts his big arm around me and guides me into my house.

Jesus, you're shaking, he says. That's some flu.

My teeth are chattering so bad we both hear them.

The fire's almost out. Stan stokes the stove, opens the damper, lets her rip until the room is hot, then fills the stove again and closes the damper halfway so it will burn all night long.

Where are the blankets?

I can't remember. I huddle on one side of the couch under a crocheted afghan, shivering, my teeth bouncing like Chiclets.

Stan finds some upstairs and brings them down, tucks them around me. I fall asleep and when I wake, suddenly, he's still there, dozing in the recliner. When the sun comes up, he's gone. His note says *Hope you feel better. Love, Stan.*

It's cloudy still and spitting snow. I turn on the lights one by one, moving through the house from room to room. There is a deep pain running from one side of my head to the other and a lump on the back where it slammed against the wall. Or was it the floor? It doesn't matter.

It's still early when Will appears.

I'm filthy, dying for a shower. Don't let anyone in the house, I tell Will first, and he looks at me strangely.

Promise?

Sure, he says, confused.

Why are all the lights on? he asks.

Why aren't you snowboarding with Ben today?

He's sick. What's wrong with you?

Flu.

You look terrible. Want some ginger ale?

I nod.

Don't leave, I say as I head up the stairs.

Why? he says.

Just *don't*. I'm practically yelling at him.

Okay, okay. He doesn't know whether to be mad or scared.

Days pass. Everything runs together in my head. Is it Thursday or Saturday? There are two images lodged in my brain. One is of the bright light on the ceiling of Stan's parents' bathroom. The other is Alec's face, looking like he wants to kill me. No one knows it, but he has succeeded.

The images are just underneath my eyelids, blocking my view of everything else. First one, then the other: light, face, light, face. They flash on and off as they please. It is as if time stopped when I was there on the cold tiled floor, and I can't get up off of it. I'm stuck. Lodged there.

No one knows. No one even knows I was there, on the floor.

Except Alec.

When I think about him I run to the kitchen and vomit into a piece of Tupperware.

My throat hurts. It's still hard to breathe. It's like he squeezed something shut with his fingers and it can't open back up. I'm running out of clean turtlenecks. The purple finger-shaped bruises on the flesh of my neck and arms are like footprints. They are Alec saying *I Was Here*. I stare into the mirror in my room, willing them to go away. They look separate from me, detached—over *there*. They're on the neck of some other girl I don't know. I'm floating away, looking on from a distance. This is getting familiar.

Nights are long. Shadows move across the room. I've never been so tired, or so wide-awake. During the day I sleepwalk, my brain shuts down; at night I'm on high alert. My brother rolls over in his squeaky bed across the hall and I think I'm having a heart attack. A field mouse runs through the wall and my breath stops. My lamp is on the floor where I've knocked it over trying to turn it on fast. Old sounds, familiar. Now, since Stan's party, I can't sleep here anymore. *Happy new year, Martini.*

I start to fantasize about guns and tall buildings. I picture myself doing the perfect jackknife off a fifteen-story building somewhere in Portland and Matt yelling, "Ten!"

Underneath the kitchen counter, in a cabinet next to the sink, I check the bottles of wine. My stash has diminished. But there is a new jug of white my mother must have brought home. The gallon jug has no cork like the tall, slender bottles in the movies, which had been a relief the first time I stole into the kitchen late one night in August, filled a glass, and went back up to bed. It was the color of ginger ale without the bubbles. All fall when I drank it, the pictures in my head—Alec bleeding, the car smashed into the trees—blurred, then shook free and drifted away. Finally, I slept.

This can work again. It has to.

For the rest of winter break, Will stays home and takes care of me. He makes me cans of soup that I can't eat, brings me packages of saltines, plates of toast. I nibble at them while he watches me, then throw them away when he's in the bathroom or upstairs. I don't want him to think I don't need him. Then he might leave.

I refill my own "ginger ale."

I shake all the time. Will goes up to our rooms and collects blankets and heaps them on the couch, where I sit all day long. He watches TV. He thinks I do, too.

The fire Will keeps tended makes me sweat, but still my teeth chatter. I wonder if they'll shake loose and tumble out of my decomposing body like they would on any other corpse. My mother calls a couple times a day to check in. I tell her I still have a temperature—a flat-out lie. But these are extreme times and flat-out lies will be called for. There is no guilt now. The old rules are for other people. No one protected me from Alec and no one will protect me now except me. I am my own human shield. I'll do what I have to.

My mother advises fluids and sleep. I follow her instructions in the rhythm of the images that still move like flash cards through my head: fluids, sleep, fluids, sleep. I can't do one without the other. When the white wine is gone, I switch to the dark red, which I pour into my white plastic water bottle from field hockey so Will can't see.

Stan calls to check in; Will tells him I'm too sick to come to the phone. Matt tries to come over. If I'm not asleep, I pretend to be. Will sends him away. He is the guard at the gate. Cassie is still in England with her family for the Christmas holidays, having fun with her summer boyfriend.

I care about one thing: getting through the day. Will tells me it is January fifth. So far I have survived five.

Here, this will make you feel better. Will puts a bowl of Chicken and Stars on the coffee table in front of me. He has taken to looking at me like a concerned stranger helping a homeless lady on the street. Like he wants to help but he's afraid I might go mental on him.

Thanks, kiddo.

I wipe at my eyes with the back of my hand. I don't want to start crying and scare him, but it's a new stage I'm in. First I shook, now I cry. The chattering has stopped. My teeth are saved. Will's been doing this for nearly a week, taking care of me; he hasn't been snowboarding once. He knows that something is terribly wrong. The fear in his eyes makes me cry harder.

I'm fine, I say, forcing my lips into a smile. But my face is purple, my eyes red—I'm a walking bruise. My cheeks are soaked. It's too big a lie.

What do you think you have? he ventures.

Oh, just some flu. I hate being sick. It makes me depressed. I'm such a baby. I try to laugh. He stares at me.

He's talking to our mother: Something's wrong, Mom, she's acting really weird. Crying all the time.

He doesn't see me behind him.

Let me talk to her. I grab the phone.

Is something else going on? she asks.

The guy I was seeing broke up with me, I say. It's a language she can understand.

I didn't know you were dating.

How would you?

Do you want me to come home?

No, I say too quickly, then adjust my tone. You need to work, Mom, I say. I'm okay.

I've taken care of Will so many times over the years when it was just the two of us at home. I can see he wants to do the same for me. He brings me all the stuff I've always given him.

Don't forget your own dinner, I say.

He sits in the recliner across the room and watches me eat. He's grown quite a few inches this year and is just over five feet now. He's starting to look more and more like our father: fair skin and a straight nose, a few light freckles. His blond hair is getting darker. But it's his smile that matches our dad's to a T, right down to the sliver of a gap between his two front teeth.

Are you going to school tomorrow? he asks.

School is tomorrow? I have not been able to think this far

ahead. But now, as he asks it, I realize I cannot imagine leaving this house.

No, I say.

Monday is hell. I know as soon as the bus pulls away with Will on it that this is a mistake. I am alone and terror is ripping through me, stealing my breath away. The walls are coming down on me, I'm sure of it. Then, in a moment of clarity, I have a new vision. Not the light on the bathroom ceiling, not Alec's face. It's a new picture, like a cue card in front of me: the bottle of tequila sitting in the back of my closet underneath a pile of dirty clothes. I've been saving it. It's made me feel better for months knowing it was there—just in case.

That case is now.

It does not take a whole bottle of tequila to pass out, which is a good thing because I know I'll need some more again soon. I will place an order with Stan today. By the time Will's bus rolls back by at three thirty, I am awake and throwing up. One of the things I love about alcohol: You always know what to expect. If you drink enough, you'll pass out. Every time. Puking is now a small price to pay.

I wake up Tuesday to the sound of wind whipping round the eaves of the house and a snowplow droning down the road in the distance. I pull up the edge of the shade, peek out the window, and through a swirling white mass see that everything is covered with piles of fresh snow. It is an act of nature. A gift from God. After one day of school, I have a reprieve *and* company.

School's canceled! my brother calls from his room.

                    *   *   *

Matt comes tromping over in his yeti snowsuit—a string bean
in a feed bag. Will looks at me looking out the window, his eyebrows raised hopefully. He doesn't say what he is thinking: *She
smiled.*

   Can he come in? Will asks. He's on pins and needles with me.
   I shrug, stare at the TV. I'm back on the couch, wrapped up.
   Matt has brought DVDs. You *are* sick, he says when he sees me.
No shit.
   It's nine a.m. and I have a killer headache. If he'd leave, I
could start the day's festivities and be asleep by noon. But he
appears to have moved in for the long haul. Which movie do you
want to watch first? he says, and dumps them out on the couch
beside me.
   I stare at him.
   Have you lost weight? he asks.
   I point to a DVD. He settles in on the other side of the couch.
Our toes touch in the middle.

My mother is badgering me. Running through one of her speed
monologues. You seem fine. You don't have a fever. What's the
matter? Did you have a fight with—who is it you're dating? (No
one.) It's not a problem with Cassie, is it? You two never fight.
Are you and Matt on the outs again? If something's going on,
tell me, but you can't stay home any longer. This isn't like you.
You're never sick. I hope to God it's not mono.
   My eyes follow her movements across the kitchen. She is

like chain lightning striking multiple targets: grocery bag, refrigerator, cupboard. Then she ricochets back again.

Alec raped me, I mumble from across the room.

She pauses, opens the cupboard. What's that? Alec what? I thought you two weren't seeing each other anymore.

Telling my mother is a stupid idea.

If I can't stay home, I have to get myself together. I won't crumble at school, in front of Him. It will mean becoming a very good actor. School will be the theater, and I will play my former self. The marquis will read: KATIE MARTIN AS THE GIRL FORMERLY KNOWN AS KATIE MARTIN. The old me does not exist anymore, but I can remember her. I am angry that she is gone.

It will be the performance of my life.

41

"Hey, sweetheart. How you feeling?"

"Hey, Stan."

"You look beat."

We are outside the main door to the school building. His breath is like puffs of smoke in the chilly morning air. When we were kids we'd pretend we were smoking while we waited for the bus on the coldest days. Invisible cigarette between two fingers, fake inhale, blow out hard. The "smoke" would shoot straight out of our mouths. We'd blow it at each other's faces.

I look at my boots and count: three breaths, nice and easy. I will not puke on them. I'm learning to will away puke. It's one of my new skills. There is a drum inside my head, pounding. I look up at Stan. His eyes are soft and brown.

"I might have mono."

"That would suck," he says sympathetically.

He's right, but what would suck worse is if anyone noticed anything wrong with me. Not the mono thing. That is a cover—

a useful fairy tale. I mean, notice that something is *really* wrong with me. That I have changed. That I'm not myself anymore. That Katie Martin has disappeared.

I put a stick of gum into my mouth, offer one to Stan. "Thanks for staying after the party—at my house that night."

"No problem," he says. "I was worried about you."

"Hey, Stan, I've been meaning to ask you if you . . ."

"Just name it."

By the time the first bell rings he's promised to get me two more bottles of tequila and four of vodka for "friends" in another town.

I love Stan.

Inside the school, fear grips me. Alec could be lurking around any corner. Lurking is his specialty. What will I do when I see his face? Melt into the floor like the witch in *The Wizard of Oz*? Will myself to disappear? No. I will not disintegrate in front of Alec.

I fortify myself before English and history, just to be sure, in a stall in the girls' bathroom. More gum. A shot of breath spray. Vodka only for school; tequila for home. Vodka doesn't reek. Vodka can be disguised. When I walk into class just as the bell rings, I stare straight out the back windows and take my seat in the front row.

Once, my eyes brush Alec's face. He looks away.

The day develops a rhythm: "My mom thinks I might have mono," I say with a sad face. I repeat it every period, to each of my teachers. My rehearsal with Matt helped, gave me confidence. If Matt sees that I am sick, everyone else will see it, too. Plus, it's technically not a lie. My mom *does* think I might have mono. I play it to the hilt. I'm the girl with the mysterious illness, the mono victim, the poor kid who can't get well. My teachers have concerned eyes. They shake their heads.

"You look tired," they say. "Have you lost weight?"

"About ten pounds."

"You can't afford it."

One says, "Eat chocolate."

Sympathy is good.

Cassie arrives at school sometime after lunch. She is just back from England the day before. She tries to catch up with me between classes, but I'm elusive, like a cat.

The hall is nearly empty. It's 2:35 and I'm shuffling through my locker, waiting until everyone is gone. I want to weave my way out to the parking lot alone. I'm drunker than I'd planned, but I have made it through my first day back at school. Perfecting my system will come later, so I think.

Cassie is coming down the hall now, skipping stairs and landing hard on the wooden floor in her snow boots. "Hey, Kay, I've been trying to catch up with you. Are you okay? You look terrible."

"I don't feel well," I say into my locker.

When I pull my head out, Cassie is studying me. "Are you mad at me?" She's puzzled, hurt, something.

I shake my head. "No. Why would I be?"

"I don't know . . ."

"I've been really *sick.*"

"I know. I'm sorry. You don't look so good. You've lost a lot of weight."

She seems strange to me, standing there with her red hair and bright, curious eyes. She wants to talk, swap vacation stories. She's looking for her friend.

"You don't look like yourself. I think you *do* have mono. My mom says it can take six, even eight weeks to get over. When do you get your test back, anyway?"

I shrug. "I haven't seen my mom for a couple days."

Cassie's eyes roll up toward the ceiling. "Can't she take a day off work? I mean, you're sick. She's a nurse for God's sake."

"I didn't say she was working."

Cassie lets out one short, humorless laugh, but her shoulders relax. "I don't know about her," she says.

She looks at me like she's waiting for me to say something else, crack another mother joke, but I can't think of anything.

"I gotta go, Cassie. I'm tired."

"Yeah. Take a nap, girl. I'll drive you to school tomorrow. You can sleep in the car, okay?"

"Nah, I don't even know if I'm coming to school. But thanks anyway." My arms are full of books now, books I'll never open. Props are important. I drift down the hall away from her, toward the door to the outside.

"I'll see you," I say, but I don't look back.

"I'm worried about you," Cassie says into the phone. "I think there's something really wrong with you and your mom doesn't even seem to care." She's been talking to her own mother about it, her mother the MD. I don't want to talk, but Will has handed me the phone without asking my opinion. He is worried; I suspect he is calling in reinforcements.

"I told you," I say. "My mother thinks it's mono."

What Cassie doesn't know is that I still haven't had my blood drawn. I'm supposed to go to the clinic after school, and my mother keeps bugging me about it, but I keep telling her I'm too tired at the end of the school day, and she's never home to drag me there herself.

"What if it's not? My mom thinks you should have other tests done."

"I'm too tired to talk," I say, and hang up without saying good-bye.

I catch them talking about me.

I'm walking from study hall to the library, where I can hide in a cubicle against the back wall for the entire period. They are in the hallway alone. Cassie's voice carries.

"Matt, she just doesn't seem right to me."

"I know."

"I don't mean to freak you out, but I'm going crazy. She looks like a scarecrow—she has those dark circles under her eyes. Her clothes are hanging off her. I mean, I go away for two weeks and she looks like she's been in a concentration camp. What if she has cancer or something?"

"I'm here," I announce, walking past them.

Cassie looks guilty. "I'm sorry, Kay. . . . I just . . ."

"I don't have cancer."

"But how do you know?"

"I *know*," I say, and keep walking.

I don't know how many days have passed now. I'm not interested in the passing of time. Life is a game, a performance for the hell of it. See how long they can be fooled. This isn't hard. I have nearly convinced myself that my illness is real. I half expect the mono test that I still haven't taken to come back positive. Say something enough times and it becomes real. Just like that.

After that: nothing.

At lunch I stand on the sidewalk, watch the cars speed past the school, and think about stepping in front of one. I watch them and bide my time.

I float through the halls in school on a plane of perfect intoxication. I know just how much it will take to get me through each period without going so far as to get caught, and whether I have enough time to get to my locker and the bathroom between certain classes. My history teacher allows "drinks," so I can sip screwdrivers from my water bottle all through his class.

A tip for the wasted and overtired: Avoid answering questions unless called on, and just shake your head if you are. Dark circles under the eyes can make a person look pathetic, and teachers may take pity on you and leave you alone. My teachers think it's heroic that I'm sitting in class at all since it looks like I am dying. They have no idea how right they are.

Once, when we were thirteen, Cassie's mother drove us to a mall in Massachusetts where there was a glass elevator. Riding up and down in it was like moving through space: You could see everything but couldn't touch it; the people out there could see you but couldn't reach you. That is how I feel now, like I am in a glass capsule floating through school. Even Alec can't touch me. In English and history class he is invisible to me; he does not exist. He doesn't try to catch my eye or talk to me after class. It's a tacit agreement between us: We have both disappeared so far as the other is concerned.

Megan is providing me with very potent weed via her sister, and I'm grateful. It helps when my stomach can't handle the booze, and it gives me a little appetite. My throat is raw. When I drink it feels like a fire I can't put out. One day I throw up blood. This scares me. I plan to die *fast*.

Coach Riley asks to talk to me. She's heard I've been sick and she's worried about me. I know this already because she called my house, left a message for my mother.

"Your mother never called me back," she says. Coach Riley's face is concerned. She's like an older version of Cassie.

"That's my mom," I say. But I know it's because I deleted her message before my mother heard it.

"Has Coach Hollyhock called?"

"Yes."

"She says you two haven't talked in a while." This is exhausting. She's grilling me like she did at the beginning of hockey season.

"She's left messages."

"Your contract isn't final until you sign it in February."

"I have to get back to class," I say, and turn and walk away.

I splash more water on my face, then look in the mirror. It's fifth period. How can my bottle be empty? I need a second water bottle, a backup. There's one in my brother's room at home, I think. But what about the rest of *this* day? My heart flutters, a large bird trapped in my chest. Panic.

Then I see her step into view behind me. She tosses her white-blond hair to one side and starts brushing. Marcy still hasn't spoken to me since the state championship game. Hating me gives her something to do. She doesn't say a word, just watches me as I bend down, swaying slightly, to get my backpack off the floor. Its weight throws me off balance for a moment when I pick it up. I take a deep breath to steady myself, then come up and turn—

She's looking directly into my eyes. "Oh my God," she says, and her lips curl into a smile. "It's true. You're wasted."

I'm busted.

42

It is the next morning and things are moving too fast. They've hauled me into the guidance counselor's office before my first class—snatched me away the second I walked through the school's main door. I've been in here ever since, quarantined like I'm contagious and they don't want the other kids to catch what I have.

"Your mother tells me your father had a drinking problem," the guidance counselor says from behind her desk. Mrs. Bradford is a short, square woman with big, square glasses that cover too much of her face.

It is too early in the morning for this.

"Where's Mr. Hanley?" I ask. He is my guidance counselor. He is the one who helped me with my school applications and made sure the universities had all my eligibility stuff on time. This woman doesn't even know me.

The office is quiet and hot and steam is rising from the ancient radiator under the window. Once in a while it whistles or hisses at us. Sweat drips from under my arms onto my back and stomach. It is eight thirty now and I am desperate. The shaking is bad and it's her fault. I've been in here too long and they've taken my bag. She must see how much I need it. *Bitch.*

She's looking at me from behind her giant, cluttered desk. "You've been drinking in school. Can we agree on that?"

Why would I agree to that?

"Shouldn't I have a lawyer or something if you're going to interrogate me?"

She smiles faintly. "You're not under arrest, Katie."

Could've fooled me. I've been a prisoner in her overheated office for an hour now. She tells me my life story, says my father is an alcoholic, then tries to get me to confess. I'm just waiting for the cops to show up with handcuffs.

"Then can I leave?"

"A number of people have noticed it, Katie. Both other students and a teacher."

"Marcy Mattison hates me."

"Matt Fletcher does not." She looks me dead in the eye. "Neither does Coach Riley."

"You lie." My voice trembles.

"We called your mother yesterday. She searched your house and found empty bottles in your closet."

"She went through my *stuff*?" A wave of heat sweeps up my neck, flushing my cheeks.

"I asked her to when I called her yesterday. She didn't want to believe me when I told her what was going on."

"She'll tell you I'm fine. I'm *sick*. She's taking me for a mono test."

"Your mother will be here shortly. Then we can all talk together."

"She's going to work."

"No, she's coming here."

The radiator hisses and sighs.

My mother looks small in this big office with its big desk and tall window and high ceiling. I'm afraid she's going to cry. Her long, thick hair is loose and she looks like she's seventeen. It feels like we're both in trouble. Maybe we are.

"I'm not like my father," I say to Mrs. Bradford.

I look at my mother for backup. She knows. I stack the wood. I come home. I put down the storm windows and watch out for my brother. Like my *father*? It's the most wicked thing she could say. But my mother is silent. She's biting a nail.

"You're right, you're not," Bradford says. "You're younger. You still have choices."

"Yeah, and I didn't walk out on my wife and kids."

"*Katie*," my mother says. I'm embarrassing her, being rude.

"You have a choice right now. If you don't drink, you can't end up like him. So by not drinking, you'd be making a choice to take your life in a different direction. If you do choose to drink, you take a big risk. You live with a big question mark. Alcoholism, as I've said, runs in families."

She's looking me right in the eye. The woman cannot be

stared down. It doesn't help that my whole body is trembling. That my shirt is half soaked and she can see that it is. I'm not going to last in here. My nerves are shot. I feel jumpy as hell.

"What do you think?" she asks.

"I guess I shouldn't drink," I say quickly.

Mrs. Bradford draws a deep breath and stands up. "I'm glad you feel that way," she says, but she's not convinced. She rubs her arms, looks out the window behind her. Gray clouds hang heavy and low over the playing fields. A mixture of snow and freezing rain is piling up on the windowsill.

All I can see in my head is my backpack, just outside the door, with two full bottles in it. I need to get to them. "I have to go to the bathroom," I say.

"In a minute." She turns back to face me. "Your mother and I have talked about this, Katie. And we think that, in light of all that's happened, it would be best if you went away for a while."

"Away *where*?"

"There's a place for teenagers who have this kind of problem."

Would that be the rape problem or the father-who-disappeared problem? Or the chance-of-becoming-the-father-who-disappeared problem? I feel like picking up the jar of pens on her desk and throwing them at her.

"Just for a couple months," she is saying. "You'd be back in plenty of time for graduation. In time to run track, even. You were All-Conference last year, weren't you?" She offers this up like bait to hook me.

A couple months?

"I don't want to." I want to stay home and sleep. Cassie and Matt can come visit me in the afternoons and play cards. Did Matt really know? Did he really turn me in? I don't trust this woman. She's making things up.

"I'll do all my work at home." There is an awful pitch to my voice, like I am begging.

She looks at me with something resembling pity. "I don't think that would take care of the problem, Katie." She sighs, like she's the one who's exhausted. "It's all been worked out. Your mother made the decision, and the school supports her. You can't do what you've been doing here."

I look at my mother. She looks at the floor.

"Why can't Alec leave?" I blurt out.

"Katie, you're not making sense—" Mrs. Bradford starts.

"He raped me."

She blinks once, stares at me. "Alec Osborne?"

"New Year's Eve. He did, Mom." I look at her and start to cry.

Mrs. Bradford pauses and bites her lip. "You know how serious it would be to lie about something like that."

I can't speak. I've said too much already. *Shit.*

Mrs. Bradford looks at my mother. They are trying to read each other silently: *Do you believe her? I don't know, do you? Maybe she's just trying to get out of this. She's desperate, poor thing.*

I see the conversation in their eyes.

That's it. I'm gone.

They don't try to stop me. Outside the office, I grab my backpack off the floor and run down the hall. In an old wooden stall in the girls' bathroom, I open it up. Both water bottles of booze are gone. Taken by my captors.

Lori is a slut, the wall says. I grab a pen and jab it like a knife into the plywood, scraping the point up and down over the graffiti.

"Fuck you," I sputter under my breath, as though Mrs. Bradford and my mother and Alec are all there on the wall in front of me.

Fuck you.

43

It was snowing outside. Over my mother's shoulder, outside my counselor's window, rows of cars in the rehab's parking lot slowly disappeared under fluffy white flakes. I'd been here for nearly two weeks with nothing to look at from my room's window but that parking lot. The snow improved the view.

"You lost your scholarship," my mother said. "Coach Hollyhock called yesterday."

"I know," I said, my eyes fixed on the scene beyond the glass. I didn't know. But I'd expected it.

Gail swiveled slightly in her chair; she was my personal counselor. We all had one, all eighteen of us on the adolescent unit. Most of us had her. She was the youngest, or looked it, so they probably thought we'd talk to her, trust her, even. She was tiny, almost delicate, with short, wispy blond hair and a high, soft voice, but she wasn't scared of us. She was a quiet force in an innocent-looking package. Once I figured that out, I stopped tiptoeing around her. Especially when she said stupid things. If she was going to dish it out, she'd have to take it.

My mother looked at Gail and Gail at my mother. I thought of Mrs. Bradford back at school, the looks she and my mother had exchanged.

"I want you to know," my mother continued, "that I'll do anything I can to get you to school anyway." She cleared her throat. "I'll make sure you get to college this fall. And Coach Riley has been in touch with Coach Hollyhock on your behalf. She's doing what she can. She still believes in you."

"I don't want to go, anyway," I said.

"Coach Hollyhock said you're welcome to try out as a walk-on. If you can . . . handle it, there's no reason you won't make the team."

"You lost it because of the drinking," Gail chimed in. "Not because of Alec."

"Gee, Gail, thanks for the news flash."

"*Katie*," my mother said.

I shut up.

Nobody said anything.

"Time's up," I said. "Can I leave now?"

Gail nodded.

"I'll come say good-bye before I leave," I heard my mother say as I slammed the office door behind me.

"The accident is yours," Gail said. My mother had left the day before. She only came in once a week, for an hour with Gail and me.

I fixed my eyes on a snow-covered picnic table outside the

window. The sun was out, reflecting off the new snow. Inside, in Gail's little office, particles of dust floated aimlessly in a stream of light.

"You got drunk. If you weren't drunk, you wouldn't have crashed the car. And you agreed to the lie."

"I know."

"Good, because I think that's weighing you down."

"Not really." I shifted in my seat, pulling my legs up on the chair, knee to chin, and buried my face in them.

"How's that?" she asked finally.

"We're even now."

"It's not about being even, Katie."

I didn't say anything. My chest felt tight, the way it always did when she tried to force me to see things her way. It's not counseling; it's indoctrination. They let you go if you agree with them—or if your insurance runs out. Whichever comes first.

"Life isn't about getting even," Gail said. "If you make it that way . . . well, it's a painful way to go."

"I don't make it that way. It's the way it is. They fly into our buildings; we bomb their villages—right?"

You owe me, he'd said. Those were his exact words. She didn't get it. No one did; they all thought it was my fault. My fault he raped me. That's why they sent me away, right? To get rid of the evidence. Let Alec the big man roam the halls, free to do whatever he pleased.

The walls of Gail's office were closing in on me; I couldn't get enough oxygen to breathe.

"It wasn't my fault," I said, and jumped up, slamming the door of her office behind me before she could say one more word about my life.

Gail was in my room now. She had knocked quietly about half an hour later. She didn't ask if she could come in, just strolled through the door when I didn't answer.

"You can't always run when things get tough, Katie."

Wanna bet? I thought. *Watch me.*

"It's one of the things we're trying to teach you here. Running doesn't work."

Really? I thought. Running might have helped the night Alec grabbed me. But I was too stupid to do it in time. At least in the right direction. The bathroom. What had I been thinking?

"I didn't ask to come here. I was forced. Just like I'm forced to talk to you every day. Any idea what it's like to be *forced*, Gail?"

She didn't say anything.

"I didn't think so," I spit out under my breath. *"Bitch."* And then I started to cry, the tears coming fast and hard, the kind of crying where you can hardly breathe and you don't care anymore who sees you or what they think because you're way past that—past everything that makes sense.

It shut Gail up. She must have felt bad, because she came over and sat next to me on the bed, and put her hand on my back and kind of rubbed it a little. She was brave, I'll give her that. I'd rather kill someone than have them sit that close to me—never mind touch me. But when she put her hand on me, I just cried harder. I wanted my mother.

"I'm sorry, Kate," she said softly. "I'm really sorry that he hurt you. *Nobody* deserves that."

I do, I thought.

That's how crazy I was.

After I had been there for two more weeks and had played by their rules, I was allowed visits from non-family members. Gail told me that the counselor at school had reported the rape—she had to, whether she believed me or not. It was the law. The thought of Alec knowing I'd told people terrified me. I was sure he'd come after me now in revenge. They'd never let him in this place; still, I was nervous all the time, shaking, jumpy.

I didn't want to see anyone. Matt understood. He sent me a bunch of yellow roses with a note in his crooked handwriting:

Dear Katie,
I just wanted you to be okay. That's still all I want.
Love,
Matt

I sent him back a postcard with a picture of the ugly, flat building I lived in now with *I'm not mad at you. Love, Katie* scrawled on the back.

*   *   *

I didn't want Cassie to come either, but she insisted and finally I gave in. That's Cassie: never gives up. And now she was here, sitting across from me, studying my face.

In a way, I was a stranger to her now, an enigma, a puzzle to solve, where before there had just been the friend she thought she knew everything about.

"School's different without you."

She looked bleak—pale, washed out behind her freckles, her spark just not there. She perched on the edge of an avocado-green armchair and looked around the bare room. "It's been hard not talking to you. It was hard even before you came here—since Christmas."

I got up off the bed and walked toward the window, pulled the cord, watched the burnt-orange curtains sway and close, sealing the room from daylight. The sun reflecting off the snow was unbearable. Every day I wished for gray clouds, a storm to mirror how I felt.

"Simon broke up with me," she said.

"What happened?"

"I don't know. He just e-mailed me and broke up. He didn't even call." Her eyes were shining.

I knew I should feel something, but I didn't. I was blank, empty.

"I'm sorry," I said, but it wasn't convincing.

She took a tissue out of the box near my bed and blew her nose. "I should have known sooner," she said.

"You said you had a great time with him."

"Not about that. About you. What you were doing. I should have known sooner."

"Nobody knew."

She wiped the back of her hand across her face. "They did. I was the last one. People had been saying for a while that you were high in school or whatever, and I'd get so mad and say you were just sick. . . . Matt knew, of course, but I wouldn't even listen to him."

Her eyes followed me as I crossed the room and sat back down on my bed. They were dark blue today. Arctic blue.

"Stanfield got suspended this week," Cassie said. "But so did *Alec*."

"For what?"

"Fighting. Stan jumped him. Alec said something at lunch and Stan beat him up."

"I wonder what he said."

"Stan's always had a crush on you." Cassie studied my face. "He feels like shit, you know, Stan does."

"It wasn't his fault."

Neither one of us spoke.

"Why didn't you just tell me, Kay?" she said finally.

I shook my head and looked back at where the window had been, at the terrible orange curtains. "Too embarrassed. I mean, shit like this—it would never happen to you."

She looked surprised. "It could have. It still could. It could happen to *anyone*."

"No," I said. "You wouldn't have given Alec the time of day. You're too *smart* for that."

"Being smart won't stop some lunatic from jumping out of the bushes at me someday."

"Yeah, but that lunatic? At least you'd know that you didn't invite him into your *life*. That you didn't make out with the guy, or let him into your house, or let him convince you for even five minutes that he was normal and maybe even *nice*. You're not that stupid, Cassie. You never have been."

Cassie's pale face glowed in the light of the small lamp beside her chair. The rest of the room lay dark. "I'm thirsty," she said.

"There's a soda machine in the hall."

"I lost my scholarship, you know, because of the drinking," I said when she came back with a Coke for her and a ginger ale for me. I set mine down on my bedside table, unopened.

"They can't blame you, can they? After what happened."

I let out a short, hollow laugh. "Sure they can. I can."

"Even after Alec—he's such a *pig*." Her eyes darted around the room.

"Not everybody who is . . . *raped* . . . not everybody, you know, drinks a fifth of vodka or whatever it was every day."

"A lot of people would."

"You wouldn't have." I let out another short, humorless laugh. Gail liked to point out that I laughed when things weren't funny, like it was a cover or something. But did it count as a laugh if there was no humor, no glee, not a shred of happiness behind it? They should be called something else, these sounds I made.

"You don't know that. I might have."

I shook my head. "No, not you. You would have told your mother, brought the asshole up on charges. That's what you would've done." It was almost an accusation.

Cassie flinched.

"No, wait—you also wouldn't have showered, so that the charges would *stick*. Your mom probably has a rape kit at home, in her little black *bag*."

Cassie looked tiny at that moment, curled up in the plastic armchair with her knees tucked under her chin. Her eyes were rimmed red, but I didn't care. I was on a roll.

"Frankly, Cassie, you'd never get yourself into this situation, so I don't know what the fuck I'm even talking about."

Cassie looked stunned. But there was fire back in her eyes.

"You know what else I wouldn't have done, since you think you know me so well? I wouldn't have lied to you," she said. "You don't lie to your *best friend*."

You don't know the half of it, I thought.

She wiped the sleeve of her fleece across her cheeks. She looked like hell—but fierce now, too. "I don't know what I'm supposed to say to you," she said finally.

"There's nothing to say. It's over. I fucked up and it's over."

Gail was getting on my nerves. I didn't hate her anymore—
actually, I kind of liked her—but she was pushy sometimes. She
wanted me to talk about things I didn't want to talk about. I'd
been here more than a month now, and since I'd been sober all
that time, she said it was time to get at what she called "the
underlying causes."

"Causes of what?"

"Why you drank."

"It tasted good?"

Gail smiled. "You're funny, but it's not getting you out of
this."

I flipped a slipper off my toe and into the air. They made
us get dressed every morning, but appropriate footwear was
optional. I liked padding around in these old things, mainly
because Will had sent them for me from home.

"Why do you think you drank?"

"Alec."

"At the end, maybe, partly. Before that."

"You tell me." She was like a teacher trying to get me to guess the right answer, the one she already had in her head.

"You drank before Alec. You said Matt used to get mad at you about it. Yet you did it anyway. Why?"

"Matt's a Puritan. He doesn't think anybody should drink."

Gail swiveled slightly in her chair, first one way, then the other. She did that when she was thinking hard.

"Do you want to stay sober, Katie?"

"Yes."

"Really?"

I shrugged, looked away. "Some days I do, some days I don't."

"Thanks for being honest."

"Honest won't get me out of here."

"Is here so bad?"

I shook my head and wiped my eyes with my shirtsleeve. I was always crying at the weirdest times. I couldn't predict it.

"Here." She handed me a tissue box. "Let's say for today that you want to stay sober," she said softly. "The first thing you've got to do? You've got to learn to like yourself."

"Ha." Half the time I was in her office, I felt like I was on some tearjerker episode of *Oprah*.

"Is that funny?"

"Not really." I shook my head. But it was like saying I had to fly to Mars and back without a space suit. "What's to like?"

"You tell me," she said.

I sighed loudly.

"Try," she said.

"Let's see—I have excellent taste in guys, I'm a drunk like my delinquent father, I ruined my chance of success at the one thing I'm good at. . . . How am I doing?"

Silence.

Now I was mad. "You want me to *lie* to you? I don't like myself, okay? *Satisfied?*"

"I think this goes back a long way for you. I think it goes back to your dad."

"Well, how would you feel if your dad didn't bother to hang around? If he didn't bother to visit or pick up the phone or pop a birthday card in the mail? Would that make you feel special, Gail? 'Cause I just don't feel that special."

"It was a lousy thing to do to his kids."

She let me sit in peace for a while, blowing my nose. I pulled my stocking feet up onto her couch, curling them under my legs. My slippers lay abandoned on her floor.

"Remember you told me last session how your good friend Cassie came to visit recently and how mean you were to her?"

I nodded.

"Was it because you think she's a loser who doesn't deserve your friendship?"

"Yeah, right."

"What did we talk about?"

"How I've never felt good enough for her."

"Even though she's always cared about you, and she's never judged you, you still felt that way."

I nodded.

"Your father is an alcoholic, too, Katie. An alcoholic's think-ing sometimes doesn't make much sense. Maybe," she said, and swiveled her chair ever so slightly, "maybe your father never felt he was good enough for *you*.

"It's a lot to take in, I know," she said. "Just give it some thought."

And my session was over.

I'd like to tell you this: that I strolled back into school a month or two later with my head up, the old Katie back again, strong, defiant—cured. I'd like to tell you that I didn't care what people said, that I sat right down next to Alec in class, that I didn't care about what had happened.

But that would be a lie.

I made my peace with Gail. She helped me, even though I wasn't easy. She told me over and over that Alec is the one who carries all the shame for the rape, not me. After sixty days, she allowed me to move into the Transitions wing, a place where we had more privileges and did our schoolwork so we didn't flunk out. I still met with her every day; most days I looked forward to it.

We had some free time there, and group meetings with other kids with the same problems. Lots of girls had it worse than me: They'd run away or been abused by someone in their own family. Some of them had nowhere to go back to, no friends who called. Even so, I was still so depressed sometimes that I thought the only way out—the only way to stop feeling so bad—was to die or to drink. Sometimes I wanted to drink so bad I could almost taste it: the burn down my throat from a single shot of tequila, a whisper of salt on the tip of my tongue. But who was I kidding? I wasn't exactly mixing margaritas there at the end. And the counselors told me if I felt like crap now, they'd guarantee I'd feel worse if I got drunk.

"Did it work last time you tried it?" one would say.

Sometimes I hated them.

One day a fourteen-year-old named Bethany came up to me after a group meeting where I'd admitted I wanted to drink or kill myself, and I didn't care which. We were in a deserted hallway near our wing; fluorescent lights glared on the concrete walls and grungy linoleum.

"How can you let him do that to you?" she asked. Her face was pale above her narrow shoulders, her eyes big and haunted.

"What are you talking about?"

"That guy, Alex," she said.

"Alec . . . ," I said.

She nodded. "Don't hurt yourself. Don't let him win."

If anyone back home had said that to me, I'd have told them where to go. But I knew Bethany's story: that her stepfather had been molesting her for three years before she finally ran away because her mother didn't believe her. That she'd lived on the street by doing things I didn't even want to think about. That she'd been puking when she first got here—dope sick from withdrawal. I'd watched her struggle to get herself out of bed in the morning. She'd been in a psych ward once for slitting her wrists. Her scars were inside *and* out.

She was walking down the hall now, but she looked back to where I stood, like a deer caught in headlights.

"My stepfather—he's not winning this time."

I could see from her eyes that she meant it.

The counselors tried to get us ready to go back to the "real world." We had to learn how to deal with "life on life's terms," they said, and they spent quite a bit of time helping us figure out exactly what they meant by that.

What it meant in a nutshell: You can't avoid *shit*. Using drugs or alcohol isn't a fallback position. Hiding out isn't an option. Stuff happens and you have to deal with it. You run, you lose. Your best thinking got you here. And *here* is not a place you have to end up again. The choice is yours.

It was time to grow up.

There was something I had to do before I could go home, and the longer I lived in that place, with those girls and those counselors, the more I knew it. Gail agreed. I had two letters to write and one secret left to let go of—one lie left to own.

No matter how scared I was to do it.

No matter what might happen when I did.

I took out two envelopes. I addressed one to Matt and one to Cassie.

Then I began to write.

spring

45

Pale green and crimson buds speckled the tree branches like confetti. In our yard, next to the decrepit barn, an apple tree blossomed. Petals from its fluffy white flowers lay strewn across the grass like an untimely, delicate snow.

Will stood on the porch, his eyes following me.

"I won't be long. I'm just going to see Cassie," I said.

"Want me to tell Mom?"

"I told her," I said. "She'll be right back. She just went down to the store to get some milk." I turned to go.

"Katie . . . ?" Will had been my shadow all morning, sticking so close that if I stopped in my tracks he'd practically run into me.

"I'll be back in an hour, Will. I *promise*," I said gently.

"Okay," he said, but his eyes were uncertain.

I wheeled my bicycle out of the barn, brushed the winter's dust off the seat with my hand, and climbed on. The air in the tires was low. The rubber spread out slightly on the pavement under my weight, but I didn't care. I had arrived home just the night before; I needed to see Cassie.

The sun shone warm on my head, but the air was still cold. The wind blew hard against my face and through my hair as I pedaled toward the lake, goose bumps rising on my arms.

Cassie was expecting me. She was in her yard, digging up flower beds with her father; she looked up and waved. Not one of her usual enthusiastic waves, but a somber, one-hand-up-by-the-shoulder-then-straight-back-down waves, the kind you give a passing car in Westland when you don't know who's in it. She laid down her spade and walked slowly toward me.

Her father smiled and said hello, then looked back at his garden. I climbed off my bike and leaned it against their fence and Cassie and I walked away from her house, farther down the quiet road toward the deserted public beach.

We'd never had a real fight before, and my heart was racing. Cassie stared at the road ahead of us, avoiding my eyes, my face. Neither of us said a word. The five minutes it took to walk to the beach felt like eternity.

"I'm sorry, Cassie." My voice cracked and I cleared my throat. We were sitting side by side now, legs dangling off the dock.

She just nodded, flicked a toe in the water, and studied the little ripple she'd set off.

"I don't know why I did it. I know that's what you want to know—why I did everything I did—but I can't explain it."

She still didn't say anything, just played with her toes in the water, then finally shook her head. "That's not it," she said, so quiet I could barely hear her.

"What is it?"

Cassie stared straight ahead. Her lips trembled.

"Tell me, Cass—"

She held one palm up to stop me from talking. Whatever she had to say to me, I could take it. I knew that now. I could see how hard it was for her, too.

"Do you know how scared I was when I came home last summer and you'd been in that car accident?"

I shook my head slowly.

"*Very.*" She still wasn't looking at me. "*Very* scared. All I could think was what if you'd died. . . . I couldn't handle that." She flicked the water again with her toe.

"But then I thought, well, why dwell on it? It's over. You know? She didn't die. . . ."

"I'm sorry, Cass—"

"You remember last May—it was maybe a whole year ago—after that party at Cheryl's camp? You were so drunk you could hardly walk, and I had to drape your arm over me just so I could get you into the house that night. You didn't make it to the bathroom, you know—you peed your pants. I never told anyone you did that, not even you. I didn't know if you would remember in the morning. I was hoping you wouldn't." She took her feet out of the water, pulled her damp legs up to her chest, and hugged them in, chin on her knees. "I brought you back to my house that night. I was scared to leave you alone. My mom turned you on your side in case you threw up again so you wouldn't choke on it. . . .

"My mom thought you had a drinking problem back then. She said that people who get in trouble when they drink or do drugs have a problem." She laughed once, without humor. "I told my mom, *It's just what kids do.* Totally defended you.

"*Do* you *do it?* my mom asked me. I had to say no. I mean, I never had. She knew that." She shook her head. "But I didn't *want* you to be in trouble, so . . ."

"What?"

"So I convinced myself that you weren't—that you *weren't* in trouble." She stared out at the water. Tears ran over her freckles like tiny rivers, and she let them. They sparkled in the sun and dropped off her chin. "I'm *so sorry* about that. For letting you down."

I was stunned. *"Cassie."*

"I feel like such a loser."

"Cassie, you are the *opposite* of a loser."

"I know you were mad at me in rehab. You weren't really hiding it, you know?"

I dug in my pockets for a tissue, found a crumpled one, and handed it to her.

"I came to apologize to *you* for that, Cassie. And believe me, you don't have to explain to me how you can deny something that's right in front of your face—how you can pretend something isn't happening when it is."

Cassie smiled weakly. "I guess you know a little bit about that."

"Are you kidding? I'm an expert," I said. I pulled my feet out of the icy water and rubbed the cold flesh with my hands. "Listen to me, Cassie. Nothing, *nothing* you could have done would have changed me. It wasn't your fault."

She tilted her head toward me and studied my eyes; she could see that I meant it. "That's what my mom said," she said softly.

"She's right."

"So why were you mad at me?" she asked.

"I wasn't mad at you. I was mad at myself. I was just mad at myself."

We were quiet on the walk back to her house. It was a relief that her parents' cars were gone, that I wouldn't have to talk to them.

We stood on the McPhersons' lawn, newly green. Cassie bit her lip. "Can I ask you something?"

"Anything."

"What's going to happen to Alec, Kay? I can't stand it, seeing him at school every day."

"Nothing." I looked at my feet.

"That's not right."

"I know, but there's nothing I can do."

Cassie dug her foot into the soft earth of a flower bed. "My mom says the state has to investigate because you're a minor."

"I talked to them." My eyes scanned Cassie's familiar yard, then focused on the lake. The deep blue water shimmered in the sun. "There's no proof, no physical evidence. It's his word against mine. With my drinking and everything . . . going to court would be like suicide. Even Gail agreed."

"Gail?"

"My counselor. And my mom talked to Ron Bailey about it. Mom says he's livid, but he agreed. They're right."

"I'm sorry, Kay. Sometimes I just want to kill Alec."

"I want to kill him all the time."

Inside her empty house, we made sandwiches and opened a bag of chips. Cassie grew quiet, moving around the kitchen without saying a word, her eyes on the tile, on the food, anywhere but on me. We sat down with our plates in front of a large window overlooking the lake, but she didn't eat a thing; something was on her mind.

"It hurt," she said suddenly. She looked at me then; her eyes flashed. "After Christmas, when you'd hardly talk to me, when you avoided me in school, and then didn't want to see me in rehab . . ." Her hand gripped the arm of her chair, her knuckles white. "When I told you about Simon and you didn't even care, the way you talked to me the day I visited you." Her voice was trembling, the words tumbling out. "When you finally wrote me and told me you were driving Alec's car and I realized how much I didn't know. It hurt, Kay. It hurt a *lot*.

"I thought I had no right to be mad—after what happened to you and everything, after Alec . . . I mean, nothing's worse than that, right? But . . ."

"I don't blame you for being mad, Cassie."

"I just want to be honest," she went on. "When we were making lunch I just got so angry inside. Something exploded in me. I mean, I didn't even know it was there, but all I could think was, *How could she lie to me? How could she just blow me off after all these years? How could she not care, not tell me things that were so* important? *She's my* best friend. *Why did she treat me like that?* It all just kept spinning around in my head. I tried to stop it but I couldn't. . . .

"But then I thought: If I don't tell you what I'm thinking right now, it would be like doing the *same thing* that I was mad at you for doing. Because how I feel . . . This is important." She looked at me and took a deep breath. "Do you know what I'm talking about?"

"Yeah," I said. "I think I do."

"Good," she said, and her face relaxed, her eyes shining. "Because you're my best friend." We were both crying now. "And I'm not letting go of that."

46

"Ready?" Matt asked.

We picked up the canoe, flipped it right side up, and lowered it into the water next to the dock. My hands trembled as I strapped on my life jacket and stepped carefully into the boat. I was glad to be in the bow facing the lake rather than facing Matt. Maybe it was because, even though he knew me better than anyone did, he was still a guy. Or because he'd warned me away from Alec way back last summer. Or simply because he knew what had happened to me, knew what Alec had done, something so personal and so terrible that having *anyone* know—and everyone did—was almost as horrible as the rape itself.

Alec had spread it around, what he called my "bullshit allegations." Said I was just trying to cover up that I was a lush, a drunk, a slut. He made the whole thing public, as if proving he had nothing to hide. Now it was as if everyone could see through me, to the most private part of myself. It was like a second invasion.

I didn't have to go to school, and I chose not to. We'd arranged all that before I came home. Starting on Monday, Cassie and Matt would bring my work home; when I was done, they'd take it back. Gail agreed it wasn't avoidance; it was self-preservation. Why slap a bull's-eye on my back and walk into the woods?

Matt was my oldest friend, and I thought that would some-how make it easier to see him, but it didn't. With people around town, I could shut down, stay aloof, pretend I didn't care. But that didn't fly with Matt and Cassie. If we were going to be friends, I'd have to show up and tell the truth. Otherwise it was a joke; there was nothing between us. Cassie and Gail had helped me see that.

Matt slung the strap of one of his cameras over his shoulder and climbed into the canoe.

"No pictures of me today, okay?" I didn't look back at him.

"Okay." In the past he would sneak pictures of me, and tease me when I got mad, but I could tell from his voice that today he meant it.

The water was a wide, smooth mirror. Puffy clouds and a fine blue sky stretched out over our heads. We paddled past Cassie's house. In her yard, forsythia had blossomed: tiny, delicate, gold.

"I can't believe how warm it is," Matt said.

I pulled my paddle through the water, sending ripples through reflections of trees and sky. The lake was so still, so quiet in May. There were no motorboats buzzing in the distance, no kids' voices echoing from the beach, just the sound of our wooden paddles bumping against the canoe, the gentle splatter of water across the lake's calm surface.

Our island, small and familiar, drew closer with every stroke. The grove of towering pine trees that grew there creaked and swayed when it was windy, but today they stood powerful and still. We stepped into the cold, shallow water and tied the boat firmly to a tree.

I slipped off my rubber sandals and walked barefoot on the warm, rust-colored pine needles that covered the earth like a soft carpet. The branches on the old trees were sparse and the pines well spaced out; there was plenty of sunshine between them. I took off my sweatshirt and made a pillow, then lay down on my back, eyes closed, face to the sun. Matt left his camera in the canoe and sat down beside me.

"You okay?" he asked.

I shook my head.

"Don't cry," he said gently.

"I can't help it," I whispered, and covered my eyes with one arm. "I'm sorry, Matt."

"Why are you sorry?" he said.

"Just—for everything. For being such an idiot."

Matt reached over and took my hand.

"Thanks for the letter you sent," he said quietly.

I squeezed his hand, my eyes on the sky over our heads. For what seemed like forever, we lay there in silence, side by side in the sunshine.

*   *   *

Matt walked around the water's edge taking pictures, then lay on the ground and focused the lens up into the tops of the trees. *Click, click, click.* The sound was so familiar it was comforting. I had missed this: the lake, my home, my friend.

He put his camera down and looked over at me. "Are you going to graduation?"

"I don't know," I said, and sat up, pushing my hands into the warm pine needles.

It had been on my mind every single day. It was only three weeks away now, and never in my life had I imagined that I wouldn't be there, marching across the stage with the friends I'd known since kindergarten and the few who had moved here since. It seemed impossible to do it—and impossible not to.

"I don't know, Matt. I'd like to say that I could walk in there and sit on the bleachers with him and not care, but I don't know if I can do it."

I picked up a pinecone and chucked it at the water.

I wanted more than anything to be tough. Every day I fantasized about walking into the school gymnasium in my cap and gown with my head up. I wanted to look Alec in the eye and not blink. But who was I kidding? Seeing him right now would feel like losing everything all over again.

"The way they line us up by height, I'd probably end up paired with Alec for the procession." I was only half joking, but both of us knew it wasn't funny.

"They'd never do that."

"Why wouldn't they? He's walking around school, isn't he? Nobody believes me."

"That's not true. A lot of people do."

"And most of them don't."

Matt looked at me, his brown eyes soft but his lips pursed tight. He was angry at them, too. Whoever *they* were. Whoever believed Alec over me, or called me a slut or a lush or worse. The worst part was, they were half-right. I didn't lie about the rape, but the drinking part—that was me. No one had poured it down my throat.

"I wish I didn't care." I took a deep breath.

"Are you okay?"

I shook my head no. Feeling like this had become familiar. I just had to breathe slowly, wait until it passed. I fixed my eyes on the large twisted root of a pine tree. One, two, one, two. Finally, the nausea subsided.

"You don't need to go," Matt said.

"I know."

"But if you do, Cassie and I will stick to you like glue. And I can ask to be paired with you. We're both tall."

"Coach Riley encouraged me to go, too. She came by the house, you know." I looked at Matt and he nodded. "She believes me." My eyes welled up thinking about her.

"Of course she does," Matt said.

"She said, *You're a tough girl, Katie. You've been through a lot, but you'll get through this. You're stronger than most. And there are a lot of people rooting for you.* I just sat there and cried."

"She's cool."

"Yeah, she's the best. But I just can't decide right now about graduation."

He nodded and looked at me carefully. "I don't know if this will help. I mean, it's not the biggest thing in the world, but . . ."

"What?"

"Well, Alec—"

"*What?* What about Alec?"

"He got suspended yesterday. For five days. I know it's nothing compared to what he did, but . . ." Matt shook his head. "It just made me so damn happy to see *some*thing happen to him, you know?"

"What happened?"

"He was opening up his backpack in the hall between classes. It was stuffed full of books and junk, and when he unzipped it, these three unopened beers came tumbling out. Right there on the floor!" Matt's face lit up. "The hall was packed. Everyone saw it: lots of kids, Mr. Tenney, another teacher. Alec was going, *What the hell is this bullshit?* but Mr. Tenney hustled him off to the office and that was it. The whole thing flew around school in about two seconds." Matt's eyes gleamed.

"Oh, and he's going to miss three track meets during his suspension, so he can't qualify for the States no matter what. For him, that's the worst part. You know, he placed third in the state in shot put last year. " Matt looked at me now, gauging my response.

"Why didn't you tell me before?"

"It only happened yesterday."

"You know what I mean—today, earlier."

"I guess I was saving it—for when you really needed it or something."

"I need it now."

"I know."

Just picturing Alec, the guy who'd never paid for a single crappy thing he'd done his whole life—and I was sure there were plenty of things he'd done I didn't know about—in trouble thrilled me, if only for a moment.

"Somebody must have set him up." I turned and looked at Matt. "He's a lot of things, but one thing he's not is stupid."

"That's what he said all the way to the office: *Somebody set me up!*" Matt smiled.

My mind raced with the possibilities. There weren't many. "I wonder if it was Stan. I bet it was Stan."

"Maybe." Matt pursed his lips and looked intently at an ant making its way over the pine needles.

I stared at him. "You know, don't you?"

"No." He didn't look at me.

"You're a horrible liar, Matt. Why won't you tell me? Why shouldn't I know?"

"I was sworn to secrecy."

"Tell me!"

"It was Cassie."

"Ha! *Cassie?* Right."

"If you say a word, she'll kill me. She is going to tell you after graduation. She can't risk getting caught."

"*Cassie* did this," I said skeptically. "My best friend,

do-the-right-thing, play-by-the-book Cassie." I laughed briefly, incredulous. "Wow."

Matt nodded. "I know. When she told me she was thinking about it, I was pretty surprised. But you know, it *is* the right thing, if you think about it."

"How did she even pull it off?"

"She's pretty smart."

"You're right, it's nothing compared to what he did. But it's the best thing I've heard in a long time."

We stayed there all day under the pine trees until hunger started to gnaw at our insides. It was way past lunchtime. Matt took an apple out of his pack and tossed it to me. We had sat for a long time without saying anything at all. I'd always liked that about us. We didn't need to talk all the time. Even when we were younger, we'd sometimes walk all the way up Pitcher Mountain without saying a word.

A gentle wind had picked up, and water bumped against the shore in tiny waves. The sun was high in the sky now, its warm rays stronger. Beads of sweat had gathered on my forehead and dampened my shirt. We moved into the shade, under the wide boughs of an ancient evergreen.

"I've been meaning to tell you," he said finally. "I called my grandma in New Hampshire the other day."

"How is she?" His grandfather had died during the winter.

"She's doing better. She's used to being alone now—more used to it, anyway."

I nodded.

"Anyway," he said slowly, "I hope you don't mind—I asked her if she'd mind if we both came and lived with her this summer." Matt looked at me, once again trying to gauge my reaction. "I mean, if you don't want to, that's no problem, either. I was planning to stay here. I just wanted you to know. Just . . . if you need to get out of here."

"Maybe I should get out of here," I said, looking out across the water.

"I'm not trying to tell you what to do. I'm done doing that."

I smiled. "Yeah, right."

"I just want to help."

"I know."

We were quiet again for a while.

"Thanks," I said.

"It's nice without the mosquitoes, isn't it?" I sighed. "And look at the trees, the colors." All around the lake, the trees were covered with light green: shoots, buds, and half leaves just beginning to grow.

"It's amazing," he replied.

"I love it here. I don't want to leave—I just got back. Fuck Alec."

Matt looked at me, surprised.

"What?" I said. "I think you've heard me swear before."

"It's not that." He was smiling.

"We're staying here this summer. Or I am, anyway."

"*I'm* not going anywhere," he said.

"Good." I looked him in the eye.

"Good." He looked back at me.

"I'll probably change my mind tomorrow."

"Whatever." Matt was still smiling, studying my face.

"What are you looking at?"

He shook his head. "You. You seem—I don't know—different than I expected."

"Whatever it is," I said, "it's all a bluff."

He shook his head. "I don't think so."

"Well, you're making me nervous, looking at me like that."

"And I don't even have my camera out. . . ."

"Good thing for you you don't. So, you want to go in the water?" It was a dare.

"You're kidding, right? It's freezing cold still."

"Bet I can swim farther underwater than you!" I said, and jumped up suddenly, running down to the water's edge. If I hesitated for an instant, I'd never do it.

"Hah!" was all he said, then he caught my eye, whipped off his shirt, and we both ran into the water screaming.